"THERE'S NO ONE HERE BUT US."

Walker's voice combined relief with passion.

He lowered his mouth and touched his tongue lightly to Miranda's lips, testing, teasing, inviting her to return the intimacy. She parted her lips and welcomed him at last.

"No one's ever gotten to me the way you have," he said quietly, adding, "I'm not sure if that's good or bad."

"You don't have to decide now," Miranda teased.

"Right," he said, lowering her gently onto the water bed.

Miranda slipped her arms around him, feeling the tension in his body as he held her to him. In moments they would join in primal harmony. A harmony that confirmed what Miranda already knew....

You've gotten to me, too, Walker Hall.
You've gotten to me, too.

ABOUT THE AUTHOR

When Christina Crockett decided to use the S.O.R.C. as background for her fourth Superromance, she took up sailing. Now she is an avid sailor and can often be seen in her sixteen-foot Falcon, tacking along the Florida coast.

Books by Christina Crockett

HARLEQUIN SUPERROMANCE

55–TO TOUCH A DREAM
103–A MOMENT OF MAGIC
146–SONG OF THE SEABIRD
171–WINDWARD PASSAGE

These books may be available at your local bookseller.

Don't miss any of our special offers. Write to us at the following address for information on our newest releases.

Harlequin Reader Service
P.O. Box 52040, Phoenix, AZ 85072-2040
Canadian address: P.O. Box 2800, Postal Station A,
5170 Yonge St., Willowdale, Ont. M2N 6J3

Christina Crockett

WINDWARD PASSAGE

Harlequin Books

TORONTO • NEW YORK • LONDON
AMSTERDAM • PARIS • SYDNEY • HAMBURG
STOCKHOLM • ATHENS • TOKYO • MILAN

Published July 1985

First printing May 1985

ISBN 0-373-70171-3

Copyright © 1985 by Christina Crockett. All rights reserved.
Philippine copyright 1985. Australian copyright 1985.
Except for use in any review, the reproduction or utilization of this work in whole or in part in any form by any electronic, mechanical or other means, now known or hereafter invented, including xerography, photocopying and recording, or in any information storage or retrieval system, is forbidden without the permission of the publisher, Harlequin Enterprises Limited, 225 Duncan Mill Road, Don Mills, Ontario, Canada M3B 3K9.

All the characters in this book have no existence outside the imagination of the author and have no relation whatsoever to anyone bearing the same name or names. They are not even distantly inspired by any individual known or unknown to the author, and all the incidents are pure invention.

The Superromance design trademark consisting of the words HARLEQUIN SUPERROMANCE and the portrayal of a Harlequin, and the Superromance trademark consisting of the words HARLEQUIN SUPERROMANCE are trademarks of Harlequin Enterprises Limited. The Superromance design trademark and the portrayal of a Harlequin are registered in the United States Patent Office.

Printed in Canada

To my friends who made sailing and sailboats less of a mystery: P. K. Baxter and family, Wilson Barnes at the St. Pete Sailing Center, Cliff at USF, King, Karl at Schoeppner Marine, Darlene, and my three intrepid crewpersons, Jaisen, Jaimee and Juli.

CHAPTER ONE

"HAPPY NEW YEAR!"

Miranda cut her small sailboat toward the inlet the minute she saw the large sailing yacht listing precariously to one side. Pushed by the waves, the elegant craft had drifted sideways against some submerged obstacle.

"Hey, we got company."

"Happy New Year, honey!" One of the men aboard yelled, raising his glass as Miranda skimmed in for a closer look. New Year's Eve was still hours away, but apparently he and his two companions had started celebrating early. Oblivious to the danger they were in, they were having a party at barely ten in the morning.

"Looks like you could use a little help." Miranda lowered her sail and glided up next to them.

"I'll tell you what I could use..." one of them began, leering at the dark-haired lady who'd appeared out of nowhere. But before he could finish his comment, his friend nudged him into abrupt silence.

"We are having some trouble," the blond fellow admitted. "Climb aboard and have a drink." He rocked forward and almost nose-dived over the lifeline railing, trying to get a better view of Miranda in her shorts, braided headband and striped T-shirt.

Miranda had no intention of joining the premature New Year's festivities with the drunken trio. She'd come out sailing alone to think things over, to consider an offer that would mean going back to a far different world than this tranquil lagoon in the British Virgin Islands. But Miranda couldn't ignore what was happening here. Already she was flinching at the sound of the hull, the curved underside of their boat, grating against the hard, uneven rocky reef. The chartered vessel was *Pixie*, a beautiful thirty-foot sailing yacht Miranda recognized from the fleet of a local company.

Caught by the current, *Pixie* was wedged against a ridge formed by jagged chunks of volcanic stone. With each wave the boat rocked up against the treacherous rocks. In the clear waters of the Caribbean, and especially in the inlets along the northern side of Tortola and Beef Island in the British Virgin Islands, these formations were all marked on the charts. But boaters could be preoccupied with the beauty of the tropical setting. This unsuspecting crew had blundered into danger, but right now it was the boat that was suffering.

Pixie was in big trouble. The tide was going out. Soon she would have even less water in which to negotiate. Already the boat's side would be gouged and scraped, but unless someone did something quickly, *Pixie* could be ripped apart on the rocks. From the hopeless condition of the trio aboard, Miranda knew she was going to be the "someone" doing the rescuing. She tied her little craft to the back of *Pixie* and climbed up the swimming ladder.

"Have you radioed in for assistance?" Miranda's

matter-of-fact calm avoided any indication that she was being critical.

"We called in," the blond guy replied, "but we didn't know where we were, so we sorta told them where we thought we were. The motor conked out, the damn anchor came loose and we've been drifting."

"I'll give them a call." Miranda reached past the blond man and radioed the precise location and a quick summary of the situation to the owner, Virgin Isles Cruises. Then she started working on dislodging *Pixie* from the reef. Time was running out.

"I think our engine's flooded," the blonde said with a sheepish look. "None of us is too good with machinery." He spoke with a slight slurring of his words. "We're lawyers. Down here on vacation from Michigan." He was following Miranda as she moved about the deck, checking out the lines needed to raise the sails. "Bob is the only real sailor in the group, but he's passed out down below. My name is Mark. What's your name?"

Miranda stopped for a second and looked at him stonily. She didn't care what his occupation was or who he was. She had work to do. But she resisted the impulse to tell him what she was thinking. Forty thousand dollars worth of boat and four human lives had depended on someone named Bob—but Bob was out of commission and the boys had decided to get drunk.

"My name is Miranda. I think we'd better concentrate on getting you out of here. Now." She made it sound sufficiently urgent to back him off, but not cause him to panic.

"Sure, honey." Mark grinned at her through an alcoholic haze. *Pixie* lurched as the wind picked up, and Miranda had to grab Mark to steady him.

"Could you all sit together on this side of the boat?" Miranda said, wincing as the rocks scraped away on *Pixie*'s hull. "If we can get her far enough over on her side, I may be able to sail her clear of here."

"You want us to tip her over even more?" A short fellow sporting a gold chain and a diamond pinky ring challenged Miranda.

"Just a bit." The relentless scraping continued. "Please, fellas..." Miranda coaxed them sweetly, employing a bit of feminine strategy. There was no point in an angry confrontation with them in their condition, and getting them to move quickly, then stay put, was necessary.

"Come on, guys. Let's cooperate with the lady." Mark was the first to comply. Rather unsteadily, the others came and sat next to him until the three men were lined up by the lifeline railing, clinging to the upright stanchion posts. When the water began lapping over their feet, the party spirit subsided, and three solemn faces turned to stare at Miranda. Somewhere below, sailor Bob slumbered on.

"She won't capsize," Miranda assured them. "Just hold on."

Pixie heaved over farther on her side. Immobile, the three men watched the water, their grips white-knuckle tight on the stanchions.

Carefully Miranda raised the mainsail so it would catch the brisk, steady breeze. Then she moved to the back of the boat, turning the wheel slightly, hoping to ease the boat ahead into deeper water. The wind in the sails along with the shift in the weight of the three men had rolled *Pixie* well onto her side. Now the deep keel wasn't sticking straight down where the rocks could ensnare it, and more surface of the boat was in the water, so she floated higher. Gradually as the wind pushed *Pixie* even farther over, the grating noises on the underside almost stopped and the boat inched forward. With a low rumble, almost a growl of relief, *Pixie* shuddered and with the next wave, slipped off the rocks and away to freedom.

Almost immediately, the boat righted itself and picked up speed.

"Yahoo. . . !" Three male voices were jubilant again.

"Son of a gun, she did it!"

"I'm wet. Look at me. Soaked!"

"Now how about that drink, honey?"

Miranda didn't even bother answering. Instead she pulled the mainsail in even tighter as the power of the wind moved the boat along briskly. Locking the wheel in place, she went forward and raised the jib, a second smaller sail extending over the bow. Then she quickly returned to the back and took the wheel again, heading around the island as she caught a glimpse of the incoming rescue boat from Virgin Island Cruises. In a few minutes she had turned the damaged boat and the well-lubricated lawyers over to the boat hand, Billy, and was ready to get on her way again.

"We owe you one, Miranda," Billy called after her.

As the rescue boat eased away with *Pixie* in tow,

Miranda turned her sailboat for home. Her shoulders ached from the strain of setting the sails of *Pixie* alone. Her face felt rigid from maintaining the appearance of calm when she was seething with anger over their negligence. But now she was able to relax. Miranda's straight black hair glistened in the sunlight. Her boat's rainbow sails spread brilliantly against the blue-green water as she whisked along. Things shifted again into a natural order.

AN HOUR LATER, when Miranda sailed into the marina on the north side of Tortola, her brother Jeff, in his wheelchair, was on the outside dock. Shirtless and preoccupied, he was hosing off *Island Princess*, their thirty-five-foot Pearson sailing yacht. *Princess* had just returned from a two-week charter, one without any of the misfortune that *Pixie* had endured. Without needing to consult the schedule, Miranda knew that *Princess* was chartered again for the following week. Vincent, their boat cleaner, had taken the chase powerboat off to pick up some provisions. Jeff apparently chose to do the housecleaning job on *Princess* himself so he could check her very closely and speed up the process of restocking and readying her for the next charterers. As Miranda watched, it was clear that her brother had it all under control. On the surface, everything seemed just like normal.

Yet from the moment the package from Sibyl Albrecht arrived a few weeks earlier, just before Christmas, both Jeff and Miranda had found it increasingly difficult to concentrate on the routine at their marina.

Back in the States, unfinished business beckoned to them, summoning them back to a world they had known years before.

Before the wheelchair. Before Tortola. Before Calvert Charters.

Here, two thousand miles from their childhood home, they had created their own business—a marina and sailboat-charter operation in a quiet bay in the British Virgin Islands. With the insurance settlement from Jeff's accident, their fleet had grown from two thirty-five-foot sailing yachts to seven identical boats that they leased for charters. But there were the old ties, old feelings and old relationships still unresolved.

Unfinished business. The past had haunted Miranda all week. Maybe it was because the old year was ending. The start of the new year on the tranquil curve of Brewer's Bay would be marked by the usual festivities—a few friends, good food and lots of laughter. The unbroken flow of warm days and cool nights on Tortola would resume the next morning as if nothing had changed. But it had.

Miranda Calvert tied up her boat, waved to Jeff, walked into the office, barely glancing at the light-green screen of the computer. The restlessness that had characterized the past year was turning into something more severe. Miranda slipped off her headband and ran her long fingers through her arrow-straight black hair. She lifted it back from her face and let it sift gently down onto her shoulders.

Catching a glimpse of her reflection in the office window, Miranda frowned slightly. Her dark velvet-brown eyes, narrowed speculatively, stared back from beneath wide arched brows. Miranda cocked one eye at the image. She'd changed. This version of Miranda was far from the civilized appearance she once had. Hard physical work around the marina had trimmed away her earlier debutante softness. Deeply tanned and firm-muscled, Miranda looked like a primitive islander—a pagan beauty, sultry and untamed. She was almost twenty-eight now, five years older than when she left the States. Five years had improved her, and Miranda liked the woman she saw. But she wondered how the old crowd convening in Florida for a world-class regatta would relate to this emancipated lady.

What Sibyl Albrecht had sent along with the two presents in the pre-Christmas package was the information kit and class specifications for the Southern Ocean Racing Conference, the annual Florida-to-Bahamas sailing race scheduled for February. She'd also included a tempting invitation. She wanted Miranda and Jeff to be there. Then Sibyl had called to wish them season's greetings and to pull all the old heartstrings.

"How about it?" Sibyl had pressed for an answer during that holiday phone call. "We desperately need you both, Mandy, darling. Vinnie has to have a second-watch navigator for his new entry *Prophecy*. It's just for the last few races, and Jeff is top-notch with all that computer stuff. I need a writer who can put together an insider's account of the races. These are tailor-made assignments for you and Jeff."

Sibyl hardly took a breath during the first part of the

conversation, hitting her with a hurricane of words. "I can't think of a single female who can follow offshore racing as expertly as you—and write about it. Before you say a thing about being too busy with your marina down there, let me warn you that I've done some snooping. According to my sources, you have an excellent staff. Very reliable. You and Jeff can make that operation function without your being there. I'm amazed you don't get bored sometimes."

At the time Miranda had fleetingly wondered whom Sibyl Albrecht had been quizzing about Calvert Charters, but the information she'd gathered was accurate. Miranda and Jeff did have more time on their hands than they used to. Now that the money from their mother's estate had been released, Jeff had been toying with the idea of expanding—building a hotel or opening a sailing school. Miranda had been looking over vacant buildings, imagining possibilities for development as a yacht-supply store. Bored wasn't the precise term, but Miranda yielded to Sibyl on that point.

She had been taking on more tasks to keep occupied. For almost two years, Miranda had been compiling and publishing a newsletter for the Charter Operators Organization. It started out informally, a simple newsletter concerned with improving the overall standards of sailboat chartering in the Virgin Islands. Then Miranda decided to tackle some problem areas. That required a certain toughness that she'd had to cultivate. Miranda surveyed members of the organization, charter owners and customers. She followed up on their complaints and recommendations, making unannounced visits to marinas and docking sites confirming her facts and exchanging information. Then she published her findings.

Occasionally Miranda's articles had stimulated controversy, particularly from outfits whose provisioning or equipment were rated substandard. But the real professionals in the business supported her efforts. The improvements within the business would benefit them all—marina operators and clients.

Then the Charter Operators Organization made Miranda their official troubleshooter and the newsletter grew to a regular monthly edition, complete with pictures—occasionally including one of the dark-eyed female editor. Miranda wasn't particularly comfortable with the attention. The writing part, she liked. She'd even submitted a few free-lance articles on cruising the Caribbean to Sibyl who acted as agent and sold them to sailing magazines.

Now Sibyl Albrecht was sure Miranda was ready for another challenge. "Someone else can take over for you on Tortola," Sibyl said simply. "I'm convinced you can do wonders with a classy article on offshore racing, one with pages of color photographs and diagrams and charts." Sibyl's Bostonian accent made each syllable of the offer sound more tantalizing. "Having you here to make sense out of all the race results would be splendid and such fun. Mandy, you can treat the assignment as a vacation. All expenses paid." She rattled off the perks to enhance her case. "About five weeks is all it would take here. Six if you can come for the trials beforehand. We only need Jeff for the last three weeks. Surely your gorgeous brother is ready to show off. It's time we all got another look at the two of you. *Everyone* is going to be there. It's time, Mandy."

The way Sibyl stressed "everyone" was the clincher. Sibyl knew which wounds still needed healing and which questions needed answering, and the timing was excellent. Miranda could imagine the outrageously red-haired, fifty-year-old Sibyl at the other end of the phone. Her aquamarine eyes would be narrowed in determination, waiting for her young friend to reply.

In spite of distance or age difference, they were still close friends. They had always been close. Six years earlier back in the States, when Sibyl Albrecht and Miranda were neighbors in Annapolis, Miranda had entered her twenty-second year as Sibyl's unofficial "princess." According to Sibyl, she had been the most marriageable young woman in the exclusive circle of yacht manufacturing and racing. Reigning as matchmaker of the Annapolis Yacht Club, Sibyl was determined to bring off the pairing of the decade. She almost succeeded. But when the racing season ended that year, tragedy had subdued the customary high spirits at the yacht club, and no wedding was in the offing.

That summer, Miranda's brother Jeff had become tangled in his safety lines and was swept overboard in a stormy regatta trial run. Sibyl lost far more than a future candidate to marry off one day to one of her other "princesses." She had seen a talented, troubled young man leave the yacht club with a drink in his hand and return on a stretcher—his back broken and his body paralyzed from the hips down. The dreams that died in that trial race were not romantic fantasies, and they were not only Sibyl's. Several futures were dramatically altered in that one blustery afternoon.

"This year's S.O.R.C. is shaping up to be a real battle," Sibyl commented during that holiday phone conversation. For a moment it sounded as if she was going off on a tangent, casually discussing yachts long-distance. But Sibyl knew precisely what she was doing. The S.O.R.C. was the annual Southern Ocean Racing Conference—six individual sailboat races that took five weeks from beginning to completion. The event, the Grand Prix of offshore racing, had always been Miranda's favorite.

"I'm sure you saw from the brochure that your dad is on the judging committee again this year. He knows that I'm calling you about this."

"And...?"

"I know he'd like to see you two." Sibyl said it gently. Persuasively. The breach between Howard Vaughn and his children still remained unmended. Only hours after Jeff's accident there had been another tragedy. Word of Jeff's injury reached his mother at a cocktail party, an elite gathering of regatta sponsors at which Amanda Vaughn, like other corporate wives, was expected to make an appearance as a representative of Vaughn Marine. Amanda had been drinking and dutifully mingling with the guests. Then she received the phone call about Jeff. In her haste to get to her injured son, Amanda Calvert Vaughn had run her car off the road and into a bridge abutment. She died instantly.

Howard Vaughn did what he had always done; he

took charge and gave orders. "For Jeff's sake, don't fall apart, Mandy." White-faced and tense, he had met her in the hospital corridor. "We've got to get through this calmly."

Miranda did what her father asked. She held everything inside.

After that day, Howard Vaughn tried even more forcefully to dictate his children's lives. Unable to accept the fact that Jeff's injuries were permanent, Vaughn was determined that Jeff, the reluctant heir apparent to the Vaughn Marine empire, would recover. For months, he shuffled Jeff from one specialist to the next, while Miranda ran Vaughn Marine Hardware. Too busy to feel any real emotion, she stood in for her father, overseeing the business with a strength she never realized she had.

Finally she understood she had to redirect that strength to fight for herself and her brother. "He's had enough." She had stood by Jeff and defied Howard Vaughn for the first time. Tired and bitter, Jeff only asked to get away. No more hospitals and medical contraptions. He wanted time to get used to being what he was—crippled. Exhausted from hoping for miracles, Jeff needed peace. With only the faintest trace of a smile, Miranda had squeezed Jeff's hand and left him that morning. The next afternoon, they were packed and flying to the Caribbean island of Tortola.

For the first few months, to make the break from Vaughn Marine and their influential father more complete, they used their mother's family name—Calvert. The name had stuck. Through Sibyl, Miranda remained in touch, sending her father brief but regular accounts of their progress. After a year, they had started their charter business, and Miranda wrote her father directly, asking him to come down to visit. Howard Vaughn had written back, formal letters typed by his secretary, often enclosing checks that Miranda put into a separate account for an emergency. But in the five years, there had been no emergency, no visit and no reconciliation. That rift was more unfinished business that could only be settled face-to-face.

They could meet on safe ground at the S.O.R.C.

"I'd like to see my dad," Miranda said to acknowledge Sibyl's last comment. That admission voiced an emptiness that had haunted her. Before she could recover her equilibrium, Sibyl pressed her advantage.

"There's someone else who'd like to see you. Phil Pittman is racing. His divorce was settled four months ago."

At the mention of Phil, Miranda felt an involuntary tremor in her stomach. If she had been the chosen princess six years ago, Pittman had been the prince-elect. Handsome and ambitious, Pittman had not possessed the old family money that the ideal prince should have, but he had the drive to acquire it. He had taken one look at Miranda Calvert Vaughn, the pretty, well-bred, ebony-haired daughter of the marine-hardware king, and set about to win her with a determination that even Sibyl found too romantic to oppose.

Jeff's injury changed everything. When Miranda took Jeff to Tortola, she hadn't intended to stay there forever. But her ardent prince hadn't been patient nor had he come after her as he promised he would. Within that first year, Phil Pittman had reassessed his priorities, redirected his passions and married another princess, Charlotte "Charlie" Birmingham of the Birmingham Yacht Brokerage firm in Annapolis. Charlie's father made Phil a vice-president of the company.

Even after all this time, it still hurt when Miranda thought of Phil Pittman. Ardent, seductive and gorgeous, he had come on like a steamroller. Miranda believed what everyone, including Phil, told her. They would be perfect for each other. The night they first became lovers, Phil swept away her inhibitions skillfully, tenderly, promising her this was only the beginning. From then on, he proceeded to convince her how exquisitely their bodies were attuned to each other. With an unrestrained richness of passion, Miranda responded. She loved him. And she loved making love with him.

She had felt that way about no one else since. Still, the sight of a striped spinnaker or the shimmer on the water at twilight could remind her of that season they'd sailed together, the times he had led her below deck, caressed her body and made her float on his touch. For that magical season, he had been everything, promised everything, taught everything and taken everything. But when she left Annapolis, she never saw him again.

Miranda could never understand how quickly and easily Phil had shifted paths and partners, replacing her with someone else. She hadn't been able to shake the memories nor let go of the longing that still haunted her. The possibility of being replaced again stood between her and any other intimate commitment. She'd never entrusted herself so completely to another man. In many ways, she was a new woman, no longer the obedient princess, the daughter of the king. But that former "Mandy" was still inside, still distrustful, still remembering. Phil was divorced, free again. Miranda had to see him. They had unfinished business.

Now as Miranda stared out over the marina, watching her brother hoist himself from the deck onto the dock, his arms hard and muscular, his face tanned and smiling, she braced herself for what was to come. On Tortola, Miranda threw everything into the marina project on Brewer's Bay. She had lost herself in the sheer physical demands of work and repressed the pent-up emotions. She never let Jeff see her really down. She was his cheerleader, and cheerleaders didn't cry.

Matching his sister's we-can-do-it attitude, Jeff had determinedly become a "wheelie wonder," skillfully maneuvering his wheelchair along docks, rigging pulleys and ramps to make every corner of boat or storeroom accessible. In the corporate world of Howard Vaughn, they'd been taught the importance of success. But here, Jeff and Miranda redefined the term. In this Caribbean paradise of natural tranquility, they regained their love for the beauty and peace of sailing—and their independence.

Miranda knew Howard Vaughn had to see his son like this—strong, confident, happy and whole—wheels and all. For them, Miranda would play the peacemaker. With Phil Pittman, she would play it by ear.

"Well...?" Jeff wheeled into the office a few minutes later. "Have you made up your mind about the

S.O.R.C.?" His eyes, brown like Miranda's, met hers steadily. "For what it's worth, I'd really like to get you out of here for a few weeks. The guys and I could talk dirty, grow beards and throw wild parties." His full mouth quivered, holding back a smile.

"That would really be good for business," Miranda said, laughing. "With the exception of the beards, I've heard you guys do that every Saturday as it is." Then her smile faded and she turned the question back on him. "How about you? Have you decided if you'll take time off and crew for Vinnie Albrecht?" Miranda knew that Jeff would attract attention—the handsome yachtsman in a wheelchair. Unlike her, at the S.O.R.C. he'd be in the spotlight, participating rather than observing.

"If you're going, I guess I'll have to show up, too." But there was a glimmer of something more than brotherly duty in his eyes.

"It might be time to put a few old ghosts to rest," Miranda said quietly. Jeff breathed an audible sigh. He was too much like his dad to admit how deeply he needed to put together what remained of their family. But Miranda knew.

"You book the tickets, I'll start making the arrangements here," Jeff said as he whirled around and headed out the door again.

Miranda flipped through the phone book for the number of the airline. In the midst of the madness that characterized the weeks of the Southern Ocean Racing Conference, she and her brother would be quietly building bridges. Bridges between their brave new world and the past they could no longer ignore.

THEY WERE LIKE EXPECTANT FATHERS, all four of them, pacing back and forth at the foot of the stairway—nervously waiting. Dennis was wearing his good-luck shirt, a faded T-shirt with a barely recognizable Harley Davidson eagle on the chest. Circumscribing it were the words, "Ride Hard. Die Free." But there was no sense of that free spirit in Dennis's somber expression. Like his Fu Manchu mustache and shoulder-length hair, the T-shirt was left over from a few years back when Dennis crisscrossed the country on a low-slung cycle, pursuing other passions and other dreams. Now slim-hipped and rangy, he paced like the others, waiting for Walker. Looking down at his four friends from the one-way glass of his office loft, Walker Hall managed a tight smile; he knew just how they felt. He had the butterflies in his stomach, too—since well before dawn.

Walker glanced at his watch, then propped on his wire-rimmed glasses, settling them across the bridge of his straight classic nose. He didn't really need them this morning; there were no minute columns of figures to decipher nor pale design sketches to follow, but the eyeglasses did serve a purpose. If nothing else, they added an executive quality to his features that made him appear more businesslike. Today was strictly business.

"Good morning, gentlemen." Walker greeted the fellows with good-natured formality as he stepped out of his private domain at the top of the stairway. Four pairs of eyes focused intently on him as he descended toward them. Looking more like a slightly bemused college professor than the owner of a boat-building operation, Walker moved with conscious ease, intent on dispelling the tension of the morning. "You're early. Payday already?" he joked. His keen eyes scanned the impatient expressions on their faces.

No response. "You guys just have too much panache to ask for your checks?" The glasses did not conceal the devilish glimmer in his eyes.

Dennis's bushy mustache twitched, signaling the presence of a brief smile, but Harry's brows drew together in an agonized expression. Walker's comic relief wasn't working. Not today. However motley a crew they might appear, there was too much at stake for each of them. Dennis had been a biker—a drifter, working on boats when he needed the money, shifting jobs with the seasons. But he'd stuck out a full year with Walker already. A part of him still longed to hit the road, but another part desperately wanted a reason to stay on.

And Harry needed security. After seventeen years with another boat maker, Harry had anticipated trouble in the economy and the shrinking demand for large expensive sailing yachts. Just as the bottom was dropping out of that big-boat market, he had taken the risk of coming over to work with Walker on a new line of smaller one-design sailboats. He had a son in college and he wanted to keep him there. Today he'd know if his instincts had been right.

For Hall Marine, the occasion they had assembled for—the unmolding of the first series of small high-tech sailing boats—was a crucial one. A new contender would be struggling for a niche in competitive sailing—a market that didn't welcome newcomers. To have a fighting chance on the racing scene, excellence of design was not enough; the new sailboat had to hit the market and the media with a big splash. An expensive splash.

But Walker Hall intended to get that press attention—without spending a cent of Hall Marine's meager financial reserves. Timing. That's what he counted on. He'd deliberately kept the entire project top secret, hidden away in a small industrial park in Tampa, Florida, until he was ready to go public. Now the months of intensive planning, research and labor were over. It was time to deliver.

Behind his wire-rimmed glasses, Walker's steely gray eyes glinted eagerly. "So what are we waiting for?" He tilted his head toward the closed doors across the cavernous warehouse that he'd transformed into a boat-manufacturing plant. Overhead, the rising sun threw diagonal streaks of gold through the skylights left open overnight for ventilation. Only the slightest trace of resin, sickly sweet and faintly reassuring, still remained in the air.

Walker's thick curly brown hair caught the light, accenting the few streaks of gray that only recently had appeared at his temples. Like the glasses, the silvery touches added a touch of distinction, an element of seriousness that he liked. There were times when this new mature image was helpful. Meanwhile, his well-worn faded jeans clung to lean, smooth muscled thighs. A loose knit shirt hung casually from straight shoulders more powerful than they first appeared. He seemed to be in no hurry, but there was a subtle energy in his movements and a startling intelligence in his eyes. He was a man often misread, sometimes by his own choosing.

"Let's break out the fleet," he said without giving away his underlying excitement.

Brandishing a rubber hammer, Walker led the small procession to the padlocked inner sanctum, the heart of the boat-production plant, where concepts became reality. Sliding open the doors, Walker headed straight for the first of four large wooden frames, each of which supported a sixteen-foot-long inverted mold. The molds contained either the hull or upper deck of two Phantoms—the first two production models of his prototype fiberglass sailing craft. With the hammer, he tapped a few strategic locations on the boat mold to loosen the form. Nothing budged.

Three pairs of callused hands grasped the sharp upper edges of the fiberglass hull.

"Come to poppa, baby," Harry whispered low. He switched on the pressure pump, sending a stream of air through a tube between the mold and the boat hull. For a moment, the two shapes clung fast to each other, then gradually the air insinuated its way along curves and crevices, easing them apart.

Walker pressed the heel of his hand against a captive air bubble, pushing hard and forcing it to spread. With a soft, dull popping sound, the two pieces—mold and hull—became separate. Streamlined and gleaming, the Phantom, with its clean lines and chocolate-brown hull, rose easily in the hands of its creators.

"Slick as butter on the bedroom doorknob," Jack Davis said, winking and grinning from ear to ear. All eyes scanned the newborn sailboat, examining the body for the most minute flaw as they hoisted and carried it like an offering toward the skeletal work rack. Turning it upside down on the rack, they all ran their fingertips over the lines and curves, grinning nervously as they studied her anxiously. Then their glances shifted to Hall, who bent low, studying her with a critical eye.

When Walker Hall placed his hands on her, he glided his fingertips lightly, knowingly, over her surface. With a slow spreading smile, he looked up at the foreman, his eyes shining with satisfaction and relief. They'd done it. She'd come off the design pages and into their midst just as he'd envisioned her. The Phantom had life. Structurally she was perfect.

"We got us a beauty," Dennis whispered at last, and patted the Harley eagle just over his heart. The rapid pulsing there was the lone symptom of excitement that he hadn't been able to suppress. More than anything, he'd wanted this lady to be good.

"Hallelujah," Harry sang, relief etched in his smooth dark skin.

Ross Cornelius said nothing. He rarely did. His blue eyes narrowed contemplatively. He crooked one eyebrow and nodded silently. Of the four craftsmen recruited by Walker for the Phantom team, Ross was the least talkative. Even quieter than Dennis. Somewhat shy, patient and whisper thin, Ross was part chemist, part artist, but all perfectionist, who worked at Walker's side as they tested and refined, helping to transform a mere sailboat into a work of art.

The Phantom definitely was art. State of the art in small racing sailboats. Dennis, Harry, Jack and Ross had all been surrogate fathers as well as midwives in the birthing process, and in the development of the newcomer each contributed a genius of his own. Dennis's forte still lay ahead. His expertise was in the finishing, the trimming and buffing. This would be his time to show off.

But it was Walker Hall who had conceived the Phantom. From initial drawings to computer-tested design, from casting of the two identical sets of production molds to the blending of resin and layering of the fiberglass, this had been Walker's baby. However, he shared her with her four very carefully chosen godfathers.

"Let's see the rest of her," Dennis said with an impatient tug of his mustache. Without a word the others moved with him to the next mold, repeating the same process as they lifted the sleek upper deck from the narrow mold that had given it a streamlined shape. Putting them together, top and bottom, made the boat complete.

When the parts had been temporarily assembled, there were two matching Phantoms sitting beneath the morning sun streaming through the overhead skylights. The five men stood around the still-unfinished yet unmistakably distinctive racing craft and toasted her—with a half-gallon of Florida orange juice. "To the Phantom..." Walker Hall poured the chilled juice into Styrofoam cups and broke the standing rule that no one eat, drink or smoke inside the factory. Today was worthy of an exception. But not a lengthy one. "Let's get to it," he said with icy determination as he held his cup aloft. "Let's finish them off."

"When do you think we can take 'em out for a test

run?" Jack shifted his eyes eagerly from the two Phantoms to Walker. There was still a lot of detail work left including adding the rigging and sails.

"We'll have them in the water this weekend," Walker insisted. He had taken off the wire-rimmed glasses and tucked them away in the pocket of his shirt. With the prospect of performance testing—of finally sailing them, another persona of Walker Hall was emerging. Now the lanky boat builder demonstrated the aggressiveness that had gained him a reputation over the years as a disciplined, competitive sailor. "I want both boats completely finished by Friday. If she sails like I think she will, then we've got a month to get the rest of our act in shape."

Ross looked at him uneasily. He'd heard that tension in Walker's voice before, and he knew it marked the end of a phase. Like an offshore racing yacht responding to a sudden shift in the wind, he was taking off in a new direction.

Walker had stuck to the legal restrictions of the contract he'd had with the boat company he left two years earlier. He had timed it all carefully—including the Phantom's debut, tying it all into the February Southern Ocean Racing Conference, thirty days off. Now they were all about to step into the whirlwind.

"Then let's get to it," Dennis said quietly. He dumped the empty cup into the trash can, crossed the room and flicked a cassette into the stereo tape player. This morning the raspy sounds of Willie Nelson filled the warehouse as each man moved in silence to a work station. By afternoon it might be Mozart.

"I've got some phone calls to make." Walker was grinning as he started back to his office. In more ways than one, he was making a comeback. The Phantom was just the beginning. He had another sailboat he'd labored over and a spectacular race on his agenda. For two years, Walker had virtually disappeared from the forefront of Florida's boat-building industry, and he had not competed with his former colleagues. Welcome or not, he was coming out of his retreat with a few surprises to show off. Once he sailed across Tampa Bay to St. Petersburg and into the S.O.R.C., the entire spectrum of the sailing community would feel the impact.

CHAPTER TWO

STANDING IN THE COOL BREEZE beneath the blue-and-white striped canopy at the members' entrance of the St. Petersburg Yacht Club Marina, Miranda was struck by a peculiar feeling of homecoming. The last time she had stood in this spot was at the S.O.R.C. six years before when she and Jeff had crewed aboard Sibyl and Bernie Albrecht's racing yacht, *Scimitar*.

The time between then and now seemed insignificant. The same cool wind was rippling the sails and sending the musical tapping and clicking sounds of sailboat rigging across the marina. The sailor's symphony filled the air: the flap of flags, the whine of tight lines in the wind, the rapping of halyards on a mast, the soft slap of water on the hulls of the boats. The spectacle Miranda surveyed was much as she remembered, unmistakably big-time regatta. This year there were at least ninety boats competing in the six classes—far more than in the past.

"Comin' through. Watch it."

Miranda stepped aside as a pushcart laden with bags of North sails came past. A few seconds later, a second sail shipment, boasting the emblem of Hood, was whisked along the dock. The fellow steering the second cart looked like a male model—blond, muscular, smiling and wearing a brilliant-blue shirt with the Hood sail logo.

Instantly this was all-too-familiar territory, complete with rules and pecking order. Beneath the casual sporting facade of the S.O.R.C., Miranda knew there was another kind of gamesmanship under way—involving power, prestige and very big business. But she was here to report on the races, not on what was going on behind the scenes. She had even made a few civilized concessions with her appearance so she'd blend in with the usual visitors. For one thing, her dark hair was now little more than chin length and styled so she looked less like a buccaneer's wench. Dressed in tawny shades of gold—a pale striped silk jacket, designer scarf looped casually inside the collar, slim slacks, soft knit sweater, she hadn't forgotten how to dress like the yachting set. No one would doubt that she belonged here.

Miranda flipped out the preliminary list of entries, silently focusing her thoughts on the multitude of boats moored before her. Fortunately, just as Sibyl had suggested, Miranda flew in early to be around for the week of trials, the preconference training runs. She'd arrived in St. Petersburg, dropped her suitcases off in the yacht club where Sibyl said they'd meet later, then she'd cut across the street to see the boats. She needed this first look around the marina to get the feel of the place and plan her strategy. For the two articles Sibyl requested, Miranda needed details, enough to avoid repetition, and there were a lot of entries to get to know.

For that week, Miranda would have plenty to keep

her busy. Sibyl was setting it up for her to go out on a few of the boats to watch the crews practicing together, working on technique before actual races began. All the parties and official social gatherings came later, once the scheduled S.O.R.C. briefings started. Then the magic show would begin.

"Phone call for any crew member from *Loving Cup*." The loudspeaker still sputtered with the same static sounds Miranda recalled.

"Will the owner of the white van parked in the road by the dock entrance please move it." More static.

"Who took my screwdriver?" A disembodied voice came from below the deck of a boat Miranda was passing. Miranda smiled, knowing the repairs would be going on endlessly, throughout the races. It was an inescapable part of sailing. Something was always getting lost, breaking or coming loose.

Already around the marina, the tension in the air made voices aboard the boats especially sharp and the movements of preoccupied crew members seemed overly efficient. Veteran sailors, first-timers, unassigned would-be crew members of every shape, size and age were milling about the docks. Some were attending to chores. Housekeeping. Some were new arrivals like herself, only they roamed past carrying duffel bags, hoping to sign on with crews still having open posts. Others were simply enjoying being seen aboard impressive boats. Everyone was coming on stage and the curtain was about to go up.

Miranda scanned the network of cement docks and wooden walkways between which the ocean-racing yachts were moored in colorful disarray. Like heraldic banners of knights attending a tournament, brightly colored flags flapped crisply overhead, suspended from masts, some towering more than a hundred feet into the air. Patches of color were everywhere. Mainsail booms, not needed presently for their intended function of spreading sails, served as makeshift clotheslines, airing out damp gear—towels, foul-weather suits, and miscellaneous clothing used that day by crews on practice maneuvers.

Jeff had once said that the clutter looked like an explosion in a high-class Laundromat. He was right.

Methodically Miranda made her way along the wider permanent walkways of gray cement, admiring one boat after another. Then she turned on to one of the adjacent walkways. Deftly she stepped around open toolboxes, bags of sails and stacks of gear and provisions waiting to be stored below decks. The St. Pete dockmaster had done a skillful job of fitting all the visiting S.O.R.C. boats into the limited spaces without displacing too many of the hundreds of other sailboats regularly moored there. Every slip was occupied by several boats tied on to one other, as far as the horseshoe-shaped marina spread. It looked as if hundreds of bright-feathered birds had settled into a small lagoon and crowded together wing to wing. Temporarily grounded, they would eye one another curiously until it was time to be airborne again.

The names on the sides and sterns of the boats summoned up bits of information in Miranda's mind. She recalled details of technical construction, races won and lost and the reputations of owners and crewmen. *Kialoa. Sorcery.* The two eighty-foot-long world-class maxiboats were anchored off from the others like royalty holding court with the lesser nobles. These were the largest competitors, the elite of class A. *The Shadow* and Vinnie Albrecht's new boat *Prophecy* were moored nearby, also competitors in class A. Miranda moved on smiling slightly as the boats she had been reading about took on personality before her eyes. Eventually she'd know them all by sight, but right now she'd take advantage of the open-house atmosphere to absorb what she could.

From a distance she could see the sixty-footer *Hambone*, the Birmingham yacht brokers' entry that Phil Pittman would be skippering in the class-A category. Sibyl had been careful to mention that Pittman himself was scheduled to fly in sometime that night. So was Miranda's father. But Miranda was relieved not to be facing either of them yet. That time would come soon enough.

Miranda turned in the opposite direction, away from *Hambone* and its impressive neighbors, feeling overwhelmed by both their size and equipment. Massive hydraulic systems to adjust sails and computerized electronic navigation guides made the mammoth maxis impersonal and mechanical—expensive and impressive triumphs of technology. Even the smaller boats now had similar sophisticated apparatus inside and out, but these boats didn't fit Miranda's idea of sailing. She preferred the smaller racing yachts, simply equipped, where manpower not machinery made the difference. In simpler boats, the human factor was critical. From choosing the right sail to maneuvering for position, the variables were excitingly personal.

"Now that's my kind of boat." Miranda smiled suddenly as she made her way toward one entry, a forty-three-footer—midnight blue with a brilliant-yellow side stripe. It stood out from the others because not all its equipment was brand-new. There was nothing shabby or makeshift about it, but the fact that certain parts had been recycled from other boats was unusual enough to be intriguing. The teak toe rail caught her attention first. Instead of expensive aluminum extrusions where the hull joined the deck, beautiful aged teak had been cut and skillfully set in place. The fit was flawless, but the wood grain didn't match perfectly. Some pieces were a few shades darker than others.

Miranda moved closer. The leather handgrip on the huge steering wheel was dark with age, oiled so it was still pliant and serviceable, but the expensive leather was crisscrossed with rows of neat stitches where cracks had been patched. The metal binnacle post that supported the huge destroyer wheel was shiny but scratched in several places, and the plate mounting it onto the deck had too many holes, indicating it, too, had been salvaged from some other boat.

Obviously she was someone's very personal project, someone who knew what he was doing—he just hadn't had the money for the cosmetic touches to make the boat a dazzler. Knowing what care had been taken outfitting the boat reminded Miranda of the first year at Calvert Charters. She and Jeff had spent hours laboring on the used boats they bought, purchasing scrap-yard parts in order to get the most mileage out of every cent they had. Someone had done the same with this one, put her together on a tight budget. What he lacked in money, he had compensated for in time and skill. Moored amid other official entries, the forty-three-foot midsize boat had a spunky appeal, a definite personality. Miranda couldn't find it on her list, so she wrote down its name.

Persistence.

She was apparently a late entry, one that hadn't made it into the preview information package Miranda had received before she left Tortola. Enthralled, Miranda knew she'd found a favorite to watch throughout the S.O.R.C.

Hastily she sketched the layout of the boat on her note pad, then backed away a few paces, shielding her eyes as she looked up at the rigging. On the rigging there were the obligatory hydraulics to bend the mast and help shape the sail. Those devices were competitive necessities. But even the hydraulics didn't detract from the other human touches. She was a beauty.

Walker had been watching the lady in gold for several minutes. He'd seen her earlier on his way to the marina office. Then on his return trip, he spotted her again, moving from one boat to another, curious and unhurried but distinctly aloof. But when she zeroed in on his boat, he stepped to the opposite side of the dock, peeled off his shirt and pretended to be soaking up the sun. But he was lying in wait. Frankly, he'd had about enough. The first time, the race committee had taken eight hours to measure *Persistence*. Then they came back the next week, two officials this time, and he'd hauled her out of the water again while they started all over. *Persistence* was still in the class-E range with ten other boats, but someone didn't want her to stay there.

Walker Hall suspected his former partner, Mason Porter. Porter had been highly visible, politicking with everyone from the yacht-club commodore to the members of the judging panel, but it was the times he wasn't visible that made Walker uneasy. Porter's entry *Elan* was up against *Persistence*, and Porter's reputation as a boat builder was in jeopardy if Walker could beat him with a boat from the identical mold, but with modifications that Walker made himself. That was exactly what Walker intended to do.

Walker had taken apart the rule book and turned it inside out, examining every nuance and condition. If he needed to, he could turn the tables, quoting rule, amendment and subsection by page and line number. He knew it might come to that. Walker Hall's tactics were ungentlemanly, and the old regime did have a tendency to close ranks and protect their own.

Now they were sending in a spy, Mata Hari in tawny tweed.

With that shadow of a smile, she had given herself away. Like a tigress, in for the kill, she had prowled the area, spotting and closing in on *Persistence*. Solitary. Predatory. She had a sense of purpose about her. Walker recognized something in the aristocratic face that was vaguely familiar. He couldn't place her, and he wanted to know who sent her and what she was looking for.

He waited until she backed up another step, almost

bumping into him, before he spoke to her—abruptly. He spoke clearly and deliberately, without moving from his spot. "It's a mast," he said in a tone that was clearly patronizing. "And the shorter horizontal one is called a boom. As in 'lowering the...'"

He liked the way he caught her off guard. Her dark silky hair swung as she spun toward him, her expression one of obvious irritation.

"Thank you, but I do know what the parts of the rigging are called." She didn't intend to sound as curt as she did, but Miranda didn't appreciate the distraction or the unsolicited information. Slightly embarrassed at being treated like a novice, she smoothed back her hair and opened her note pad. She wanted to look efficient.

"Are you with the spot-check team?" Walker persisted in talking to her.

"Oh no, I'm not with the inspection committee. I just happen to be very impressed by this boat." This time Miranda's reply simply sounded polite.

"Shows you've got taste," he quipped, pulling his visor down over his eyes as he stepped down onto *Persistence*.

"So does whoever built this boat." Her remark came out a bit too glib, even though Miranda meant it.

Walker stopped, turning to look up at her. "Who are you, lady?" Walker's tone was civil enough but his full, straight mouth was expressionless. His eyes were masked by the shade. "What do you really want?"

"I'm just an observer," Miranda answered, bewildered by the undercurrent of hostility.

"Your observation technique isn't particularly subtle." Again his comment hovered between humor and cynicism. Clearly he was the one doing the close scrutiny now, studying her with a trace of defiance in the tilt of his chin, his eyes still obscured by shadow. He could have been taken for one of any number of young crewmen making themselves conspicuous on the dockside. Posing. Showing off the body. Miranda had seen the type before. The Boat Coolie. B.C. for short.

There were other less-respectable names for the position, but from his cocky attitude, Miranda knew she'd encountered a B.C.—the full-time boat hand, Jack-of-all-trades, acting as if he owned the boat he was hired to look after. A vagabond breed, B.C.'s traveled the racing circuits from season to season maintaining the boats. During the races, they crewed. When a race ended, they dismantled the boat for transporting, made sure it got to its next destination, then they readied it in its new location for the next competition. Like a watchdog, this boat coolie was bristling because she was poking about his territory.

"I keep thinking I've seen you somewhere." He stepped forward, bracing his hands on his hips, studying her. Miranda almost laughed out loud. That was a typical male opening line. If he thought she was one of the available and accommodating yachting groupies, "boat bunnies" who frequented the marina to look at the men instead of the boats, he was mistaken. Miranda had seen enough of regattas to avoid getting involved with any crewman. The touches of gray in this one's unruly brown hair suggested he was a bit older than the customary B.C.'s. Mid-thirties, Miranda guessed, but the maturity was deceptive. He was still acting like a kid, following the racing circuit, looking for action on or off the water.

"That's a line I've heard before," Miranda said dryly, shaking her head. "Your technique isn't particularly subtle, either."

"Lady, if I were interested in lines, I could have come up with a better one than that." His response was quick and not playful at all. He crossed the deck, approaching the dock where Miranda stood. With one leap, he landed beside her. Standing an even six feet, he moved to one side so his shadow fell across her, blocking the bright rays of the morning sun and casting her in cool shade. His shade. Silhouetted against the sky, his tanned shoulders, covered with a faint film of perspiration in spite of the cool air, were like satin, edged in light. In a coarse, purely physical way, he was attractive. Obviously he knew it. Miranda stepped back to put a little distance between them.

"I won't attack you in public," he teased, coolly amused that she yielded some space. "I remember faces, and I've seen yours somewhere," he insisted. "I'm trying to place you. It's nothing personal." The edge of impatience in his voice made her feel foolish, like a presumptuous child who had spoken out of turn.

"I think I'd have remembered if we met. We haven't." Miranda answered quietly, trying to ease out of an unnecessary confrontation that threatened to become distinctly personal. She had no intention of getting into a dispute with this man, nor did she want to encourage his attention. There would be plenty of other females passing by who would be more receptive. "I still think this is an exceptionally fine boat." As she directed the conversation back to a safe subject, she met his gaze, and held it. Her message was the same as his—nothing personal.

Gray eyes, remote as a smoke screen, didn't waver from hers. He crossed his arms over his bare chest, turning his attention to *Persistence*. He got the point. "She is exceptional," he acknowledged with unqualified pride.

Miranda felt a little guilty that she'd been so brusque. Glancing sideways, she made a quick appraisal of his face, which was now more visible beneath the visor. Up close, the charcoal eyes revealed flecks of blue like deep water in a stormy winter sea. The only suggestion of softness was in the thick lashes, brown like his hair. The rest of his features—straight nose, full mouth, creases in his cheeks that would turn into dimples—were distinctive.

The face was striking. Not handsome, but interesting. Even with the ridiculous visor forcing his unruly dark curls over his ears and pressing strands of hair against his forehead, it was the kind of good-looking face that would turn women's heads. Then there was the body. Nicely proportioned, trim, yet well defined in all the right places. Being objective, Miranda had to admit he had a certain virile appeal. But he wasn't the kind of man she could take seriously. He was a boat coolie.

Suddenly he turned and glanced at her again, his eyes twinkling with amusement because she was studying him. So he took a good look at her, not surreptitiously as she'd been looking at him. The fellow was bolder than she was. His eyes traveled tip to toe, slowing at strategic points. He did not miss a thing.

"Will you stop staring!" Miranda sputtered, her brown eyes flashing indignantly. "Your observation techniques could do with a little refining."

"Maybe I just need more practice." He tugged the visor off his head and looked down at her. "If you really aren't on the race committee, what's your reason for checking *Persistence* so meticulously?" He leaned closer, his bare shoulder brushing against her jacketed one. Then, to make sure she didn't think the contact was accidental, he nudged her again. "Well...?"

Miranda smiled. The man had a sense of humor and a certain tenacity that she respected. Even though he pretended to be playful, he was still concerned primarily with the boat.

"I was just taking some notes for an article about the S.O.R.C."

His eyes shifted, taking in her tawny outfit in another head-to-toe sweep. When their eyes met, she knew he didn't believe her. "What were you sketching on your note pad?" His question was conversational, and he was even smiling slightly, but there was wariness, not humor, in the steely gray eyes. His breath fluttered over her cheek and rippled against her throat.

Instinctively Miranda pressed the note pad against her chest, feeling her color rise when his eyes followed her movement. Everything she'd jotted down so far was hasty, amateurish, intended for her alone.

"Since I like accurate press coverage, I'd be glad to

check your facts so far." He held out his hand, challenging her to relinquish the note pad. From the set of his jaw to the cynical smile, she knew unless she passed him the notes, the civility he'd been showing was about to end. Wanting to reassure him, she handed him the note pad.

He barely glanced at it. He simply skimmed the page, cocked one eyebrow in apparent satisfaction, then thrust the open notebook back at her. "The owner's name is Walker Hall." He waited while she wrote it down. "He also modified the design and built the boat."

"Walker Hall." Miranda nodded as she wrote. At some time in her years with her father at Vaughn Marine Hardware, she'd heard that name. She'd been Vaughn's liaison between top executives for the larger yacht-building companies and the numerous suppliers of marine hardware. "I must know him," she noted. "What company is he with?" She hesitated a moment, then looked up when he didn't answer.

"He used to be with Porter Yachts. Now he owns his own company." Again suspicion clouded the gray eyes.

"That Walker Hall..." Now Miranda remembered. Mason Porter was an associate of her father, and Porter Yachts had always been a big account. She'd heard of a shake-up in that company a couple of years earlier, and Walker Hall was the man who caused it. In passing on the gossip, Sibyl had said only that Hall was an ungrateful fellow, an upstart, who'd moved up through the Porter company, then left Mason Porter in a huff when business hit a slump.

"Now what does that mean? That Walker Hall?" he said irritably. "If we've never met, as you insist, then why is my name so familiar?"

"Your name." Miranda almost choked. "You're Walker Hall?" It was more of a statement than a question. The half-naked man who stood next to her was no boat coolie after all, and neither he nor the boat he'd crafted fit the image of an upstart.

"I know who I am," he said calmly. "It's you and your information I'm not sure about." And from the chill in his voice, she knew they were heading for another confrontation.

"I'm Miranda Calvert." She introduced herself with more composure than she felt. "I really am doing articles, one for *Racing* and one for *Offshore* magazine. My interest in your boat is strictly professional." That wasn't quite the truth. Her initial attraction to *Persistence* might have been objective and businesslike, but it had hastily turned personal. The affection Miranda felt for the boat was instinctive. And now Miranda felt a similar admiration for the man whose hands had built her and whose possessiveness now seemed perfectly justified.

"Then you'd better learn to spell her name. You'll be using it a lot," he added confidently. "You spelled it with an *A*. It should be *E*."

He was right.

"I'll fix that." With a tight smile, Miranda corrected her error. She already felt foolish enough mistaking Hall for a boat coolie. Having the handsome boat builder correct her spelling made it worse. If he was deliberately trying to fluster her, he was succeeding.

The creases framing Hall's self-satisfied grin deepened into the dimples she suspected he had. Instead of adding a childlike innocence to his smile, they gave him a rakish look, almost devilish. His laughing eyes told her he knew she had thought he was a boat coolie, but no amount of distance she put between them would dampen their mutual attraction.

Miranda forced a nonchalant smile and fought the urge to bolt from his presence. Boat coolie or boat builder, she didn't want to get involved. "Good luck with the races, Mr. Hall. Thank you for your time. Perhaps we'll talk again." She was taking control by concluding the unsolicited interview.

Walker reached out and grasped her upper arm gently, but firmly enough to bring her closer to him. "We're not through. We'll talk now." Again his low voice caused an unexpected rush of pleasure. "You seem to know something about my background. But I don't know yours. Let's solve the mystery."

Miranda indignantly began peeling his hand from her arm. "I can see that *Persistence* is a trait both you and your boat share. But there's no need to get physical, Mr. Hall." As she spoke, her fingertips touched his skin, the roughness of the calluses oddly delighting her. They were a sailor's hands, tanned and leathery. Like the boat he had built, the hands revealed imperfections, but they possessed a competence and strength, a sensuous eloquence that made her feel strangely excited. Miranda looked up at him, uncertainly, disturbed by his ability to trigger such a confusion of feeling with just a touch. Abruptly the amusement that had sparkled in Walker Hall's eyes turned to something darker.

"Relax, Miranda," he said as if he'd read her mind. "If I were after your body, I'd let you know it." He pulled the visor back over the crop of curly dark hair and the expression in his smoky eyes was again lost in the shadows. "You underestimate me." With a terse nod, Walker released her. "Information is what I want."

"Surely we can talk—civilly," Miranda said, determined to end this encounter on a more genteel note. "I don't like caveman tactics."

Walker Hall was no longer looking at her. He stood on the deck and stared out over the marina. "Then make some connections."

Miranda knew what he wanted. "You did business with Vaughn Marine a few years ago," she explained. "I handled the important transactions. Porter Yachts was one of our accounts." He turned and stared at her.

"I'm Miranda Calvert Vaughn. Howard Vaughn is my father." Miranda knew that fact alone would provide a focus for anyone involved with yachting. Vaughn's name meant money, power and the finest in marine equipment. It was possible Hall had seen her somewhere with her father. But she didn't like the peculiar light in the gray eyes.

"Howard Vaughn..." Walker Hall contemplated her features as if trying to recognize the image of the marine-hardware king in his daughter's face. But Miranda knew the similarity wasn't there. The face was pure Calvert, elegant and finely boned. Walker's expression underwent a subtle change. Smoke screen. The remoteness was back. Walker's earlier caution surfaced. He'd finally been able to slip her into a category. She was a Vaughn—again.

Miranda had almost forgotten what it was like to be pigeonholed that way. In the islands, she'd become her own person. Here, she was part of a tradition. Now it was as if everything else about her didn't count. Combing her long fingers through her hair in a gesture of frustration, she sighed and shifted her gaze away from his.

"Why did you drop the Vaughn?"

He was prying into her personal affairs, and Miranda knew she could cut him off with a curt comment. That would end that. But she looked closely at the man whose callused hands had built *Persistence*, the same hands that had held her arm so firmly and sent waves of warmth coursing through her. In spite of her instinct to be cautious, she wasn't sure she wanted to end the encounter at all. "I'm not being evasive, but that is a long and involved story," Miranda spoke at last.

"Did you drop it as a declaration of independence?" Walker's slight smile seemed more sympathetic than mocking. "Howard Vaughn can be quite a dictator."

"I noticed that about him myself," Miranda admitted with a rueful smile. "However my father prefers to think of himself as an enlightened despot. He insists he rules for the good of his people, whether they agree or not."

Walker smiled at that. She was quick, very clever.

"Apparently he wasn't enlightened enough in your case."

"True. A few years back, my father and I reached an impasse." Miranda kept the tone light, but her brown eyes were definitely serious. "We couldn't agree on which of us was leading my life."

Again an amused smile softened Hall's expression. "I felt something similar to that at Porter Yachts," he added. "And how are things now between you and your father?" His inquiry was too pointed to be simple curiosity. Something told Miranda that Walker Hall's interest was more than casual.

"My relationship with my father is a little uncertain. I haven't seen him face-to-face for five years. Neither has my brother, Jeff." She could tell this information had short-circuited whatever scenario Walker had been envisioning. "Coming here to the S.O.R.C. puts us on neutral ground. We have to see what we can work out in order to come up with a mutually agreeable family package. The bitterness between us was temporary," Miranda said cautiously. "My independence is not." For a few seconds they eyed each other like adversaries appraising the opposition. They both knew they were in sensitive territory.

"Good luck with the negotiations," Walker said with sincerity. "I've had my differences with your father, but as long as we're going to be traveling the same route for a few weeks, maybe you and I can be friends." Walker reached toward her and offered his hand.

"Friendly, perhaps," Miranda agreed up to a point. She tried not to register any sign of sensual pleasure when his rough hand enveloped hers and held it. But the warmth spread through her, and he didn't relax his grip until her eyes met his—straight on, like equals. The transformation in his expression was gradual. A slow grin spread, deepening the creases in his cheeks into parentheses framing his dazzling smile.

"If you've got a few minutes, come on aboard, Miranda," Walker said, inviting her onto his prized possession. The man had an uncanny knack of finding the chinks in her emotional armor, and getting a closer look at *Persistence* was one. With the invitation, Miranda felt as if she'd been promoted to a higher level of regard in his estimation. Without understanding why, that respect was suddenly important to her—and so was Walker Hall. She considered him aggressively territorial, brash, even arrogant. He certainly had a way of getting to the point promptly. But now he was smiling as she boarded *Persistence*, and Miranda didn't mind his straight talk. Instead, she was finding him fascinating and increasingly disconcerting.

Walker was finding something else—a thermos. Then he sat cross-legged on the deck, and poured each of them a cup of hot tea. When he held one cup out to her, she sat next to him. "So what have you been doing the last few years?" he asked. "Apparently you're not still working with Vaughn Marine." He leaned forward, cupping his mug of tea between his hands. "It hasn't been years since I've seen that face and it doesn't have anything to do with Howard Vaughn." This time Miranda accepted his remark without comment.

"My brother and I run a sailboat-chartering operation in Tortola." Miranda barely had the words out when Walker's eyes seemed to light up.

"Tortola." He'd found the missing connection.

"You've been there?"

He shook his head. "No, but I was in the Bahamas. And I remember some kind of clipping." He nodded. "That's it. I've seen your picture. You're the vigilante editor."

Miranda's mouth dropped open slightly.

"I'm the what...?"

"You're the one who made such a commotion over Jack Flint's boathouse in Tortola that he pulled up stakes and moved." Walker's laughter washed over her. Miranda was surprised how delighted he was to place her. "Flint has an article you wrote raking him over the coals. Your picture was with it, posted on his bait-house wall. That's where I've seen you, complete with a nasty caption he'd scribbled under your picture."

Miranda felt the heat in her cheeks, recalling the Flint incident. "I can imagine the kind of graffiti he'd come up with. He said quite a few nasty things right to my face when I confronted him with a list of customers' complaints." She bit her lip thoughtfully, remembering having to face Flint's torrent of expletives without registering the alarm she had felt. The man's outburst had frightened her, but she had not flinched, at least not outwardly, and she had not backed down.

"Flint overpriced his goods." Miranda stated the facts. "It was as clear-cut as that. Customers complained. I checked it out. I advised Flint that the Charter Operators would take action if he didn't become more reasonable with his pricing. I won't tell you what his response was." Anyone who knew Jack Flint would guess his reply was both crude and explicit.

"So you closed him down." Walker's expression was inscrutable.

"I didn't close Flint down," she answered evenly. "I reported my findings in the newsletter you saw. The Charter Board issued an advisory urging people to avoid dealing with Flint. His business dropped off, so he left Tortola. I can't say I'm particularly sorry."

"I know a few folks who are sorry," Walker countered. "His new clientele. Flint moved to Nassau," he informed her. "He's set up business in a marina there and is still overpricing things. And he's still got your picture pinned up on the wall of the bait house. Of course his side of the story is that some hysterical broad got angry when he threw her over for another woman, so she made trouble for him by lying about his business." Walker held up one hand to silence her protest. "You don't even have to dignify his story with a rebuttal."

"The issue was a local one. It should have stayed that way." Miranda fell silent, brooding over the outrage of being put on display. "He has no right to spread lies about me."

"No right at all," Walker agreed.

Miranda stared into her cup of tea, preoccupied and stinging from Flint's revenge.

"You aren't thinking of playing vigilante and going after him again?" The look Walker gave her was thoughtful, almost challenging. When she hesitated before answering, Walker looked slightly disappointed.

"I've got enough to do with these articles to keep me busy," Miranda said simply. The thought of confronting Flint once they got to Nassau had crossed her mind. "One round with Flint was sufficiently traumatic," Miranda declared.

"Too bad. Sometimes being civilized has its limitations," he teased.

"I've got too many people I need to interview about the S.O.R.C. to give any time to Flint," Miranda replied, defending her decision. Walker looked at her then shrugged, letting the matter drop.

"You might be able to pry a secret or two out of me if you put your mind to it." Now Walker's tone was openly seductive.

Miranda shot him a cautious look. "I'm not interested in secrets. I'm interested in facts that I can use publicly."

"Do you mean you're not intrigued by the comeback of the turncoat Walker Hall and a showdown between him and the blue bloods of yachting?" The cynicism in his voice had an immediate effect on Miranda. She recognized the slick PR package he'd constructed out of the Porter Yachts split, and she wanted no part of it.

"Is that the angle you're using? The outcast returns?"

"That's one of them," Walker said enigmatically.

"A bit melodramatic perhaps, but maybe it will catch on with some other reporter." She patted his shoulder playfully, but the effect was not one of lighthearted camaraderie that she planned. Instead Walker captured her hand beneath his, holding it there. He rubbed his roughened thumb over her smooth fingers, skimming the polished sculpted nails, another civilized concession she'd made for the trip there. While her palm pressed against the cool curve of his shoulder, they both remained motionless. Suddenly when their eyes met, the coolness was gone. The innocent act of friendship became far more intimate.

"I could get to like this." He drew her hand onto his chest where the mat of silky dark hairs tickled her palm. The air around them seemed electrified. The energy of their cross-fire conversation had led them into something physical and undeniably charged with sensuous voltage.

"I couldn't." She lied. Her senses were flooded with aching reminders of another body, another man, and the few who had tried to fill that emptiness and failed. Yet this man suddenly awakened possibilities. "I'm not looking for anything, Walker." She spoke calmly in spite of the slowly rising body heat she felt. "I came here to tie up the loose ends of some memories I left behind."

"Well, I'll be honest with you. I came here to tie up a few loose ends of my own. I'm here to win the S.O.R.C." The reply was blunt. Determined. "I can't let anyone or anything get in the way. I need the win."

Miranda had seen this kind of competitiveness before—in regattas, in her father, in Phil Pittman. Winning was everything. Other priorities were adjusted accordingly. And after the S.O.R.C. there would be other races. The America's Cup. The Admiral's Cup.

The Canadian Cup. The Sardinia Cup. There was always another competition.

"I certainly don't intend to get in anyone's way."

"You already have, lady." With infinite care, Walker Hall lifted her hand and pressed a kiss into her palm. Then reluctantly, he let go. "I just don't know what we're going to do about it." This time, when the gray eyes fixed upon her, the message was clear. Walker was issuing both a warning and an invitation that would be impossible to forget.

"This is ridiculous." Miranda threw her hands into the air. "I don't even know you and you don't know me. I came here to see someone else." She had to tell him the truth.

Walker considered her words a moment, then shrugged. "Maybe that's best for both of us." He leaned back, pensive but apparently unflustered by the emotional roller-coaster ride they'd been on. Miranda was once more struck by the similarities between this man and his boat. *Persistence*, like its owner, seemed self-possessed, confident and at ease. But the readiness was there, a precision and power that could be activated in an instant.

"What's the next move?" he asked point-blank, trying to decipher Miranda's expression.

"I know what my next move is." She stood and stared down at him. "I say bon voyage, get off this boat and go on with my business." Her words were perfectly rational, her features composed, but neither she nor Walker moved. Miranda's heart pounded in her chest as a confusion of thoughts tumbled from the shadows of her mind. Effortlessly Walker had reactivated the desire deep inside her. Until now, it had only been a memory. Looking at his bare chest, Miranda could imagine nestling against him, stretched out under the brilliant-blue sky, watching the powder-puff clouds. It would be idyllic, romantic and foolish. Wanting someone and being able to keep him were not the same. In six weeks they would be going separate ways. And Miranda remembered the sadness that came with endings.

Walker sat up immediately and reached toward her.

"What are you going to do?" Miranda asked apprehensively.

"I am going to spare you the embarrassment of being thrown to the deck and ravished in public. I'm a quick learner, and I remember what you said about caveman tactics." He held her hand and led her toward the dock. "But I find you hard to resist. You take care of your business, and I'll take care of mine. Then we'll see what happens." His fingers slipped loose of hers as she took the giant step onto the dock. "If you need an excuse to get away from your other commitments anytime, remember I'm very good at checking your spelling."

Miranda did not answer. She walked away from the mooring without looking back, her heart hammering a protest.

Across the marina aboard *Limelight*, Sibyl Albrecht would be waiting for her with an itinerary of cocktail parties and press conferences and a closet full of designer dresses to remind Miranda how luxurious civilization could be. Miranda suspected her old friend would be opening up her entire bag of tricks in an effort to lure her back to the States permanently. Then there was Phil Pittman and her father, with whatever they might have up their sleeves.

Walker Hall had appeared in the midst of all of them with his own bag of tricks, and Miranda had no idea what he might pull out of it. But she knew it would be fascinating. On her way back to the castle, the princess had wandered far from the high walls and had fallen under the spell of a seafaring gypsy with smoky eyes. One with callused hands and persistence, and a penchant for winning.

CHAPTER THREE

WALKER PILOTED *Persistence* through the narrow opening, inching past other moored boats in the marina, aiming for Tampa Bay. Cloaked from head to toe in foul-weather gear, his crew crouched on the deck, keeping out of the chilly wind and sporadic showers that had skipped across the area since sunrise. It wasn't typical Florida weather, but they needed a shakedown run. He decided on a quick trip from Tampa Bay under the double-arched Sunshine Skyway Bridge into the Gulf of Mexico. This course was the same as they'd sail at the start of the first S.O.R.C. race.

"Don't show off too much," Walker had cautioned the men aboard. "We'll try it with the one-point-five-ounce spinnaker, just to get the feel of it. Save the big chute for Saturday." Even now he didn't want anyone to know how well *Persistence* could perform. To win the overall S.O.R.C., they only needed to place high in their class in a couple of the six events and to be consistent enough and lucky enough not to have a disaster in the others. The overall average was what counted. Even that was adjusted according to the handicap indicated by the International Offshore Rating. On adjusted time, a steady performance by a smaller boat could win over an uneven performance by a huge magnificent maxi. Walker just couldn't afford any mistakes. Pushing too hard in a trial run in this fluky weather was taking an unnecessary risk with the equipment as well as the crew. They'd hold back until it really counted.

As *Persistence* passed the warning beacon on the jetty protecting the marina entrance, Walker could see the miles of sails of other racing yachts scattered across the dull-gray horizon. A lot of other competitors were out refining their techniques and testing equipment. Amid them all, he spotted the red maxi *Prophecy*, and he knew the slim figure aboard, the one in the yellow slicker, was she. He'd seen Miranda climb aboard the big boat hours ago with binoculars, cameras and rain gear. She was easy to spot. Everyone else aboard wore scarlet foul-weather gear with the *Prophecy* logo. Miranda stood out like a spot of sunshine in their midst.

"Well, are we going to raise 'em?" Dennis bellowed from his position on the foredeck. Braced against the metal railings of the pulpit, he'd been facing seaward, looking like a mustachioed figurehead decorating the prow of the boat. Until now, they'd had to keep the sails down, but they were in open water and it was time to turn off the engine and use the wind.

"Let's do it," Walker responded, and instantly the eight men above deck shifted to their posts. Voices called out directions, massive sails rustled in the breeze and pulleys made ratchet sounds as the billowing sails leaped to full height. There were a few seconds of wild flapping as the men called "grinders" cranked the lines tight on the winches and pulled the sails into tight winglike shapes. Then the hectic sounds subsided; there was nothing but the soothing rush of the wind and the sweep of water against the hull. The sense of being in touch with the primitive natural forces sent a shiver of relief through Walker's body. It was like breaking free from civilization, and Walker loved his freedom.

Scanning the boats ahead, Walker could see *Prophecy* turning back toward him, apparently finished for the morning. He held his course knowing they would pass close to him, trying to tell himself that it was the boat he wanted to get a closer look at. But it was the lady, Miranda, a name that ran like a melody in his mind. And he knew that getting close to her was risky.

She'd already gotten under his skin with her sophistication that was softened by her almost childlike curiosity. Her enthusiasm over his boat was so darn sincere, and she'd picked up on all the modifications of *Persistence* with the insight of a pro. Yet her dark eyes radiated a sadness as eloquently as they sparkled with delight or anger. Every experience was in her eyes, carefully concealed but so close to the surface—the estrangement with her father, the abuse Jack Flint had subjected her to, this "someone else" she'd come to see—all of it hurt her, yet she carried on smoothly. She didn't like scenes—at least not public ones. He depended on them. For the next few weeks, everything Walker had to do was public—so starting anything with her didn't make sense. Besides, she had problems enough without him making more for her.

Prophecy now was almost upon them, and Miranda was there, right up front. With her feet sticking out over the edge, yellow slicker flapping, and her zoom-lens camera aimed straight at him, she sat surrounded by men in red. So he forced a grin that was decidedly photogenic and waved. Everyone aboard *Persistence* watched and hooted, posing for the camera. Miranda fired off a few shots then looked up over the camera at Walker. Her face was flushed and damp from the spray of saltwater, her smile radiant, and she didn't look vulnerable at all.

"Good lookin' boat you've got there, Mr. Hall," she yelled. Miranda's dark hair was streaming in the wind and her voice sounded clear as a bell. Walker wished he could reach out and grab her.

"Thank you, ma'am," he called back, giving a slight bow. Dennis and Jack nudged each other then bowed, too.

"Who's she?" Ross Cornelius asked from just behind Walker's shoulder.

Walker hesitated for a second, as a number of possible answers leaped to mind. Most of them were merely wishful thinking. "Howard Vaughn's daughter." Walker tried to make it sound as forbidding as it needed to be. That relationship had been strong enough to bring her back here, and her connection with Vaughn and all that implied was one obstacle that wouldn't go away.

"Geez. . .too bad." With that cryptic comment Ross summarized what Walker had been telling himself since he met her the day before. She was a Vaughn. She owned a marina and a charter fleet. He was a boat builder without a single production order on the agenda and a precarious financial situation that depended on the outcome of the S.O.R.C. They weren't in the same league at all, but he couldn't stop looking at her.

If he'd seen her like this first, vibrant and windblown, it wouldn't have been so complicated. He would have acted on impulse and not have let her leave him the previous afternoon. But he wouldn't have held on for long. He never did. They would have made a night of it, maybe more, then continued on their separate ways. Like ships that pass in the night, he thought as he watched her now. Walker would have laughed out loud at the appropriateness of the phrase, but *Prophecy* was right next to them swallowing *Persistence* in her shadow, stealing away the wind from their sails. The image of Miranda riding the waves on the massive red maxiboat with the word *Prophecy* just beneath her feet was too significant to be amusing.

Sooner or later, Walker figured he might meet a woman he wouldn't be able to shake, one whose face would linger in his mind. He just wished it had been another time and another woman, one who wouldn't take special care and who would leave him when it was time. He'd come this far alone, not wanting or needing anyone, and he couldn't have handled his life any other way. Starting over in the boat business was all right for a solitary man: no one waiting, no one expecting anything. Now, with the pressure building, he had to stumble into someone like her. Maybe he was out of her class, but *Persistence* wasn't.

"Let's get the damn spinnaker flying. Get it out," Walker snapped, unable to hold back the frustration he felt.

"What's with him?" Dennis said, jerking his thumb at the skipper.

"Yellow fever." Jack Davis chuckled. "Caught it from the gal in the slicker."

"That isn't funny." Ross Cornelius put an end to the banter. "Set the spinnaker pole. Let's see some of that precision you guys bragged about."

Dennis pushed back the hood of his jacket, letting the wind whip his hair like a pony's tail. The dampness had already plastered his mustache against his face.

"Move it, Scaramouch," Jack teased him.

"Listen, dude," Dennis said, flexing his muscles slightly, as if he were going to put his short, slim buddy off the pulpit and into the bay with one quick punch.

"Knock it off, you two," Walker bellowed. "Fly that chute and get off the foredeck."

Moving efficiently, Jack and Dennis performed the maneuver perfectly, then took their places with the others on the high side, the weather rail of the boat. Until there was another sail change, all they had to do was sit. Glumly Jack leaned over, dangling his arms between the horizontal lifelines, nudging Dennis's shoulder. "Get out your harmonica, and play us a tune. I have a feelin' we're gonna need something to cheer us up."

Walker kept *Persistence* heading downwind, her yellow-and-blue striped spinnaker puffed way out in front as she rolled gently with the uneven winds. Dennis tapped the silver harmonica against his palm then played a country-and-western song while the waves beat out the rhythm against the hull. With the double arches of the Skyway Bridge looming ahead and the sun finally breaking through the clouds, it should have been one of those remarkably synchronized moments when the entire universe seemed to work in harmony. But for Walker Hall, it wasn't. He was thinking of the dark-eyed lady and ships that pass in the night. She was sailing into a safe harbor just as he was putting out to sea.

"THE RIDE WAS WONDERFUL. Thank you, Vinnie. Tell Sibyl that I got some great photos. But I have to run. I've got to get a call in to Jeff," Miranda said in a rush the moment *Prophecy* docked. Soaking wet from the knees down, and glowing with excitement, she was anxious to head for the yacht-club phone booths to call home. In three weeks, Jeff would be meeting them in Lauderdale to help navigate on Vinnie Albrecht's boat, and Miranda had a lot to say about *Prophecy* and about the other sailboats she'd been watching. In spite of her personal preference in sailboats, she had developed more than a grudging appreciation of the huge maxiboats during the early-morning run, and Miranda needed to share her impressions with someone who would understand. She also wanted to talk about *Persistence*. Jeff would appreciate the boat's peculiarities.

The row of identical Plexiglas cubicles, specially installed to accommodate the hundreds of crewmen and boat owners at the S.O.R.C., were all in use when Miranda strode into the hallway. Her deck shoes squished with each step. Shivering from the cold, Miranda slipped her feet out of the wet shoes, rubbing her bare soles against the soft carpeting. It helped. Then she peeled off the yellow slicker, shaking off the dampness and folding it over her arm.

Gradually the warmth began to creep back into her toes as she waited her turn, catching snatches of the varied accents and languages of the people passing by. This year's S.O.R.C. had attracted entries from France, England, Sweden, Australia, Italy, Japan and Canada in addition to both the United States and a few South American countries. The influx of international accents added an exotic flair even to hallway conversations. But when the short balding fellow dressed as a Brazilian crewman slipped a few phrases of Russian into a purely Portuguese conversation, Miranda started listening in earnest. Then she heard the fellow mention *Persistence*—in English—and she moved closer.

Using the Plexiglas as a mirror, she pretended to be absorbed in applying her lipstick. The bits of Portuguese she'd mastered in order to deal with South American charterers would help her get the gist of what was being said. But entire sentences slipped by without one familiar word being used. The little fellow turned and glared at her, then gruffly signaled for her to back off while he completed his conversation. Miranda took out her blush and proceeded to rouge her cheeks, already pink from the wind, but the activity camouflaged her eavesdropping.

Then like a specter emerging from the mist, a face peered at her through the Plexiglas. For a moment she thought she was dreaming until the illusion spoke.

"Mandy...?" Phil Pittman said, stepping around the transparent barrier to greet her. "It really is you." Phil scrutinized her features, his uncertain smile widening in approval, registering a mixture of pleasure and amazement to see the subtle changes that five years had made. "You look spectacular," he declared, hesitating before reaching out to grasp her shoulders. "Welcome back to civilization."

Miranda had to concentrate to keep from staring at her old sweetheart. He was every bit as golden and gorgeous as she remembered. His smile was radiant with perfect white teeth, even more striking now against his deep tan. His blond hair, highlighted by touches of sun, was collar length, more casual than when she'd known him. But the navy jacket and open-necked yellow shirt were typically expensive, just what a yacht broker was expected to wear. Phil looked every bit as "spectacular" as he'd judged her.

"Phil, it's good to see you again." Miranda's mouth felt stiff as she smiled at him, remembering how many times she had played through this scene in her mind. The look of slightly stunned admiration on Phil's face was exactly what she had wished for, and the glow in his blue eyes recalled memories of when the desire there was dark and powerful.

"I'd hoped you'd say that," he replied smoothly, gently pulling her toward him into a tentative embrace. "Nice to see you, too," he said as he gave her a welcoming hug. "In fact, you're not only the best sight I've seen today but you're almost the first. I just got here. Got hung up with business and had to fly in on the company jet. Running across you right off is a wonderful surprise. How about having lunch with me? This is a heck of a place to try to talk."

While Phil and Miranda had been standing there, the

uneven flow of human traffic in the hallway had parted around them. Crewmen in foul-weather gear lumbered past, their damp clothing cold and dripping. There were still several people lined up and waiting to use the telephones, and a few were watching the reunion between the handsome couple with mild interest. Miranda glanced uneasily at the little Portuguese-speaking fellow who still stood, his back to them, talking into the phone. He was consulting a small note pad, apparently passing on the information it contained, but there was no hope of hearing any of his conversation now.

"I was going to try to call Jeff," Miranda said. "But I'll take you up on the lunch offer first." Unfinished business could take precedence for a while. "Let me get my shoes." Still barefoot, she stepped closer to the wall where she'd left her sodden deck shoes. Slipping her feet back into the wet shoes, she balanced on one foot while Phil steadied her, his direct blue eyes still studying her closely.

"I wasn't sure if you'd even want to speak to me," Phil confided once they'd moved from the hallway into the relative serenity of the yacht-club dining room. "I hoped it wouldn't be awkward for either of us, meeting again."

He held out the chair for Miranda as he had in those magical days long before, then he sat next to her, his hand resting on hers. "I really needed to see you." The tone of his voice sent a reassuring warmth through her. Perhaps deep inside, some traces of his feelings for her still existed. "I was afraid you'd still be angry."

"I never felt any anger toward you, Phil," Miranda said softly. "I was bewildered and hurt, maybe, but not angry. There have always been things I never could understand."

"I guess that's why I hoped to see you here." His eyes softened as they met hers. "To try to understand what we had. I'm divorced, you know. The marriage to Charlie was a mistake. I suppose I knew it all along." He glanced up self-consciously as the waiter arrived, then both he and Miranda discreetly fell silent, scanning the luncheon menu while the fellow brought their coffee.

"Still take it with cream?" Phil asked, offering her the small pewter pitcher. "And fake sugar?" He opened one package as he had years before, holding it above her cup of steaming dark coffee.

"As a matter of fact, I do," she answered. For Miranda, the scene was flowing as she had often wished it would, with her troubled lover discovering her again. But each comment, each familiar gesture seemed so perfectly rehearsed, that she felt increasingly remote instead of close to him.

"I really thought it was too good to be true with us," Phil told her after their order had been taken and they sat, sipping coffee and reminiscing. "When you left, it was like the movie had ended, and it was time to grow up and get on with real life." Miranda watched him as he spoke, vaguely pleased that his memories were as vivid as hers. For her, that fairy-tale love affair had remained perfect, making other men and other relationships uninspired by comparison.

"But somewhere along the way," Phil continued, "I began to realize that I'd been wrong. I wanted that movie, I needed that fantasy, and I'd settled for what seemed like a pale imitation." Miranda swallowed a sip of coffee, recognizing his feelings as close to her own, only she hadn't settled for anything. She had simply mourned what was lost, treasured the memory and regretted the disillusionment.

"I tried to forget you, but it didn't work. I remembered how it was with us. We really clicked." His hand tightened over hers. "And the sex was good, unbelievably good." He said it so sincerely that the bluntness of his comment was softened slightly. But now Miranda waited for the rest of it, the sensitive, insightful part that made it clear he remembered a relationship more complex than terrific sex. She'd recalled the enthusiasm they shared about sailing, the laughter, the conversations, the friends they both enjoyed. And the sex. But not separate from the rest.

"I never found anyone who could make me feel like you did." His dreamy eyes, clouded with memories, stared into space. "Mandy, I didn't know how important you were to me."

Miranda stared at him, unable to think of an appropriate reply. Phil slid his hand gently up her arm, then back again to her hand, possessively cupping it beneath his. "You're even more exciting to me now that I realize what else is out there. No one comes close to you. Sibyl says you don't have any special man in your life." He tightened his grasp. "That puts us both back where we were at the beginning. We're older but wiser, and in your case, far more beautiful," he said solemnly. "I want you to think about what we had, and give us some time to get acquainted again. We can be together here."

When the waiter appeared at that moment with their order, Miranda almost sighed with relief. "Being together" had acquired a new meaning over the intervening years. If Phil's method of getting acquainted again meant resuming the sex without too many preliminaries, Miranda wasn't ready. In spite of Phil's eagerness to pick up where they left off, for her, the chemistry wasn't working. Something was off, and she wasn't sure if it was the timing or the combination. But it didn't feel right. She had wanted to be special to him, so special that he'd never forget her. Now that he had confirmed that she was indeed irreplaceable, she wasn't in a rush to go further.

"I guess we have some catching up to do," Phil said, releasing her hand amiably. "If it seems like I'm rushing you, it's just because you look so good and we've only got a few weeks for sure. I blew it once with you, and now you're here, I don't want to take any chances." His blue eyes gleamed with a confidence she remembered, but their cool depths revealed little else.

"I don't want to take any chances, either," Miranda said softly. She knew that with the slightest sign of willingness, she could leave with him right this minute, and be in his arms the next. But she couldn't ignore the fact that in spite of their lost love, both of them had lived other lives for five years. Both had established careers. They'd become different people. And while "Mandy" and Phil eagerly became lovers again, two total strangers would be sharing that bed. And the aftermath could be disastrous.

"We'll take it easy," Phil promised, resting his arm along the back of her chair. "Talk to me. Tell me about this business of yours in the islands." The move to courteous conversation was just what Miranda needed. Phil had always been good company, listening, talking, asking questions. But as Miranda sketched in the history of Calvert Charters, Phil studied her face feature by feature, and she felt as if he wasn't interested in her marina at all.

"You must be doing well in the yacht-brokerage business," Miranda said, neatly turning the tables. "Are you here to race sailboats or to buy and sell them?"

"All of the above," Phil replied laughingly. "I have a few buyers who will be very interested in the races here. They'd like to own a winner. And I'm sure some of the owners will be approachable with an offer as we see the results of the races. I like to make people happy."

"For a commission," Miranda teased.

"Unless I'm dealing with you," he immediately countered. "I'd like to make you happy. No commission asked." Again his conversation had become highly sexual.

"Well, I'm not looking for a boat," Miranda responded.

"I'm flexible," Phil said smoothly, with an ease that made the line sound well practiced and well used. "Tell me what you want, and I'll do my best to deliver."

"Right now, I want my coffee refilled, and I could use another fake sugar." Miranda held out her hand.

With an obliging chuckle, Phil passed her a pink packet of sweetener. "I didn't remember you being so good at sidestepping the obvious," he noted with a sly wink.

"And I didn't remember you being so single-minded or so obvious," she observed dryly.

"But you do remember what it was like." He looked at her evenly.

"I remember." Miranda stirred her coffee silently, feeling more comfortable with the past than with the present.

Throughout lunch, Phil chatted easily, updating her on the marriages, children and divorces of several friends from the Annapolis area. Then they talked about boats, and Miranda was intrigued by Phil's discussion of multiple partnerships in boat ownership. Conglomerates—professional syndicates, business partnerships—were the main buyers in the large-boat market. Depending how they chose to advertise their boats or what experimental equipment they tested and endorsed, they could get significant tax breaks.

Phil explained the attraction of shared ownership, sounding increasingly like a polished professional salesman. "Forming a syndicate is the way to go. Boats are expensive playthings for one individual to maintain, but if you share you can afford a far nicer toy. Besides, owning part of a trophy-winning boat is better than owning all of a loser."

Miranda didn't agree, but she didn't choose to argue. "So who owns the boat you're racing, *Hambone*?" Miranda asked.

"The company owns fifty-one percent. Eight of us own the rest. Even Vinnie Albrecht's maxi *Prophecy* is group owned; it belongs to several doctors who practice in the same medical-arts building as Vinnie." His eyes narrowed as he talked business strategy. "If the boats win in their class, the investors can sell them off and make a profit. Then someone else can own a piece of a winner—or the whole thing if we find an Arab sheikh with a bundle to spend." Phil chuckled as if he had one in mind.

"It isn't like the old days," Miranda said, sighing. "I think I liked it better when the boats were part of the family. Everyone worked on his own boat, the family members and friends crewed it, and it wasn't auctioned off just because it won."

"Times have changed, Mandy. Skilled designers and reliable builders have to be bought like pro-ball players. Experimental materials and synthetics—Kevlar, mylar, titanium components run the cost up. Electronics cost megabucks. In the big leagues, keeping competitive is expensive." Phil leaned back and glanced about the room, his eyes stopping on one group of familiar faces. "Let me just go over there for a moment and say hello," he said, excusing himself. "Business. I'll be right back." Miranda nodded while Phil crossed the room to greet the four men seated by the window. One was Mason Porter, Walker's former boss. Another was a California millionaire who owned a maxi. The two others were sail makers. In some ways, Miranda noted, times hadn't changed so much. Business as usual.

There were two other side trips before Phil finished his lunch, and several old friends stopped by their table briefly, to greet Miranda after her long absence from the racing circuit. They also bestowed the twosome with tactful smiles.

"So nice to see you, especially together," one of Sibyl's dowager friends whispered, patting Miranda's shoulder with a ring-laden hand.

Phil basked in all the attention, enjoying the consensus that Miranda was back where she belonged. "You've been missed," he said as he leaned close to her. "How about coming over to the hotel while I unpack. We'll have a quiet drink. I'd like a little time with you alone."

"I still have that phone call to make to Jeff, remember?" Miranda felt like everything was closing in on her. "I don't think it's a good idea to rush things, Phil." His eagerness to get her alone seemed almost territorial, as if he were staking a claim that he intended to defend. "I've got plans for dinner and I need to get back to Sibyl's to clean up. I can taste the saltwater on my skin."

"I'd like to taste that myself," he whispered provocatively. He looked at her speculatively with a smile that once would have swept away her inhibitions. But by now Miranda was finding his fascination with her body more irritating than flattering.

"I really must go and try to get that call through to Jeff." She stood to leave.

"I'm at the Concourse. Where are you staying?" Phil was on his feet immediately.

"I'm staying on a cruiser in the marina. Sibyl and Vinnie chartered it so they could be near *Prophecy*. Slot 237. The boat is called *Limelight*." Miranda watched the smile on Phil's face waver as she gave him the information. Even with three full bedrooms, TV lounge, bar and assorted other compartments, there would be no privacy possible aboard a power cruiser smack in the midst of the St. Pete Yacht Club Marina.

"I have a suite to myself," Phil added pointedly. "As soon as I get settled, we'll get together. Tomorrow?"

"I'll check my agenda," Miranda promised.

He stroked her arm lightly again, smiling and shaking his head. "I was a fool, Mandy. You sure turned into one heck of a woman." He stood there watching as she walked away, then he glanced over at the four seated men, now into their postlunch discussion. When Miranda looked back, Phil was joining the men, and she felt as if she'd been given a reprieve.

Mulling over the unexpectedly negative feelings that her meeting with Phil had caused, Miranda passed through the latest influx of sailors returned from the midday shakedown runs. She didn't even notice the curly haired fellow in the midnight-blue jacket abandon the orange juice he'd been sipping while he watched her from his vantage point at the bar.

"Is that him?" Walker Hall fell in step beside her as she reached the hallway. "The guy with the perfect smile," he teased. "Is he the guy you came to see?"

"He's one of them," Miranda replied with a grin, genuinely glad to see him. "There's still my dad. He switched his flight down until tomorrow."

"And are the ashes still smoldering?" Walker asked, brushing her arm lightly with his as the milling crowd slowed their progress.

"I gather we're talking about Phil and not my father now," Miranda replied, steadily moving along the congested corridor toward the phone area. "In the first place, it's none of your business. In the second place, I haven't reached a decision on that yet."

Walker shrugged good-naturedly and continued strolling along next to her. "You can't tell if you're smoldering?" he said doubtfully. When Miranda glanced at him, Walker was frowning.

"Actually my heart is racing, my mind is reeling, and I can't wait to rush back there and throw myself into his arms." She didn't really mean any of it, but his probing made her contrary. Her comeback was a test to check his reaction.

Now the deep-gray eyes that met hers flashed with impatience. "You're too darn cautious to get carried away like that. And you're not stupid. Phil's a salesman, but with the edge he had, if he hasn't sweet-talked you out of here and into the sack by now, he's slipping."

Miranda glared at him, peeved by his presumptuous attitude and the fact that Walker had hit uncomfortably close to the truth. "We only had lunch. Give him time," Miranda replied crossly, stopping at an available phone booth and digging in her pocket for a dime—unsuccessfully.

"The important question is, are you going to give him time?" Walker stepped in close to her.

"None of your business, and I haven't decided," Miranda repeated.

"I know Pittman, not well, but enough. I've seen how he operates. Once the charm wears off, he'll bore you to tears," Walker declared, presenting her with a dime for the phone. "He's a company man, uniformed, real pretty, urbane, civilized and plugged into the system. Programmed for success. Your father would approve." He laced his comment with sarcasm.

"Give me some room to move in here," Miranda insisted, pressing him away from her so she could reach the telephone more readily.

"Back there he wasn't giving you much room," Walker recalled. "He would be with you now if the choice were his. I watched him. He couldn't keep his hands off you, but here you are. So that means you're the one calling the shots. How intimate a relationship is this between you two?"

That did it. Emotionally and physically Miranda had been feeling increasingly cornered. Now Walker had pushed too far, and Miranda instinctively pushed back. Just as she lost her temper and tried to clout him, Walker managed to grab her wrists. He pinned her hands against her sides, keeping her from bumping into the Plexiglas partitions.

"You arrogant Neanderthal," she flung out. "What right do you have to interrogate me like this?"

"None, dammit." Walker kept his back to the hallway, blocking off the intensity of their encounter from the eyes of the passersby. "I just want to know," Walker demanded, his voice low and controlled, "what's going on between you two. Are you lovers? And don't tell me it's none of my business."

Miranda stared at the peculiar expression on Walker's face, part anger, part pain. But it was his sudden calm, waiting for her answer, that stilled her.

"We were going to get married a few years ago. That was when my brother got hurt. Jeff and I went to Tortola and Phil married someone else. He's divorced now. And we aren't lovers anymore." She felt depleted by the summary, having finally put it into words and made it real. Five years in five sentences.

"Thank you. Sorry I kept at you." Walker let her wrists free and lifted his hands, lightly stroking her hair. "When I saw him touching you, I wanted to knock that smile right off his face. But I decided you'd be a bit put out by the ungentlemanly behavior, so I just sat at the bar and watched. When you walked away from him, I didn't know whether to cheer or just be thankful it wasn't me."

"Walker, I'm exhausted. I don't want to get into this now." Miranda was still reeling from all that had been dumped on her at once. Returning to the commotion of the yacht club after the exhilarating morning out on the bay, then seeing Phil and now facing Walker had all drained her energy.

"I don't care how it was with you two once. Obviously it's gone," Walker declared with a heaviness that Miranda didn't understand. "It's not the moves, it's the magic, Miranda. Whether we want to make the moves or not, we've got the magic." He clasped her shoulders, holding her only briefly with unexpected gentleness before letting her go. "I just thought it was worth mentioning," he added. "Before things went too far."

"Are you folks ever going to use that phone?" The other booths were occupied again and one disgruntled fellow wanted to make his call.

"I'll be working tonight, but I'll be out on *Persistence* tomorrow," Walker said as he stepped back. "If you happen to be passing by and your heart starts racing and your mind reels and you need a pair of arms to throw yourself into—no explanations needed. . . ." He grinned, looking almost embarrassed as he backed away.

"Don't hold your breath." Miranda laughed softly in spite of her sagging spirits. "I'm not the impulsive type, remember?"

" Maybe. . . maybe not," he said thoughtfully. "Anyway, you're welcome for the dime." Walker reminded her of her oversight and seemed to delight in her immediate discomfort. "Tell your brother I'm looking forward to meeting him, and if he isn't betting on my boat, he should be. So should you."

"You really are obnoxious," Miranda said, sighing.

"Perhaps, but I'm not boring," he commented cheerfully as he bent forward, placed a quick kiss on her half-parted lips and walked off.

Miranda was startled by the sudden touch of his lips, light and sweet. "Show-off," she muttered under her breath, trying to concentrate on the call she had come to make.

"I'd like to call the British Virgin Islands. Tortola." Miranda glanced at her watch, adding on the time change. And when Jeff's voice came on the other end, Miranda felt as if she had connected with something real after a day that had seemed dreamlike by comparison. "You're going to hate it and you're going to love it. . ." she began immediately, pushing all other considerations aside.

THERE WERE A DOZEN RED ROSES waiting for Miranda in her cabin when she went back to the cruiser to change. Without needing to read the card, Miranda knew they were from Phil. The gift was an elegant and grand gesture, one well suited to his campaign. He'd sent them before, often. Especially after a night of lovemaking. "Dinner tomorrow?" the note said. Signed "Phil."

The voluptuous perfume of the flowers hung in the air, as Miranda dressed for the evening. First she would attend one of the obligatory cocktail parties at the beach house of a retired commodore from the Annapolis area. Dinner with a few friends followed at a French restaurant. Finally, back aboard the Albrechts' cruiser, Vinnie and Sibyl were hosting a wine-and-cheese party featuring videotapes of last year's S.O.R.C. Eventually the sleek gown she pulled on now could be traded for slacks, a sweater and bare feet for the video at ten o'clock.

Miranda brushed her hair until it shone, waiting for Sibyl to summon her. The deep-scarlet roses were reflected in the mirror. She frowned, knowing that she should be thrilled to have Phil back again, ardent and thoughtful, and lavish with his attention. But she wasn't. In fact, she resented the way he had concentrated on memories, making her reexamine them and question them as she never had before. How much simpler was that "Mandy" who had loved this man? How much of what they had shared was purely physical, she wondered. And had it all been so perfect because there had not been time enough for it to fade—like the roses would, eventually.

Miranda stared at the crimson buds, remembering the old saying she had learned as a child. "Take great care with what you wish for. Your wishes may come true." She was no child now, but she had wished for what seemed perfect years ago to be perfect again. When she saw Phil, for a little while renewing that romantic past seemed possible. But Miranda was getting a new perspective on that perfect memory, and the picture was becoming increasingly flawed. She could see too clearly that Phil Pittman's ambition had a dark side. One minute he was admiring her and the next he was checking out prospective business contacts in the yacht-club dining room. His ability to mix business with pleasure was something she had once admired in him; now it made her uneasy.

The other face that kept appearing in her thoughts was the face of a man not perfect or predictable—not even polite. They didn't suit each other at all. Miranda thought that was obvious. Walker had seemed no more anxious to get involved with her than she wanted to get involved with him. Regardless, he had come to find her. Then he'd pushed her enough to make her angry, to force her to confront the present—to admit what was there and what wasn't. He said they had magic.

He'd said "before things went too far" he wanted to mention that. Nothing more.

Holding on to Phil for all these years had kept her safe. The pain and disillusion Miranda harbored had allowed no worthy challengers inside the walls. Now one unpredictable and errant knight had arrived on the scene, without invitation—and without roses. This adventurer made his own rules.

CHAPTER FOUR

WALKER HALL WAS NOTICEABLY ABSENT from the marina area the next day. Several times Miranda passed *Persistence*, nonchalantly riding at her mooring, with only one slim fellow aboard. He had charts spread out on the deck, studying them, and making notations in a spiral notebook. Late in the day as the low clouds turned dusky rose with the disappearing sun, Miranda paused, watching *Persistence* now unoccupied and secured for the night. Soon her father would be coming to meet her, less than a hundred yards away, on the cruiser *Limelight*. She couldn't stall any longer hoping Walker would appear.

"I had to make a few changes in our dinner plans," Howard Vaughn said as he met his daughter aboard the Albrechts' boat. While Sibyl and Vinnie shook hands with him, Vaughn kissed Miranda's cheek and patted her shoulder a bit awkwardly. "I hope you won't mind, dear." Early in the day Sibyl had relayed the message that Miranda's father had finally arrived and wanted to take her to dinner. That eliminated Phil Pittman for the evening. But now as Miranda compared her casual outfit to Howard Vaughn's fine blue suit, she realized this father-daughter reunion was not going to be either informal or intimate.

"I'm a couple of days late arriving in St. Pete, so I've missed a good bit of the backstage action," Vaughn explained, his expression cordial but reserved. Miranda couldn't help but notice he seemed to be regarding her thoughtfully, as if he needed to correct his five-year-old image of her. "I know we need some time to ourselves," he acknowledged, "but if we can include a few associates at dinner for some shoptalk, I'll promise you my undivided attention afterward."

"Fine," Miranda replied, suspecting that he had arranged the additional dinner companions to give him time to feel comfortable with her. And that was all right. She could use the buffer, too. Silver-haired and ramrod straight, her father still had the elegant, athletic stance that made him look impressive in any surroundings. The few traces of aging that Miranda noticed were in the deep creases across his brow and the slight hollows in his cheeks. Vaughn was thinner than she remembered, but not at all frail. Tanned and weathered, at sixty, he was like seasoned teak on a ship, as sound and tough as ever. But right now he was employing his polished public image, and Miranda would indulge him for a while. She could only hope there were other sides to her father that would surface eventually.

"I guess I'd better change." Miranda knew what was expected at a corporate dinner party and she didn't want to make her father uneasy. But she wished she could hug him and tell him how good he looked. However, from the formality of his greeting, she knew that would be too intimate and too abrupt. In the Vaughn family, physical displays of affection were discreet and limited in public, and even Sibyl and Vinnie were considered public. "I'll just be a couple of minutes," she promised.

"We'll have a drink. Take your time," Vinnie called from the bar. But Miranda dressed hurriedly, slipping into a slim black bias-cut dress, simple but appropriately classic. Anticipating the coolness outside, she pulled on her deep-plum cashmere jacket, then stared at the combination in the mirror. Clearly the outfit needed something—a scarf, a belt—to soften the striking color combination and pull it all together, but Miranda simply brushed her hair and changed her lipstick shade. Too much time had already been lost to her and her father to spend more in the pursuit of fashion. "Understated elegance," she decreed with one parting look at her dramatic reflection.

Although Walker had been missing in person during the day, his presence at the S.O.R.C. was discussed throughout dinner. Jack Byrd of Byrd sails had seen the laser-cut sails on *Persistence*. He was impressed with the star-burst design of the spinnaker as well as the fine inset work on the less-decorative sails. "I tried to get some information on the guy who made the sails, but he's real hard to track down. No one on *Persistence* is talking. Best I heard was that some guy named Gibbs has a production plant in the center of the state, and his technique is so secret, he won't even let the boat designers in to watch. He's good."

Ted Birmingham had nodded when *Persistence* was mentioned. "Phil looked her over. She's a variation on Mason Porter's *Elan*. Apparently Hall picked up an old production mold that Porter had discarded and copied her, and there's nothing Porter can do about that. Perfectly legal. Hall's made some real interesting changes, and if *Persistence* does well, he and Porter might have a real hassle over producing more just like her."

"I thought Hall had left boating and gone into some other line." Hugh Crawford, an Australian boat designer, joined in the discussion while Miranda listened.

"Rumor has it he's been doing specialized fiberglass work, some hush-hush industrial equipment, but that might have been just a cover while he worked on this boat," Boyd disclosed. "Hall and Mason Porter split over a dispute about that boat's design in the first place. Apparently neither Porter nor Hall would back down, so Hall was forced to quit. Then the small print in his contract kept him from opening his own shop for a couple of years or competing with Porter's designs. The contract didn't say anything about modifying one for himself. He just couldn't produce a competitive line." Boyd shrugged off the contract loophole. "Hall's got one heck of a nerve entering in the S.O.R.C. right off, especially with *Elan* racing in the same class. Porter is in a real sweat," he acknowledged. "If Hall wins, we'll know who was the brains in the Porter outfit, or at least who was right about that design."

Across the table from Miranda, the only other female in the party sat sipping her wine and listening halfheartedly. Her Kewpie-doll face displayed a perpetually pleasant expression, and her wide blue eyes occasionally settled on Miranda. Charlotte Birmingham had come with her father, and every time Phil Pittman's name was mentioned, Miranda wondered what "Charlie" Birmingham knew about the former romance between Miranda and Phil—or the one that rumor said was starting again.

While dinner proceeded and the conversation revolved around boat talk, Miranda found herself watching the nervous movements of Charlie's hands and the steady emptying and refilling of her wineglass. It reminded her of countless company dinners in the past, when Miranda had sat near her mother. The conversation had been just as sophisticated and Amanda Vaughn had consumed just as much wine. Miranda had a grim sense of déjà vu as she watched the young woman across the table. The social drinking had finally led Amanda Vaughn into a shadowy existence. Gradually Miranda had stepped in as the corporate hostess when Amanda was "too ill" to attend. Even when Amanda died in the car accident, no one ever mentioned her drinking problem. It was as if it had never existed at all.

Charlie had that same quiet desperation about her, an attentiveness that seemed forced yet perfectly cordial. But the wine had glazed her eyes, and Miranda suspected that a little fresh air before dessert would help. Miranda leaned forward, intent on rescuing Charlie. "If we turn left at the ladies' room, and go into the garden, there's a glass-blower in the patio. Let's go take a look."

Charlie shifted her eyes to her father, who was too engrossed in the description of a boat he had for sale to care. "Sure," she agreed, leaving her drink and standing as Miranda did.

"I'd forgotten what it was like to be a social necessity," Miranda joked as they crossed the room. "We sit around and look nice and make small talk." Charlie seemed surprised by Miranda's openness, but she responded only with a slight smile.

Miranda was determined to make Charlie more comfortable with her. "My father insisted we keep cards on all our guests so before each gathering we could skim over the data—everything from what drink they prefer and how they like their coffee, the name of their boat, the ages and schools of their children, to details about our business dealings with them. They were handy, but I kept wondering who had cards on us and what they would say."

"If I had one on you, it would say that you're darn lucky you got away from all this," Charlie replied with an intelligence in her eyes that hadn't been evident until now. "One gets lulled into it. All the entertaining seems like such fun at the beginning, until business takes over, then gradually you find yourself becoming part of the table decorations. Or a depository for trivia, just as you said." The wine was affecting Charlie's fluency, but her perception was not impaired.

"I know the feeling," Miranda said, nodding.

"I went from being corporate daughter to corporate wife." Charlie shrugged. "Then I found out that in the climb to success, wives are necessary only up to a point. When I divorced Phil, I couldn't divorce the company or my father. Not if I wanted to continue living in the style to which I am accustomed," she added wryly. "Unlike you, I never mastered anything other than how to be a suitable dinner companion or party hostess, so count your blessings. You got out and are on your own. I hope you have sense enough not to be tempted back into all this."

Miranda studied the pretty lady as they passed through the glass doors leading out to the restaurant gardens. Old converted gas lanterns lighted the pathways leading to the glass-blower's stand, and the pale light transformed Charlie's hair into an angelic halo. Soft and gentle mannered, Charlie had to be a year or two younger than Miranda, but her advice to stay out of the corporate whirlpool was delivered with a solemn, almost motherly concern. Miranda couldn't tell if Charlie's warning was meant to include Phil Pittman or simply referred to the yachting milieu. But one thing was certain. Sweet-faced Charlie was far more complicated a woman than she had anticipated. The cool crisp evening air surrounded them and Miranda pulled her jacket closed.

"Look at that clown." Miranda bent down, peering into the glass display case holding samples of the craftsman's work. Made from clear shimmering glass, the big-footed clown was holding a fistful of balloons on strings as fragile looking as a spider's web.

"Josh would make short work of that," Charlie said, crouching next to Miranda and staring at the figure. "He's not quite four. He's into demolition and 'Does it come apart, mommy?'" The amusement in her face as she spoke of her son added an appealing quality to Charlie's slightly tipsy demeanor.

Miranda's smile faltered. Until now she had not heard the name of Phil Pittman's son. Josh. Almost four. He was real. Sibyl had noted in passing that Phil Pittman had a child. But in discussing that his marriage was "a mistake," Phil had failed to mention his son at all. Calculating hastily, Miranda noted that whatever alleged inadequacies there had been in Phil and Charlie's relationship, they hadn't interfered with having a child within a few months of their wedding. And she knew that the same thing could very well have happened to her. In fact, there had been moments when she wished it had.

The glass-blower fired up his burner, illuminating the area with a brilliant bluish light as he started on another figure. Several other restaurant patrons moved closer to watch him work, looping slender threads into a lacy pedestal. "If Josh is interested in taking things apart," Miranda said, steadying Charlie as they stood and turned back through the garden, "there was a toy shop downtown near the bay. If it's still there, it had nice, chunky wooden toys, clocks and cameras, with pieces that fit like puzzles."

"Sounds like Josh," Charlie said with a smile. Suddenly she grasped Miranda's arm as the world from her perspective began spinning crazily. "As you might guess, I'm not really much of a drinker," she apologized. "And I'm really embarrassed about all this." Her wide blue eyes glimmered with involuntary tears. "I'd heard you'd had lunch with Phil, and I knew what people were saying. I've often heard what a lovely couple you'd made, years ago. When I realized dad and I were having dinner with you, I became very self-conscious. I never did get quite as thin as I was before

Josh. I'm supposed to be watching my calories. Instead, I put away a few more drinks than I can handle. I've said some things I shouldn't have, but I feel terribly dumpy and ordinary next to you. You're so darn slim. Phil likes slender women."

Miranda would have laughed if the situation hadn't been so tragic. Miranda's purple-and-black outfit had accentuated both her height and her slender build. Oblivious to the fact that her more ample shape had a wholesome softness that suited her, Charlie had been hurt by the contrast between them. "Look, I'm really not interested in what kind of body Phil likes. We had lunch and we talked about old times. That's all. I'm not getting involved with Phil." Miranda said so with more conviction than she realized she had acquired.

"Neither am I." Charlie shrugged. "That's what's so foolish about all this. I really don't want him, either. He put me through plenty as it was. But it is a little embarrassing knowing that people are talking. I guess my pride gets wounded, even now. It was childish for me to get so upset and drink so much." She blinked at Miranda as if trying to focus. "I don't know what I expected, but you're really very nice. Granted, I'd like you a lot better if your lipstick were smeared or your panty hose had runs," she confessed with a glint of mischief in her pale-blue eyes.

Miranda laughed good-naturedly. "Then you should have seen me a couple of hours ago with soggy shoes and stringy hair. I was a real prize."

"It's hard to believe you're not always this perfect." Charlie grinned, still holding on to Miranda's arm.

"But it helps to know you're not taken in by Phil. He's very smooth, very impressive." She rushed on to qualify her comment. "He's great at romance. It's just marriage and family he's not good at."

Miranda shrugged, unwilling to invite any further discussion of Phil's personal life. She didn't need any more evidence that he was not the man for her. Her instincts already confirmed that and the realization had nothing to do with Charlie. "Let's go back and order dessert."

"I'd better just watch you eat while I drink about three cups of coffee, then I'll feel better," Charlie confided.

Inside, the men were still absorbed in boat talk. This time the focus was on the encroachment of foreign boat building on the American market. "Those Far East countries can hire an American designer, use cheap labor and undercut our prices," Ted Birmingham complained. His brokerage was offering fine yachts for sale, but some could be duplicated in the Orient for half the price.

"What bothers me is when a foreign partnership snaps up a fast American boat, changes the name, then uses it to beat us in another regatta," Howard Vaughn commented. "It happened with a Sardinia Cup winner and one out of the Mackinac Race. It could happen here at the S.O.R.C. They could pick up a winner and run her against us at the Admiral's cup."

"Let's hope I catch wind of it early enough to get in on the deal," Ted Birmingham said, chuckling. "I could pick up a nice commission on one of these beauties."

"Really, dad..." Charlie made her disapproval apparent. For a brief moment Charlie's eyes met Miranda's, apologetically.

"Only kidding," Birmingham said, laughing. "I'd do my darndest to keep a boat flying the flag of the good old U.S. of A." The other men nodded politely, but the somberness lingered in their eyes.

After dessert, Boyd and Hugh Crawford hurried off to another party. Birmingham and his daughter stood, getting ready to leave, and Miranda finally was to have her father to herself.

"I have to stop in at the yacht club for a few minutes," Howard Vaughn explained. "We'll drive over there and have a nightcap. Then we'll talk." But from the moment they entered the club, Miranda had the sinking feeling that the interruptions would never end. While her father stepped into an office to go over some official forms, Miranda ordered coffee at the bar where cigarette smoke hung like a low fog over the room. Wearily she slid into an end booth to wait, feeling very alienated from the scene.

The room was already well populated with crewmen and a collection of locals and visitors who'd dropped in for a drink and to look up old friends. Miranda watched the comings and goings in smoky solitude, accepting a refill when the waiter passed her way.

"Hey, Stasch, come here." Three fellows near the entrance summoned the wiry Portuguese seaman whose conversation Miranda had tried to overhear the day before. Certain that no Portuguese native had a name like Stasch, she wondered what he was up to. Stasch and his three companions huddled over the table, sketching on napkins and passing them back and forth, adding details and talking animatedly.

When Walker Hall came in, Miranda started to wave him over, but as soon as he saw Stasch and his friends, Walker joined them, his back to her. Uncertain what to do next, she simply watched.

As her father entered the room, several heads swiveled to look at him, including Walker Hall's. Glancing over the seated customers, Howard Vaughn finally located Miranda, indicating for her to stay put while he made a phone call. Miranda nodded just as Walker Hall turned and looked at her. After saying something to his companions, he came to join her.

"Some enchanted evening..." He began singing softly as he moved into the booth and sat next to her. "You may see a stranger...across a smoky room."

"Ah, more evidence of the multitalents of Walker Hall," Miranda joked. "I suppose you dance, too."

"Is that an invitation?" Slowly and boldly his gaze shifted downward, following the cut of the jacket lapels to the softly draped neckline of her dress. "Is that why you're done up fancy? You're considering throwing yourself into my arms, but you want it to seem casual, as if we're dancing?"

"Walker, it's almost midnight. My mind isn't working fast enough to be that clever or devious. Besides, there's no music." But as she looked at him, she wished it was possible that he could hold her, just for a while.

He leaned closer, pressing his shoulder against hers. "Music can be arranged," he assured her. He was watching her lips as she smiled as if he fully intended to kiss her right there.

"You seem to have an affinity for small crowded cubicles in public places," Miranda quipped, but she was well aware that whatever happened here between her and Walker, there would be gossip.

"That depends on the crowd," he answered with a grin. "If the crowd is you and me, I like it. I know it's only been a day, but I sure have missed seeing that face of yours." He lowered his voice obligingly. "Not that I'm partial to one aspect of anatomy over another. I have noticed your body is very nice," he added. "You haven't been out tempting Mr. Perfect Pittman, have you?"

"You're exasperating..." Miranda said, sighing, knowing he was trying to provoke her. "I was out with my dad."

"Just checking," he said, summoning his most innocent and appealing smile. "I got called away today. I hoped I hadn't missed anything earthshaking. Frankly I'm surprised you're here. Hanging around in a bar. You have to be real careful or you might attract some disreputable low-life, someone who might get real turned on looking at you." He inched a little closer as he spoke. "You smell lovely, too."

"Walker..." She didn't dare look at him, suspecting he'd do something embarrassing in front of everyone. But her resistance was weakening. Just feeling his shoulder gently nudging hers and his thigh brushing against her leg sent a very disturbing wave of pleasure through her. She hoped he was going to go no further.

However safe and playful the contact, there was a provocative element that promised more.

"I want to take you out on my boat. Tomorrow," he said suddenly. "We deserve equal time, and you can add a touch of class to my crew." He looked at her brown eyes, now fixed on him and sparkling with interest.

"I don't want to compromise your reporter's integrity," he continued. "We'll talk all that nautical stuff and act real nice right out in the open. You can see how it goes. It's a business trip. Interview me for the articles you're doing. You're going to need to know a lot about me." The maddening touches of arrogance were balanced by the clear conviction in his gray eyes. "I just don't want either of us to miss out on something important," he continued.

His smile softened while she considered the personal message in his words. "I'd like to go out in your boat." As she accepted his invitation, Miranda caught a glimpse of her father returning, finally free to give his attention to her. For once she wished he'd been diverted longer.

"How's it going with you two?" Walker asked hastily, rising to relinquish his place. "Is his favorite song still 'Hail to the Chief'?"

"I don't know yet." Miranda smiled at his remark. "My private audience with him is just coming up."

"Good luck, then," Walker whispered, then stood. "Good evening, Mr. Vaughn." Walker stuck out his hand and greeted the elder gentleman who didn't seem pleased with his daughter's choice of company. "Walker

Hall," he said with a deliberate self-effacing quality that caught Vaughn off guard.

"Yes, Hall. You're looking well. I heard you were back in the business," Vaughn replied, keeping his expression amiable in spite of the wariness in his eyes. Miranda knew she'd have some explaining to do once Hall left.

"I'm just small potatoes here, at least for now," Walker noted. "As for the interview, Miss Vaughn," Walker said, turning to her with the same formality he'd shown her father, "I'll expect you at ten tomorrow, prepared to sail." The flicker of a smile suggested that he was deliberately giving her a motive her father would accept. "I appreciate your interest in putting something about the boat in your articles." Without altering his ingratiating manner, he excused himself and returned to his companions.

"You're going to interview him?" Vaughn asked with interest. "You might start by asking him what he's doing with that headhunter."

"Who's the headhunter?" Miranda followed her father's line of vision.

"The one on Hall's right. Dark-haired tall guy named Benjamin. He calls himself a vocational consultant, but he's a recruiter for businesses. They tell him what they want, he finds a top-notch employee who fits the job. Then he finds out what it takes to lure him away from his current employer. He hunts heads," Vaughn said simply. "I've known a couple of good men he enticed out of the boat industry here who are now in Japan."

"If a person chooses to switch jobs and gets a better

offer, then I can't see what's wrong with that. Maybe Walker needs somebody's head," Miranda speculated, finding the terminology amusing.

Vaughn gave his daughter an impatient look. "I wonder..." Vaughn considered a moment. "I do know that a headhunter can sabotage the hierarchy of a firm. You don't know who is loyal and who isn't. A company can't function without stability."

"Then that company had better make its pay and benefits competitive," Miranda insisted. "Being loyal shouldn't mean you are expected to take lower pay for your work."

"Well, it looks like your friend Walker is either hunting heads or being hunted," Vaughn muttered as the foursome stood to leave. "And I'd be interested to know which it is. He's a damn good boat builder. Started off in Porter's shop laminating fiberglass, then worked up to a top executive slot. I'd like to know if he's selling himself or trying to buy." He turned his attention to Miranda and looked at her expectantly.

"If you're asking me to find out and tell you, you've got the wrong gal." There wasn't the least trace of hostility in her tone, which was subdued and slightly bewildered. "I'm not covering personnel espionage. I'm not a spy, and I don't work for you, dad." She felt her color deepen knowing what she considered improper journalistic conduct, her father could interpret as mere family loyalty. "I'm doing articles about boats. That's it. If you want to find out what Mr. Hall says to me, you'll have to read it when it comes out."

"There probably isn't anything to it anyway,"

Vaughn declared, but his gaze lingered on the door that Walker and his international entourage had used to exit. Then he looked at her uncertainly. He'd run out of diversions. "Now how about that drink?" he finally asked.

"Make it brandy and you've got a deal."

"Brandy. Two." Vaughn signaled for the drinks. "So, where do we start?" he asked.

"Let's start with me saying how good it is to see you, dad," Miranda replied. "I know we've never been much for the mushy stuff, but I just want you to know I have missed you. I didn't always agree with you, and obviously I still don't, but I do care about you. Jeff misses you, too." Miranda said it all before her courage failed her or her voice betrayed the emotions she'd been holding back.

Vaughn looked as if the wind had gone out of his sails. His familiar smile drooped and his shoulders sagged slightly, like an actor suddenly deprived of his script who had to go on stage without lines. "We have missed a lot of each other," Vaughn said pensively. "You've changed. You were always pretty but you've turned into quite a beauty, like your mother. It took me a while to get used to your going by Calvert, but when I look at you, I know it fits. Sibyl says you prefer Miranda, not Mandy. I could give it a try." He kept his hand cupped around the brandy glass and raised it to her. "To Miranda Calvert." He paused thoughtfully. "Pretty name. Suits you."

Miranda watched him, wondering if he would be able to accept Jeff's preference for Calvert as readily as he accepted hers. His relationship with his son had been intense, volatile and burdened with expectations. With the exception of Jeff's dark eyes, he and his father were strikingly similar, and that would be more evident when they met face-to-face again. Even their gestures were alike. And so was the fierce pride both men possessed.

"I understand you and Phil Pittman have been seen together." Vaughn's comment shifted the focus of their conversation.

"We talked and we had lunch," Miranda answered.

"I'm delighted that you two have some time to get to know each other again. Phil's made quite a career for himself, and he's well worth considering, Miranda. How did you two get along?" He leaned closer, eager for the progress report.

"We got along fine except I think I was supposed to be dessert."

"Miranda!"

For the first time in her life, she saw her father blush. "You wanted to know," Miranda said dutifully, enjoying the spontaneous emotion her father had shown. "Next time, tell me if you want a straight answer or not. If you want me to edit my comments, I'll be more discreet."

"I might get accustomed to the unedited version," Vaughn confessed, realizing he'd been underestimating her. "Even though you're beginning to look more like Amanda, I'm beginning to hear more and more Vaughn and less Calvert." He seemed pleased.

"Then wait till you see Jeff," Miranda said, laughing. While she talked about her brother, Howard

Vaughn watched her closely, asking questions about the business, the boats and the prospects at Brewer's Bay. "We have an option on some property," Miranda explained, "but we're not sure what to do with it. I think that two chiefs and too few Indians is our problem. Jeff wants to start a hotel or a sailing school. I'm thinking in terms of a yacht-supply center. One of the things I wanted to talk to you about while I'm here is the marine-hardware business and the possibility of doing something in Tortola in conjunction with your main office."

"I want to talk to you about that, too," Vaughn said, picking up on that immediately. "Not in Tortola, but here in Florida. The boat industry is shifting south because of the hard winters we've had. I'm considering locating a branch office on this coast or in the Lauderdale area, and I'll need someone to run it." As he talked, Miranda could see his entire posture change. He was transforming into the president of the board, becoming more authoritative with each breath. "Once you wanted the top executive job and I said it was to be Jeff's instead," Vaughn recalled. "Only he didn't want the job. Now you both proved you're willing and able to handle a business. I want you to consider moving back here. The company is big enough for all three of us, or it will be if you two want in. Once you get over the shock, we'll talk money," he added. "But since you believe that loyalty should not determine pay and benefits, I'll have to review my offer. You've been away long enough, Miranda." Vaughn was careful to use her full name. "Now that you're back, don't be in too great a hurry to leave again."

"I don't think you understand how much we love what we're doing," Miranda cautioned him. "We like it in Tortola." It seemed as if all the events of the evening were merely polite preliminaries leading up to this business proposition.

"You both need to consider how much you can accomplish here and how rewarding it can be." Miranda knew this was the king talking again, slightly more diplomatic than he had been years before, but driven by the same single vision—his own. Rather than risk losing the gains they had made, she simply shook her head and ended the conversation.

"Let's call it a truce for tonight," she suggested. "We both have busy schedules tomorrow. Let's stop while we're still on friendly terms. But when you've got a few minutes, try to remember that working for you and for ourselves are not the same, dad."

"Just keep an open mind." He'd become the suave negotiator, and Miranda had seen his technique work innumerable times before. "I've got some plans for you to look over. There's plenty of time to think it through. And when Jeff gets here, all I ask is that you give him a chance to think for himself."

Miranda's pleasant expression darkened, and she suddenly understood how her father must have seen her role in Jeff's retreat to Tortola. The ambitious younger sister, more serious and practical, had taken charge when Jeff was weak. She had hidden the invalid brother away. Vaughn thought she was the boss. She was the dictator.

Miranda stifled any defense that would have given

away too much. The truth would be apparent when Jeff arrived. Wait till he saw this supposedly henpecked son, strong and full of humor, equal and independent in every way—with the exception of a slight limitation in mobility. Jeff was as nonconforming now as he was years ago, and heading the family business still wouldn't appeal to him. Wait till Vaughn experienced Jeff's perverse wit that became even more outrageous as he adapted to his condition and to the wheelchair.

Long live the king.... Miranda thought. *Wait till you see your son.*

WALKER SPRAWLED ON THE SOFA in his office, staring at the ceiling. He remembered her joke about crowded cubicles. And the way she avoided his eyes when he got personal, especially in public. But he recalled just as vividly how her eyes had sparkled when he'd offered her a trial run, and the gratitude in her eyes when he had handled her father so smoothly. They were on the same wavelength whether they liked it or not. And he was setting her up. He was going to use her in a very public sailing demonstration. Knowing Howard Vaughn's daughter, who coincidentally was a very beautiful woman, would add more drama to the performance already planned.

Walker wanted the attention. The meeting with Stasch and Benjamin in the bar that night had been no accident. It was deliberate and public and would trigger rumors. People would begin speculating, and that meant more rumors. Howard Vaughn showing up was a real coup. But having his daughter there was just too tempting for Walker to pass up.

There was only one more day before the races started, and Walker knew every photographer covering the S.O.R.C. would be at dockside tomorrow photographing the entries—all decked out in battle regalia. He was ready to spring another surprise and steal all their thunder along with a lot of front-page coverage. But it wasn't going to be with the S.O.R.C. boat at all.

Using the lady was an afterthought. He'd planned to leave her out of it. Then he saw her tonight. They'd looked at each other, like two souls in limbo. He guessed she'd been across the barroom a while before he'd come in. If she'd seen him, she hadn't made a move to let him know. Regardless, he made the move for both of them. Even with all the hassles at the shop that day and the meetings with Stasch, she was there, in his mind, all the time. One way or the other, something had to happen between them. So tomorrow, he would put her on the spot. And that would be a beginning—or an end.

PHIL PITTMAN WAS WAITING on the Albrechts' chartered cruiser when Howard Vaughn dropped Miranda off well past midnight. "It seems the roses have seen more of you than I have," Phil said, once they were alone on the deck.

"The flowers are beautiful. Thank you, Phil."

"So are you. Very chic." He nodded approvingly at her outfit. "I've been trying to catch up with you all day, and so when Sibyl invited me for a drink, I decided that this was one place you'd finally have to come back to."

In spite of the casual explanation, Miranda suspected that Sibyl was matchmaking again. "I have been on the run all day," Miranda admitted. "I even had dinner with Charlie and your former father-in-law."

Phil's face registered only the slightest sign of displeasure. "And how is Charlie? I haven't seen her in weeks." His attitude was so patronizing and civil that Miranda remembered Walker's epithet—Mr. Perfect Pittman.

"She seems fine," Miranda hedged.

"And did you two manage to discuss me?"

"Only briefly. We were also talking about kids and toy stores. It was a very pleasant evening."

"I wish I'd been invited," Phil said, resuming his congeniality. "I would have enjoyed looking at you." His eyes followed the curve of her throat down toward her breasts. The same gesture from Walker earlier had made Miranda feel warm and very sexy. Now with Phil, she closed her jacket.

"If you're chilly, I could help block the wind." He reached out and stroked her arm, drawing her against his side. "We still fit together like pieces of a puzzle," he remarked, holding her shoulders in a gentle embrace.

"Phil, I really think we'd better have a talk." Miranda spoke without moving away.

"Why does that have such an ominous sound?" He glanced down at her, his face almost ghostly in the moonlight.

"I think we better stop before we begin. We're in danger of damaging a possible friendship by trying to turn it into something else." Miranda had felt the pieces slipping into place all day, and the picture they were making was becoming clearer. "Those memories of loving you got me through some very rough times," she admitted. "They kept me from buckling under when I just didn't have the emotional stamina for anything except helping my brother and me survive. Even the hurt I felt kept me from getting into a new relationship before I really knew what I wanted. I'm ready to take some chances now. I guess I've been ready for a while, but I still had a lot unresolved about you. I don't want to be your lover again, and I don't want our memories to get messed up in the process of trying to be friends." Miranda breathed deeply, as if she was stepping out into the open after a long convalescence.

"Just what did Charlie say to you tonight?" Phil's voice took on a bitter edge, betraying his annoyance. "She talked you right out of my life. What was it that backed you off? I should have a chance for a rebuttal."

"Charlie didn't talk me out of anything," Miranda replied firmly. "I finally managed to sort things out by myself." Charlie's very open confession of damaged pride had shown Miranda something about her own vanity. Miranda had wanted Phil to confirm her uniqueness and her desirability; that was a matter of pride. But Walker had really made it crystal clear. The inescapable truth was that the magic wasn't there between her and Phil, and Miranda knew she'd have to stop using the memory to hide behind if she were going to love again.

"Don't you think that you should take a little more time? My God, Mandy, you haven't given me a chance." His voice was controlled and unnatural. "Yesterday it looked as if we were off to such a good start. . . ."

"I've given this a lot of time already," she replied with a definite wistfulness. "I've been thinking about you for five years. But it won't work. We're not the same people anymore. It can't be like it once was. Not like you want it to be."

"I think you're making a mistake." There was a barely perceptible note of anger in his voice.

"I hope not."

"That's it?" Realizing he still had his arm around her, now he withdrew it. "After all these years that I loved you?"

"The girl you loved doesn't exist anymore, Phil. And I certainly am not going to turn myself back into her. I like who I am."

"So do I," he said softly. "I thought you understood that."

"I know you like what you see, but you haven't the faintest idea of what I'm like now. Short term, I can fit in here, but I miss the independence I have on Tortola. Don't think for a moment that you're seeing the real me. I'm not a decoration. I'm not willing to be less intelligent or less possessive or less ambitious than I am. Putting it simply, I'm not your type and you're not mine."

"That's getting to the point all right," he said dryly. "I still think we could make these few weeks memorable." His voice was warm and resonant again, and he reached out, rubbing his hand persuasively over her shoulders, then down her arm, drawing her close again.

"My erogenous zone is higher up," Miranda said

evenly. "It's between my ears. At least the most important part is. Don't confuse lovemaking with manipulation, Phil, or you might make me think that's what you've done all along."

"Now that sounds like Charlie talking, not you," he said cynically. "I still have a whole suite to myself at the Concourse. How about coming back there with me, just the two of us, for old times' sake?"

"You are making this easier for me by the second," Miranda countered. "For old times' sake, I won't shove you over the side right now. But that's it. No matter how much you try, you aren't going to change how I feel. And I feel this is time to call it a night."

"Okay, okay. I'll behave." Phil stepped away from the boat railing just in case Miranda reconsidered. "I'll keep my distance. Just don't be too quick to rule me out."

"Go home, Phil," Miranda said, sighing.

"Right. But I'll see you tomorrow. You're welcome aboard *Hambone* anytime. Come out with us tomorrow and take a run." The perfect smile was in place again.

"I have plans to go out on *Persistence*."

That melted his smile. "Fine. But the invitation is open and *Hambone* is a fine boat. She's a winner."

"I'm sure she is," Miranda said politely.

"Who invited you out on *Persistence*? Did Sibyl arrange it?" Something in his blue eyes made it clear his inquiry wasn't merely personal.

"Walker Hall, the owner, invited me for a ride."

"I didn't know you had met Hall." Phil's eyes narrowed slightly at the mention of Walker Hall.

"We've been getting very close over the past few days," Miranda said enigmatically, recalling the phone booth encounter and the booth in the bar.

"You and Hall?"

Miranda knew she couldn't let her private joke go on. "I'm kidding. We've barely met. But I like his boat. Apparently she's a winner, too. Fortunately you're not in the same class." Miranda was talking about the boats, but she suppressed a mischievous grin, knowing that the comment was appropriate for the men, as well.

"Let me know how the boat works out," Phil requested. "I'd like to know what Hall intends to do with it."

"Then ask him, not me," Miranda answered testily. "I'm nobody's messenger. Do your own snooping."

"I will." Phil arched his brows thoughtfully as he studied Miranda's obstinate expression.

"Good night." She stood there waiting for him to disembark, then she pulled in the gangway. There was something final in the action—removing the bridge between them—that made the tears build in her eyes. But they weren't tears of sorrow. "Now it's my turn," she said softly, understanding at last that she'd always put someone or something else higher on her list of priorities. From the family and the company to Jeff and the marina, something else always came first. But no longer. It was her turn, and she was going to enjoy every moment.

CHAPTER FIVE

AT TEN MINUTES TO TEN, Miranda followed Howard Vaughn through the hallways of the yacht club, listening to the latest dispute that morning. This issue was nothing as significant as a measuring violation or a questionable modification, it was a problem over spectator space. Who got to ride on what boat and who would make the worst scene if they were left behind?

The officials' boats were restricted to judges and club officers and "guests," but there were fewer power cruisers available than in previous years. That meant guests' space was limited. Even the press flotilla had diminished to one large power cruiser.

"We're short of spectator boats, Howard. It's embarrassing, but we can't take the usual observers out tomorrow to watch the race start. We've actually had to make rosters of the approved committee members and spectators, and some very influential names have been bumped." The fellow talking to Vaughn sounded desolate.

"Get on the phone and start calling around," a second official recommended. "If you can't get a couple of cruisers donated, then find out what we can charter them for."

Miranda shook her head, recognizing this same scene or one similar from every regatta she could remember. There were always the flocks of prominent club members and industry representatives who came for the events without boats but with the expectation and often a well-intentioned promise of a free ride. However, the number of willing powerboat owners had dwindled. Now came the frenzied last-minute search for transportation to keep feelings from being hurt and embarrassing omissions from spoiling the sporting atmosphere.

"It isn't my problem," Vaughn said, effectively cutting off the complaining. "I've got my officials situated. And I made no commitments to anyone. Those who want to ride along can take care of themselves."

"We don't want a lot of unauthorized boats out there crowding around the starting lines. We could end up with a real mess," Vaughn's shorter colleague noted. Occasionally amateur boaters and overeager fans with cameras and binoculars had blundered too close and impeded the start of a race. Some had even caused collisions by failing to follow one critical rule of the sea—boats under power were always obliged to yield right of way to those under sail. All the S.O.R.C. yachts would be under sail only.

"Then call the coast guard and have them keep out the small spectator boats," Vaughn snapped. "Try the university marine-studies division. They have a couple of cruisers they use for research. See if they'll carry passengers. Or suggest chartering one of the riverboats that make dinner cruises. But don't come griping to me," he stressed. "I'm judging, not playing social director."

"I have to go, dad," Miranda called over Vaughn's shoulder. There had been no time at all for any personal talk that day, but she did get a judge's view of the day-before-the-race activity. Vaughn was getting everything set up for the huge meeting in the club ballroom that night, the prerace briefing that all crew representatives would attend. She'd been privileged to sit in on a couple of smaller meetings with him already, but it was almost time for her appointment with Walker. "See you tonight." She wasn't even sure he could hear her in the congested corridor.

Vaughn stopped long enough to acknowledge her farewell, then immediately was distracted by another complainant, this one wearing a crew jacket and a very displeased expression. Miranda eased through the crowd, eager to get away from the haggling and out to the dock.

As she stepped out the yacht-club door, the burst of cool air enveloped her, but the spectacular Florida sunshine managed to make the February chill seem refreshing. Overhead, brilliant international flags snapped in the brisk wind, marking the nations whose boats had come to compete, and Miranda could feel the escalating excitement for the next day's race. The grassy park areas all along the St. Pete waterfront were carpeted with vividly colored sails, carefully being dried, folded and bagged, ready for action. Everywhere seamen and a few crewwomen had abandoned their previous work clothes for their colorful matching crew outfits, boasting the logo of the boat they were with. Photographers, amateur and professional, were everywhere.

Miranda was crossing to the marina entrance when a biker in a black jacket pulled up to the curb, the roar of his chrome-and-black Harley obliterating the normal marina sounds. The biker wore a black T-shirt, had a huge mustache, and his long hair streamed out under his helmet. The tall muscular man parked the massive cycle, then tucked an instrument case under his arm and strode out onto the docks. Like the music case containing a machine gun in an old gangster movie, the scarred violin case drew some apprehensive looks.

Miranda fell in step a few paces behind him, curious to see where he was going. Secretly, she was enjoying the startled expressions on people as they noticed the awesome biker strolling in their midst. When he cut along the finger dock toward *Persistence* and several other class-E boats, she slowed her pace. She thought back to the crewmen she had seen on Walker Hall's boat. One had a mustache. He had been the tallest one aboard, she recalled. Grimly she admitted this could be part of the crew that Walker had told her could use some of her "class." The biker was heading straight for *Persistence* all right.

All the action on the neighboring boats ceased as the biker lunged aboard, placing the music case in the shade. He stripped off his leather jacket and shirt, exposing magnificent pectoral muscles and an assortment of tattoos including one of a coiled rattlesnake. Grinning as if he knew how much attention he'd attracted and was thoroughly enjoying it, the biker continued to strip off his heavy boots, replacing them with worn deck shoes. As Miranda stood across the dock, she watched the gradual transformation from Hell's Angel to buccaneer and suspected Walker Hall had staged it all. What worried her was what part in the performance he'd planned for her.

When the biker climbed onto the bow of *Persistence*, and looked toward the bay expectantly, Miranda, and everyone at that end of the marina, followed his lead.

As soon as the twin boats tacked into the open, Miranda let a soft groan escape. "Oh no..." she whispered, wondering if it was too late to simply disappear into the crowd of bystanders. The two boats coming toward her were not S.O.R.C. competitors. Dwarfed by the sailing yachts at least twice their length, these visitors were small, perhaps sixteen-foot, open-deck racing dinghies, unlike any Miranda had seen before. Beautiful striped sails in oranges and golds spread from twenty-foot masts, and the sylphlike boats cut around the larger sailing yachts like butterflies skimming through a flower garden. The helmsman and sole occupant of the first butterfly was Walker Hall. At the helm of the second boat was an unlikely sailor who looked like a Rastafarian mystic, complete with beaded dreadlocks and chocolate skin. All he needed was the reggae music to capture the island spirit.

Photographers who had been eager spectators of the minidrama unfolding, suddenly remembered their cameras. The whirr and click that followed broke the near-silence that had fallen over the marina. A video unit, eager for some unusual footage on the S.O.R.C. action, moved in to capture the unique scene and make it history. Walker smiled and cut toward the dock while crewmen on the adjacent boats looked on, bellowing questions and whistling appreciatively at his boats.

"Hey, where'd you get them?"

"Nice boat. What's it called?"

"How much for one of those?"

"How about a demo ride?"

Others stared in sullen silence at the interlopers.

Miranda felt the firm pressure of a hand on her arm. "How about it?" The biker had located her in the midst of the spectators. "Walker said you're going out with us. Are you ready to go?" Above the huge droopy mustache, the blue-gray eyes were steady and cautious, but there was an unexpected gentleness in his voice.

"I'm a bit overdressed," she tried to joke, indicating her nylon jacket, knit sweater and slim flannel slacks. With the exception of the biker in his jeans, the others were wearing bathing suits.

"What gets wet can dry," the biker said philosophically.

Miranda dreaded having all those cameras aimed at her, and she knew they would be if she moved closer. But she caught a glimpse of Walker as he fielded questions and scanned the crowd. He was looking for her. When their eyes met, Walker shrugged slightly and smiled, leaving the choice up to her. Bold, arrogant, pushy and outrageous—he was all of those. But there was something more to him, an almost perverse pleasure in doing the unexpected and doing it well. Miranda took a deep breath and steeled herself. Whatever it was about him that charged her with a vibrant energy for living, she was willing to make a spectacle of herself to be close to him again.

"Come on aboard." Walker steadied the boat as Miranda sat on the edge of the dock so her feet nearly touched the deck.

"This wasn't exactly what I had in mind," Miranda muttered, bracing herself on his shoulder, then easing down next to him.

"Who's the lady?" Now the comments were about her.

"Hey, don't get her wet. I hear they melt."

Walker ignored the onlookers' gibes and signaled for Miranda to move up front. "Here's a brochure on the boat." He handed the video reporter a printed pamphlet. "If you want to talk later, I'll be available. The name's Walker Hall and the boat is the Phantom. She's making her debut today, and the lady gets the first dance." He waited while the biker climbed into the second boat, then they cast off, the exotic foursome drawing more camera fire from all sides.

"Ready about..."

Almost mechanically Miranda grasped the jib lines, ready to switch sides as the boat got under sail. In the midst of the too-public spectacle, the familiarity of tacking calmed her. She concentrated on the maneuvering, anxious for the silence and solitude that would be waiting out beyond the congestion of the marina.

"Miranda, meet Dennis," Walker called to her as the biker nodded, "and Lloyd."

Lloyd, the Rastafarian look-alike glanced at her briefly. "Nice to meet you, Miranda." Then it was back to business, as the two boats sliced between the pilings and a moored maxiboat weaving out into the bay.

"You built these?" Miranda asked.

"Sure did," Walker replied, his gray eyes gleaming with pride. "I kept thinking about the kind of boat I wished I'd had when I was younger. Something fast but sloop rigged like the big boats so you could really develop good sailing techniques. I couldn't compete against Porter Marine for two years, but since they don't make small boats, I dreamed up this one. Actually I'd been wanting to do it for years and couldn't get Mason Porter to put any research into it. So I sketched out the boat myself and built in a little pizzazz. State of the art in design and construction but without the high price tag. Let me show you what she can do."

With very little further conversation, Walker piloted the high-tech boat into the wavy waters of Tampa Bay, shaping the sails so the Phantom sped forward, heeling over to the side. Hastily Miranda slipped her feet under the sturdy hiking straps fastened to the cockpit floor and followed Walker's example, leaning out over the side of the boat, equalizing the weight. With the boat poised at a thirty-degree angle, they skimmed along, moving in wordless harmony with each shift in direction or variance in the wind.

Dennis and Lloyd in the second Phantom inched up behind them.

"We can't let 'em beat us," Walker yelled, hiking out even farther.

"Then I suggest you prepare to get very wet, or should I say wetter." Miranda stayed calm as the cool bay water swept over the lower rim of the side deck. Already she was soaked up to her knees, and the spray from the boat hitting the waves had streaked her nylon jacket and dampened the seat of her pants. But she was having great fun doing the balancing act, testing the Phantom's prowess now at forty degrees of heel.

"Don't worry," Walker said, laughing. "She'll make it to fifty before she tips, and I'm not anxious to drop her in. That isn't the kind of debut I want her to make."

Miranda's spirits sagged abruptly, realizing Walker was very conscious of being scrutinized by those aboard every nearby boat and those still watching from shore. Adding a dark-haired lady, pretty enough to make a striking foil for the three men, yet sufficiently skilled as a sailor to impress the spectators seemed cold-blooded and calculating—and strictly exploitive.

"Listen," Walker said as he released one line, letting the boat point straight into the wind. Abruptly all movement stopped and the sails fluttered lifelessly. He'd seen Miranda's gleeful smile disappear. "This show was already planned. You weren't. I could have gone through with this unveiling with or without you. I preferred with. I'm not sorry, and I wish you weren't."

"I just wish you'd have told me what you had orchestrated. Really, Walker, the biker and the violin case and the Rastafarian with the muscles. And then me. Not at all subtle," she said by way of a reprimand.

"We've already agreed I'm not a subtle man," he replied, hesitating as he assessed her. "If I told you about the Phantom or about Dennis and Lloyd, would you have showed up?" His mouth curved into a smug smile as he challenged her.

"Probably not."

"Then we would have missed a lot." He shrugged. "We're not just testing the boat today, and we both know it, Miranda. I said you and I shouldn't miss anything, even if we do have to make certain adjustments in our plans." The sensual warmth in his voice and the way his eyes locked with hers made her oblivious to the chill issuing up from her soggy feet. "I don't have time to be gentlemanly, Miranda. Now let's get back to what we were doing," he added with an amused but indulgent chuckle.

"You take the helm," he ordered her. "You skipper and I'll be crew. And let's catch up with Lloyd and Dennis and see how good you are." Immediately he shifted weight, moving toward the front of the boat while she inched toward the rear. "You're lucky we're in public and I'm such a decent guy," he teased. Just to prove his point, as they brushed past each other at midship, his hand grazed the curve of her leg and briefly glided over her derriere.

"You're lucky that I have enough respect for what's at stake here to refrain from lowering the boom, literally," she snapped, conscious that his touch had been deliberate. He was counting on her restraint.

"I know, I'm a barbarian." He laughed low in his throat. "But from certain angles, you do bring out the primitive in me."

"Then grab the jib lines, caveman," Miranda commanded. "And hold on to your loincloth." She turned the boat abruptly, heeling out over the water with her hair flying as the wind caught them. Walker scrambled out over the side as the boat streamed up in line with the other Phantom.

"You wanna race?" Dennis saw Miranda closing in. "Round the orange float, then end up back here?" He set the course. With a thumbs-up sign, he let out a war whoop and took off with Lloyd crouched like a panther in the foredeck, handling the jib lines.

Under the midday sun, the brilliant-colored Phantoms were two flashes of fire against the bright-blue water. Tacking back and forth in a zigzag course toward the marker, Miranda issued quick commands, nearly breathless from the exertion. Walker shifted with her, side to side, laughing maniacally as she stole inches on the other Phantom on every tack. "You got 'em." He shook his fist enthusiastically as they neared the turn mark.

Miranda waited until the last possible moment before reversing directions, nudging the marker's anchor line in the process of cutting around it.

"Ain't that illegal or something?" Dennis yelled.

"Not as long as you don't touch the marker itself or drag it with you. It's legal to bump the anchor line," Miranda yelled back.

"We'll catch you anyway."

"Wing on wing," Miranda called out, letting the large mainsail out full on her side. Walker pulled the jib out the other, so the boat planed over the tips of the waves like a bird with one wing spread on either side. With the wind at her back, Miranda held on, her teeth clenched to keep from screaming—thrilled, terrified and totally drenched. It was a straight run back and she led all the way.

"Nice work." Lloyd stretched his hand out to shake Miranda's once the victory was complete and the second Phantom coasted up beside her. Soaked like her and genuinely impressed by her daring, Lloyd looked less foreboding than he had before. His dreadlocks glistened with water droplets, and his innocent smile was disarming.

Dennis looked like a bedraggled puppy, long hair and mustache dripping salty water. "Not bad, for a woman," he muttered good-naturedly, flexing so his tattoos undulated in the sunlight. But the macho routine was purely an act, Miranda realized as he lowered his voice and winked at her. "If you aren't busy the next few weeks, we could always use another hand."

"These hands are in bad shape already," Miranda said, rubbing her reddened palms together. "There's a cold front creeping in, and my blood is too thin for that kind of sailing. I'll be snug in the officials' boat cheering you on."

"The officials' boat? Special privileges..." Walker pointed an accusing finger at her. "Howard Vaughn has been pulling strings, I see."

"He pulls other people's strings, not mine," Miranda replied testily. "I'll earn my space aboard the officials' cruiser by helping to spot boats," she insisted.

"Sure you will." Walker feigned a knowing expression. "You expect us to believe it has nothing to do with your being the daughter of the chairman of the judging committee?" He was enjoying harassing her.

"It's a compromise," Miranda admitted unflinchingly. "Just like my being here with you. I want to be near my dad. If that means accepting privileges and sitting on a boat with a bunch of men, I'll bear up somehow. Between the paperwork, the hot chocolate and the box lunches, my dad and I might get a chance to talk. I don't want to miss a chance—with him." She added the last words with just enough emphasis to make Walker realize he was pushing too hard.

"Okay. Truce." Walker conceded. "Let's take you back in so you can dry off, and we'll have another chance to show off."

The sail back into the marina was smooth and easy, and the crowd that had been there before had dissipated substantially. "Looks like the show's over," Miranda observed dryly.

"Honey, it's just beginning," Walker responded. "Drop by tonight after the briefing. We're having a briefing of our own. You don't want to miss it."

"Another performance?" she questioned. "Lights, camera, action?"

"Just drop by. I promise you won't get wet."

"I'll think about it..." Miranda barely had the words out when Sibyl's throaty voice hailed her. "Miranda. What on earth happened to you? We have a luncheon scheduled in an hour and you look...wet." She settled for the least of a series of possible descriptions.

"Sibyl, I'd like you to meet Walker Hall and his associates Dennis and Lloyd." Miranda smoothly disregarded her own appearance and introduced the short red-haired woman to her bare-chested sailing companions.

Sibyl's turquoise eyes narrowed warily as she looked from one man to the other. "I'd heard about this outing you were on, but I really didn't believe it," she commented. "You gentlemen have created quite a stir with your flamboyance. Perhaps you felt it was a bit too sedate here this year," she added with a forced smile.

"We're just doing a public service, ma'am," Walker said gravely with a chivalrous bow. "Wouldn't want anyone to get bored." Sibyl eyed him closely, looking for a trace of humor in his dead-pan eyes. When his gaze shifted to Miranda, Sibyl looked from one to the other suspiciously.

"Really, dear, we must be going," Sibyl insisted, catching Miranda by the arm and urging her along. "A bit caustic, but he really is a handsome devil," Sibyl whispered, glancing back over her shoulder fleetingly at Walker as his entourage began to attract a crowd once more. "However, those other two are absolutely garish."

"They're also very good sailors," Miranda informed her friend. "The garish part is only a smoke screen. If the rest of Walker's menagerie is anything like those two, he has good reason to be sure of himself."

"Oh he does, does he?" Sibyl squeezed Miranda's arm. "Is that a professional assessment or something more?"

"Down, Sibyl. Don't poke your nose into my business."

"I knew things would pick up if we could ever get you off that island," Sibyl cracked. "I just knew you'd thrive on the excitement."

"I thought you invited me here for professional reasons," Miranda said, stopping abruptly. Sibyl's guilty expression confirmed an uneasiness Miranda had felt all along. More than a writing assignment had prompted the invitation.

Sibyl fluttered her hands in panic. "I did have professional reasons. I needed the articles. Strictly business," she promised, her pouf of russet hair matching the flush appearing on her cheeks. "But as long as you're here, as Mr. Hall says, we don't want anyone to be bored." Her overeager expression was making Miranda extremely nervous.

"Don't start scheming," Miranda warned her companion. "This time, I plan to make my own decisions with no help from the cheering section."

"Rah, rah!" Sibyl teased. "I told you this was going to be such fun."

FUN WAS DEFINITELY LACKING at the two-hour briefing that evening. Miranda sat with her note pad open on the table, jotting down details about weather conditions and course markers. The cold front had stalled along the Suncoast, bringing fluctuating winds and choppy seas, and the temperature had dropped to the forties. If the front edged closer, the chill factor sailing on the Gulf of Mexico would be a disappointment to crews that had come hoping for balmy breezes.

Walker Hall and his thin solemn-faced companion, Ross Cornelius, sat across the room with Dennis right behind them. Dennis hunched over in his chair, staring at his hands as he listened to the committee advisors. The general mood was black but Miranda felt strangely detached as she watched the skippers and crewmen of the eighty-nine boats that would begin the first race the next morning—weather permitting.

"I saw you on the news this evening." Phil Pittman moved in behind Miranda and spoke to her over her shoulder. "You and Hall and his bizarre buddies."

Miranda nodded. She'd been told about it already by numerous people who stopped her on her way into the meeting.

"I suppose you know he had some little guy roaming the dock passing out sales brochures all day while he was showing off that boat of his?" Phil's disapproval was evident in the tone of his voice. "Quite a hustler, my dear. But of course," he added sarcastically, "you hardly know him."

Miranda sighed and finally turned in her chair to face him. "I know a number of hustlers around here. A few who pride themselves on civility and subtlety. But a hustler is a hustler, Phil, and before you put both feet into your mouth, remember how many times you've passed out your nicely engraved business cards from the brokerage while you've been here." His haughty smile was still frozen in place, while Miranda turned around and resumed her note taking, trying to ignore the heat she felt in her cheeks.

Across the room, Walker looked at her, then his gaze shifted briefly to Phil. The inscrutable expression when he turned his attention back to the speaker made Miranda even more uncomfortable. She didn't like the feeling that no matter which way she turned, someone expected an explanation or someone needed appeasing. Her father. Phil. Sibyl. Walker. They all tugged at her in their own ways.

"If I promise not to give you my business card," Phil persisted, leaning close again, "can I buy you a drink when this meeting lets out?"

"I'm afraid not," Miranda declined politely. "I promised to give my dad a hand clearing everything away here, then I plan to go back to the boat and get some sleep. I want to get up early for the race." She was still considering Walker's invitation to come aboard *Persistence* after the briefing, but until she knew for sure precisely what he had planned, she wasn't going to complicate the evening with other commitments. She'd been accommodating others all day, and she was taking time out for herself.

"Then how about breakfast?" Phil asked. "The *Hambone* crowd is convening at eight at the Concourse. It might look more equitable if you spend a little time with us instead of Hall and his questionable crew. There has been quite a bit of talk, Miranda, and with your father as head of the judging..." He didn't complete the thought, but his meaning was clear. Any sign of favoritism was inappropriate for the judge's daughter.

"I doubt if anyone thinks I could sway my father on a ruling," Miranda contended. "I wouldn't even try. Who wins is not that important to me."

"It's important to a lot of other people. I'm just suggesting you employ a little diplomacy."

"Is Charlie going to be at this breakfast?" Miranda inquired.

"I suppose so. Everyone from the crew and the company generally shows up." Phil seemed disconcerted by her interest in his ex-wife.

"Will Josh be there?" Miranda's question caught him by surprise.

"He's not coming down until next week." Phil sounded increasingly defensive. "Why all the interest in them?"

"As long as I'm being diplomatic, we don't want to add fuel to any unsubstantiated rumors that may be floating around," Miranda said, her dark eyes gleaming deviously. "If we're all there, you and Charlie and me, behaving like good friends, that might eliminate speculation of another sort."

"Breakfast for three wasn't what I had in mind," Phil said irritably, knowing that Miranda was outmaneuvering him.

"I'll see how my schedule is in the morning," Miranda concluded. "I'll be there if I feel awake enough to be charming."

"Sure. Charming." Phil didn't sound hopeful at all.

THE MUSIC THAT DRIFTED over the lighted marina that night wasn't the usual rock and roll that generally accompanied prerace parties. The on-deck sound systems that had been blaring occasionally during the trial week were shut off. Instead of letting off steam in the customary high-spirited way, people assembled on the decks of surrounding sailboats listening to the soft reggae music issuing from *Persistence*. After the tension of the meeting, this contrast seemed almost like spiritual restoration.

The cold spell had prompted the appearance of sleeping bags, heavy jackets and blankets, and the steamy spirals from coffee and hot chocolate added feathery touches to the scene. Warm breaths made little clouds in the air, and noses sunburned and windburned from earlier in the week now turned deep pink from the chilly moist night air. Pulling her jacket collar up, Miranda strolled to a point across from *Persistence* where she could watch the music makers without getting caught up in the crowd seated closer to the boat.

Anonymous and apart, Miranda sat in the darkness on top of a piling, listening to the strangely beautiful combination of sounds. Dennis, cross-legged on the foredeck of *Persistence*, had a silver harmonica resting on his knee, but the music he was making came from an electric violin, tucked under his chin. With a poignant eloquence, his rough fingers pressed the strings and his muscular biceps, with tattoos bared by his sleeveless sweat shirt, arced in the air, pulling out the melody.

Walker Hall leaned back against the cabin, knees bent up, playing a harmonica larger than the one Dennis had in reserve. Lloyd supplied the percussion, alternating between drums, metal cylinders and wooden blocks. But it was the small, slightly built fellow, the one Miranda had seen aboard *Persistence*, who produced the most exquisite sounds, strumming on a dulcimer, an instrument Miranda had only seen in museums and read about in fairy tales. But the angelic sound was breathtaking.

Framed by the overhead spotlights, the foursome had apparently been playing for some time before Miranda came by. And now, as she watched the poetic scene created by these four unusual players, she didn't wish to break the spell by moving closer. It was their show. Walker might have invited her earlier, but she had nothing to add to the moment.

Lloyd grinned to his companions and broke into a naughty reggae song with a catchy chorus that soon was chanted back to him by the crowd. Then he switched to a Jamaican melody, his solitary voice, gentle and pure, subduing the prerace jitters of the crowd. "Become as the calm before the gathering storm," Lloyd sang. "Let peace of spirit keep you from harm."

Miranda listened, hypnotized by the tranquility of the scene. As lovely as it was, she knew Walker had planned it all for publicity. She hoped that no one would be passing through the crowd handing out those brochures Phil had mentioned. Walker was a hustler all right, but Miranda didn't want that part of him to spoil this moment. "Let the wind in the sails lift you out of your earthly troubles...."

Lloyd's song floated through the air as a photographer with a huge flash apparatus moved in close, picking out the best angle to shoot from. Wrinkling her nose in distress, Miranda wished he would just leave. But he didn't. When a second cameraman carrying a shoulder video pack arrived, she decided it was time to go, before anything more was ruined.

WALKER ONLY CAUGHT A GLIMPSE of her as she headed back along the dock. The smooth dark hair, swaying just above her shoulders as she walked, and the long purposeful strides reminded him of the first time he'd ever seen her. That time she had clearly been interested in *Persistence* and curious about her captain. But this time she was leaving, and he hadn't even known she'd been there, watching and listening from somewhere out beyond the lights.

He'd seen her twice since their ride on the Phantom that day. Passing through the yacht-club foyer, he'd watched her getting into a limo with Sibyl Albrecht. Both of them had been wearing classy suits with hats and gloves. Then she was gone. What bothered him was that Miranda seemed to fit so well into the whole thing—the clothes, the limo, the ladies' luncheon scene. Then, at the briefing, he'd seen the more familiar version of Miranda. She was dressed casually in slim slacks and a sweater. During the briefing she had taken notes, and afterward she had stuck close to her father. Pittman had tried to catch her attention, leaning over her shoulder like a vulture. But Miranda seemed to be having none of it—whatever it was she said, it was obviously meant to discourage him.

During the briefing, Miranda and Walker exchanged several looks. Cautious. Curious. But neither one actually made a move. He really hadn't known what to expect tonight. He wanted her there, to listen and to enjoy the music. Sure it was a show, but there was no harm in it. This was for fun—mostly. Yet there was method to his madness. This image of his men offered an alternate impression. Just as the gossip caused by motorcycles, beads and dreadlocks was subsiding, he'd give them something else to talk about. The key was to keep 'em talking because that meant they'd be talking about *Persistence*, the Phantom and Hall himself. Every media person around was looking for the hottest story, and that meant coverage.

Walker watched as she turned at the end of the marina, walking alone along the sidewalk toward the Albrechts' power cruiser. She wasn't more than a hundred yards away, the length of a football field. That was all. But tonight it felt like a hundred miles. Until the pressure was off and unless he pulled off his schemes, they would remain worlds apart.

> She is the daughter of the king,
> Just cannot get away.
> The way the people crowd the streets
> Just to see her play.

Walker had heard Lloyd sing that song before, but this time it touched him as it never had before. Jack played along on the dulcimer, and Walker watched, almost enchanted, as the phrases crept into his mind.

> And when the time comes,
> She must take her place down in the throne room.
> And when the time comes,
> She must live a life that's not her own.

Lloyd sang to a silent audience. The words spoke of limitations, of separateness, of a solitary path dictated by duty.

Walker leaned forward, trying to see how far Miranda had gone, wondering what had kept her from coming close enough for him to talk to her or touch her. He could go after her, but that wouldn't change anything. He couldn't shake the sadness of the lone phrase, "And when the time comes..." For two years he'd put everything he had and all he could borrow into this effort. The time had come. And for the next five weeks he had to live a life that wasn't really his own. Then there was Miranda and this song and her life, one that he didn't fit into. Walker did not know what would happen in five weeks when the S.O.R.C. ended and their separate worlds claimed them. But there was a growing emptiness each time he let her in, only to let her go again.

From the deck of *Persistence* he could see the light in the stateroom window of the cabin cruiser where Miranda was staying. Then a moment later, the light went out. That other world claimed her tonight, but Walker wasn't ready to surrender her completely. It wasn't yet time for that.

STANDING IN THE DARK ROOM, looking out the window at the gathering across the water, Miranda refused to give in to tears. She had listened to the song, every silver-edged word, as it carried over the marina and pierced through the night. If that was what Walker wanted her there for, to hear that song, to compare her to a princess tied by duty and blood to "a life that's not her own," then he had misread her completely. She wasn't being drawn back into the old life. She was only building bridges, trying to salvage part of her past and create a future. Yet the song did disturb her because she knew it was partially true. She did try to please everyone who was important to her.

And they will love her,
And adore her,
The daughter of the king.

The words could have been about her—once. Once she had dreamed of serving in Howard Vaughn's place after he retired—abdicating to his heir. But that was years ago. Now all she wanted was a father, a family, as complete as it could be without dark-eyed Amanda Calvert Vaughn who had not survived the pressures, excesses and temptations of the courtly life.

Lloyd sang the song again, almost from the beginning, and Miranda covered her mouth, stifling the sobs. The fairy tale was dying to the strains of a dulcimer. But Miranda stayed at the window, drawing in each pure syllable, feeling more alive than she had for a long time. She couldn't explain how a mere song could touch her so deeply, recalling old wounds, old illusions, old dreams and making her feel so totally alone. But these feelings seemed more real to her than all the feelings she'd allowed herself to show.

"Damn you Walker Hall," she murmured, cursing him for being able to pierce through all her protective walls. She dreaded what would happen if she let herself care, yet she knew some part of her hungered for the daring he possessed. He didn't see how tenaciously she held on to the independence she had found in Tortola. Like everyone else, he thought she belonged here—with the king and his court. He underestimated her.

The tears began when she thought of Charlie. Still caught up in the system, Charlie would be hostess at the

Birmingham-sponsored breakfast. Entrapped by the expectations of others, Charlie would do her part dutifully and always be in the background. Ironically they envied each other. At least they had. Miranda had wished for the life with Phil, and Charlie had wished for a way out, an escape such as the one Miranda had made.

Miranda brushed her cheek with her fingertips, relieved that in the dark no one could see she'd lost control. She'd always been the one to bear up admirably under stress. Hers was the shoulder friends and family could lean on. Now she needed someone. She'd hoped Walker could understand her attempts to reconnect, to restructure old ties into new ones. But even though his uncanny insight impressed her, she hated the unpredictability, the arbitrariness of the man. One moment he was whispering in her ear; the next he was demanding an explanation for her other allegiances.

"You're really a dummy," she whispered to the distant Walker Hall. "All the fancy stuff is what I don't want." Across the marina, Dennis was now playing a country-and-western tune and the crowd responded cheerfully. It was a change of pace they all needed. Miranda sighed in frustration. Just like the music, Walker went from sentimental to brassy and bold, and she was never sure where the performance began or left off.

The sound of Walker's harmonica joined in with Dennis's violin. Then the fellow with the dulcimer caught on and strummed along. Undressing in the dark, Miranda studied the curly-haired harmonica player. Though he was making music with his friends, he sat apart, solitary, like her. They had that in common—an aloneness that was at once their defense and their most vulnerable quality. That aloneness was somehow part of the allure of sailing. Under sail only skill mattered, and she and Walker had meshed talents almost without a need for words. Even on land, there had been times when she felt an indisputable feeling of rightness between them. But then there was now. Tonight. That song.

The final ripple of applause from the audience signaled that the serenade by Walker and his crew had ended. Gradually the crowd melted away and the lights on the moored boats blinked out, letting the night close in. Ultimately, Walker was alone on *Persistence*, standing in the darkness, staring across the water toward the Albrechts' cruiser. Miranda watched him a moment longer, wondering what he wanted of her, what he was trying to prove. He'd orchestrated this emotional tug-of-war, repeatedly setting her up, then pulling her off balance. Tonight he'd won another round. But he didn't look triumphant as he turned, little more than a moving shadow, and disappeared below.

CHAPTER SIX

SATURDAY DAWNED FAR MORE PLEASANTLY than the weather forecasters had predicted. With light and variable ten- to fifteen-knot winds and the temperature at fifty, the first race of the S.O.R.C. wasn't going to be the frigid ordeal everyone had feared.

"Couldn't have asked for better conditions if weather came made to order," Howard Vaughn proclaimed, standing in the cockpit of the officials' cruiser, surveying the fleet. All across the choppy bay, competition sailboats assembled while a cool southerly wind promised a picture-perfect start. Miranda stood next to her father, peering through binoculars at the spectacle, trying to follow the course of *Persistence* as she waited for the first class to start.

The expression on Walker's face when *Persistence* was leaving the marina had been impassive, but when he caught sight of Miranda he had grinned and waved and given her the thumbs-up sign. "I want to see you when this is over," he yelled right out loud while everyone aboard both boats looked on. Miranda had nodded and tried to look efficient, jotting down a reminder in her notebook, a reminder she certainly didn't require. She intended to see him too. She had a few questions she'd avoided asking him until now. Before he jumped to any more conclusions about her or caught her off guard again, she wanted to get some things straight, starting with that song whose words had haunted her all night long.

Miranda had a few less-personal questions, as well. She wanted some explanation of his connection to that Stasch fellow and the headhunter Benjamin. This time she wasn't kidding herself; this wasn't research for an article. She was studying Walker's ethics, sizing him up, testing him the same way he'd been testing her.

The class-A maxis—*The Shadow, Kialoa, Prophecy, Hambone* and six other boats in the fifty-five- to eighty-three-foot range—were first to approach the starting point at noon. The starts were staggered, ten minutes apart with one class passing under the Skyway Bridge before the starting signal for the next class was given. Larger boats would go first, but even with spinnakers flying, Miranda knew they wouldn't have the wind-power for record speeds. The huge maxis would lead all the way. However, when the times were adjusted according to IOR handicaps, any boat could come out the winner. The light-wind conditions favored the smaller-class boats, and Miranda paced with nervous excitement, knowing that *Persistence* could possibly take this opening round.

This opener, a 138-mile jaunt south into the Gulf of Mexico to Boca Grande, then back again, would take all night and part of Sunday. With crews split into four- or six-hour watches, all the participants would get an exercise in serious competition before tackling the longest race, the grueling 370-mile second event around the Florida Keys to Fort Lauderdale scheduled for Tuesday. The Boca Grande Race was the overture, and Miranda fidgeted with the binoculars like a child at a concert, ready to get on with the show.

When the class-E boats finally got under way, *Persistence* left Mason Porter's similarly shaped *Elan* behind. Racing side by side with the rainbow-striped *Razzle-Dazzle*, last year's fleet winner in the Boca Grande Race, *Persistence* billowed her brilliant spinnaker with the star-burst design and sailed past the officials' boat toward the Skyway Bridge. Miranda tried to maintain her objectivity, but when *Persistence* took a slight lead after clearing the bridge, Miranda wanted to follow along, monitoring the race from beginning to end. But neither she nor the officials' boat were going anywhere. The final class-F boats, thirty-three- to forty-foot racers, had yet to begin. They were jockeying for position back at the starting line, and Miranda had to record their departure times. Diligently she turned the binoculars to class F.

Once all classes were off, steady radio contact kept the details of the races coming through. At the sea buoy where Tampa Bay opened into the Gulf of Mexico, there were three class-E boats in close company, *Persistence, Razzle-Dazzle* and *Divine*, the French entry. Far ahead, in the maxi class, traditional rivals *Kialoa* and *Sorcery* held the lead with the Albrechts' *Prophecy* close behind. Back at the Yacht Club, flanked by officials and friends, Miranda transcribed the notes she'd made, listening to the accounts coming in. Bored with paperwork, she paced the corridors between the officials' conference room and the lounge like a caged panther, as the radio reports played on overhead speakers.

"If you could slow down for a few minutes, I'd like some company for dinner." Charlie Birmingham corralled her. "I was supposed to meet my father and some friends, but I've had enough business and this blow-by-blow account of the race only makes me nervous. How about both of us getting out of here? Maybe we could find that toy store you mentioned."

"Let's go," Miranda answered, knowing that unless she was out there on a boat with the competitors, nothing else would substitute. Certainly not a radio report. Getting away altogether for a few hours would break the tension. Having Charlie to spend the time with made the prospect even more pleasant.

"I feel like a kid playing hooky," Charlie admitted once they had finished prowling through the collection of unusual shops along the bay and picked out a restaurant. "This was fun."

"Very bulky fun," Miranda agreed, clasping a stuffed frog Charlie had purchased for young Josh. Gladly she handed the creature to the hostess in the restaurant foyer while Charlie followed suit. Packageless, they proceeded to a quiet corner table.

"I'm curious." Miranda broached a new subject as they sipped their coffee. "Surely you must sail. Why haven't I seen you out on *Hambone*? Why didn't you go along on the Boca Grande Race?"

"I like to sail," Charlie acknowledged. "I'm just not very good at it. I'm not strong or very agile, and I hate getting yelled at. Phil turns into Captain Bligh when he's skipper." She looked at Miranda uneasily. "I've heard what an excellent sailor you are."

"I still get yelled at," Miranda admitted. "It comes with the territory."

"I choose to stay out of that territory during races," Charlie noted. "Phil has a ruthless streak when it comes to racing. Even Josh refuses to go out in a boat with his dad. Phil is on him every minute, cramming him with information even an adult would find confusing." For a few seconds, some indefinable emotion smoldered in her eyes, then they returned to cool blue. "This summer I'd like to get Josh a little boat, a pram or a dinghy. Something he can learn on, without having Phil pressure him. But for now, the frog will have to do."

"The frog is a beauty," Miranda agreed, willingly changing subjects. "I can't wait to meet this kid."

"He'll be in Lauderdale next Friday." Charlie's voice ached with loneliness. "I do miss him," she whispered.

"My brother Jeff is flying in then, too, just in time to warm up for the last four races. You and Josh will have to meet him," Miranda insisted. "He's very good with kids. He's even started a sailing class for children on the weekends. Of course our prams are clunky old wooden ones that we rebuilt and the sails are patched, but the kids love them."

"I thought your brother was in a wheelchair," Charlie said with a trace of apprehension.

"He is. I have to keep reminding him of that." Miranda laughed, easing any discomfort over the topic. "He wheels around the marina, yanks himself on and off boats, and sometimes we both forget that his legs don't work. The kids think it's great. They figure if he can sail, so can they. And if he falls in, he floats just like the rest of us."

"I guess that's right." Charlie relaxed again, apparently relieved that their tentative bonds of friendship were not strained by discussing Jeff's handicap. "How did he get injured?"

"He fell off a boat." Miranda began the account of Jeff's accident, including the fact that he'd been quite a drinker in those days. When she talked of all the pressure on him, to do well at college, to sail in regattas on Vaughn's boat, then to work for Vaughn Marine Hardware, Miranda could see the understanding in Charlie's sad blue eyes. Jeff was a company son, just as she and Miranda had been company daughters. There were expectations and pressures, and there were innumerable occasions to drink. Some escaped, some fell into the trap. Jeff was one who fell.

Later, when they were walking through the bay-shore park on the way back to the marina, Charlie looked at Miranda slyly. "Phil says that our becoming friends is a problem. Apparently you were supposed to show up at our breakfast party and didn't. He thinks I've talked you out of seeing him."

"You didn't. I missed your breakfast because I wanted to help my dad." Miranda noticed the relief in Charlie's expression. "Phil will have to realize that you and I have more to talk about than just him," Miranda noted with an arch of her eyebrow. "Don't let him aggravate you."

"I did hear you're becoming chummy with that Walker Hall. He's the one my dad thinks is so crass and commercial." She watched as a small smile flitted over Miranda's lips.

"I seem to have been generating a lot of gossip," Miranda observed, not really all that amused.

"I just thought you might want to know what's being said," Charlie replied apologetically. "Since Mr. Hall brought those little sailboats into the marina, several of the boat builders are fuming. They think it's unethical for him to flaunt his products at a prestigious sporting event." Then before Miranda could comment, Charlie added icily, "I wonder what's the difference between that and handing out business cards? What about all the highly visible company logos, all the charming dinners and luncheons with potential clients? Their sales campaigns may be more refined, but it's still the same practice."

"Only less conspicuous," Miranda joined in. "At least Walker didn't have a For Sale banner flying from the mast, although I wouldn't put it past him."

"Then there is something to the rumors about you and Hall?" Charlie's eyes danced mischievously.

"There's something, all right. Whatever it is, it's erratic at best," Miranda admitted, pleased that she had a woman friend to talk to. "Walker is definitely the on-again-off-again type. But I don't like being treated like a yo-yo."

"I should think we both have had enough yo-yo romance after our experiences with Phil," Charlie reflected, enjoying the camaraderie and the girl talk. "Next time, I'd like to be the one pulling the string."

"I'd like not having anyone pulling strings," Miranda said thoughtfully. She'd had enough of a contest of manipulation with Walker already.

"Ah...another romantic besides me," Charlie observed, sighing sympathetically. "When you meet a nonmanipulative man, check if he has a brother."

"I have a brother," Miranda replied, feeling the matchmaking instinct beginning. "I'll introduce you. Jeff is too busy enjoying life to manipulate anyone. He's got the most bizarre sense of humor, and he can tackle anything. He may be on wheels but the rest of him is highly functional."

"It is?" Charlie looked surprised. "I thought with that kind of injury..." Charlie's color deepened.

"Jeff had always been quite a romantic himself—an active one," Miranda added. "According to the ladies he's known on Tortola, Jeff is all right. Occasionally the logistics with a paraplegic takes a little extra time and a sense of humor, but he manages." Miranda realized with a flush of embarrassment she was getting ahead of herself. Jeff didn't need a selling job, and part of her matchmaking motivation was purely selfish. She liked Charlie—for herself, for a friend. It had been a long time since she'd had a woman she felt so compatible with. "Wait till Lauderdale. See for yourself. Right now I also have to go and find a radio. Yo-yo or not, I want to know how Walker's boat is doing."

"I suppose I should show an interest in *Hambone*," Charlie conceded. "But it's difficult to stir up any affection for a boat that looks like a monolith. Let's get a drink. Hot chocolate with a sliver of cinnamon," she added quickly. "The frog and I are on the wagon."

By eleven that night, the crowd in the yacht-club lounge had thinned, and Miranda and Charlie gave up. But Miranda was awake again at dawn, anxious for the first of the boats to return. "I'm never going to make it through the series like this," she confessed to Sibyl over their coffee. "I can't stand the waiting."

"Vinnie hoped you'd say that." Sibyl smiled knowingly. "He has a post on *Prophecy* for the long race to Fort Lauderdale. Last year *The Shadow* set a course record at a little under forty hours. Vinnie hopes to stay with the leaders. That would put you in Lauderdale early enough to watch the other classes come in."

"I'll go." Miranda almost leaped out of her chair. Riding the giant red maxi, she could feel firsthand the excitement of the race around the Keys and still keep radio contact with the field. And Walker would only be hours behind. It would be the next best thing to riding on *Persistence* with him.

"We'd better take off." Howard Vaughn called for Miranda to hurry and follow him aboard the officials' cruiser. "*Kialoa* has a lead with three others in hot pursuit. Let's get out there."

Eighteen hours and thirty seconds after the 138-mile race began, at 7:50 A.M., Miranda watched the first maxi, *Kialoa*, cross the finish line. Four, five and six minutes later, the next three class-A maxiboats swept between the marks like grandes dames at the ball. From then on, sails were constantly in view on the horizon as B leaders fought off contenders from the C, D, E and F classes.

At one o'clock, *Persistence* was the first class-E boat to burst into view amid a field of bigger boats. With *Razzle-Dazzle* streaking along beside her, *Persistence* crossed the line twenty-two hours and twenty-five minutes after her start, claiming the win in her class.

"She's got it," Miranda squealed with excitement, watching through her binoculars as Dennis and Jack Davis danced a jig on the foredeck. Walker Hall hugged Lloyd, the helmsman, then threw back his head and let out a whoop she could hear all the way over on the officials' boat.

"She'll probably take the overall Boca Grande fleet trophy, as well," Howard Vaughn noted as he calculated *Persistence*'s handicap and adjusted time. "She corrects out ahead of every boat so far. *Razzle-Dazzle* takes second—in the class and over fleet. I think we've got us a new star."

Miranda's heart was pounding as she raced to the cruiser's stern to wave at the triumphant crew aboard *Persistence*. Bouncing up and down and shaking her fist in the air, she held up one finger. Number one. Just as Walker said it would happen. The next minute she had an on-board call.

"You want to stay out here or would you like to ride in with us?" Walker radioed to Miranda on the officials' boat. He was willing to swing back close enough for her to jump ship.

"I'd love to ride with you guys, but you'd have everyone in a panic if you changed course now." Miranda didn't want anything to detract from the spectacular victory. "Just get her into the marina safely. I'll catch up with you there. Congratulations, Walker. Your boat is magnificent and so is the crew."

There was a momentary silence as Walker hesitated. "Get back up on deck, Miranda. I'm coming to get you."

Like a mounted knight flying his lady's colors, Walker turned *Persistence* about and headed back toward the anchored officials' boat while Miranda squeezed through the crowd of other passengers. "Dad, he's coming up beside us," she explained hastily to Vaughn. "He wants me to ride in with them. Is it legal?" Wide-eyed and breathless from the trip below, Miranda was ready to wave Hall off if his unorthodox passenger transfer could compromise his victory. As head judge, Vaughn was the highest-ranked authority. His decision was law.

Already overhead, the helicopter carrying local video news teams moved in, filming *Persistence* for the evening news. Word was out that against a fleet of international entries, one of Florida's own had taken top honors, with *Razzle-Dazzle*, another local favorite a close second. Vaughn glanced up anxiously, not wanting anything on film that might detract from the reputations of the well-run, well-organized event. "He needs to stay clear or he could be called for interfering with the course. There's a couple of bottles of champagne in the cabinet," Vaughn said quickly as *Persistence* returned. "Take them, get in the chase boat and meet them halfway. Give them to the crew and make it look as if we planned it that way."

It was a skillful cover-up, but one Miranda really wanted to be part of. Flourishing the two bottles of champagne, she hurried to side deck. Then she leaped into the chase boat that Vaughn signaled off immediately. About seventy yards clear of the course, they stopped while *Persistence* tacked toward them. One by one she pitched the bottles to Dennis while Walker leaned over the lifelines, one arm outstretched, ready to grab her when the boats came into alignment. Lloyd eased *Persistence* close to the chase boat, Walker's hand caught hers and in an instant, Miranda was vaulting the three and a half feet of open space, landing with one foot on the teak toe rail.

Hanging on to Miranda tightly, Walker waited until *Persistence* had moved past the chase boat before letting her switch feet and climb over the lifeline rail into the cockpit. His face was damp from the spray of seawater, his curly dark hair was flecked with moisture, and his gray eyes were alive with a blazing glow of sheer triumph. When he pulled her against him with a spontaneous hug of celebration, Miranda felt his exuberance shoot through her limbs, unleashing the excitement she'd been reigning in.

"You were wonderful." Miranda laughed over his shoulder, hugging him as he swung her around. "You're all wonderful," she yelled to the crew.

"What'ya expect?" Dennis crowed. "We just look goofy," he cackled.

"Speak for yourself," Lloyd called from the helm. "Some of us aren't as weird as you are." While Miranda watched, he lifted off his massive flow of dreadlocks, sweeping them across him in an elegant courtly bow. Then he pitched the wig down the hatch.

"Why you..." Miranda tried to struggle out of Walker's bear hug, furious that all the Rastafarian business was simply part of the stage show. But Hall held on to her while she wriggled and squirmed, chuckling low and throaty as the helicopter overhead made another low pass. Miranda stopped resisting, but in the momentary lull, she looked up at Walker. "Don't you dare..." she warned, feeling his gray eyes boring into her own. Her last words were smothered on her lips. And for the Channel 8 news show, she was soundly and expertly kissed.

The effect of Walker's lips on hers was dizzying. The initial contact, sudden and firm, softened coaxingly, becoming more tantalizing as his hold on her relaxed and his arms became more caressing than viselike. Miranda no longer protested, allowing the delicious sensations he was prompting to flow through her, like a new wind clearing the clouds away. The kiss deepened, his tongue seeking and gaining entrance to the sweet warmth of her mouth. Walker purred deep in his throat, a sound at once satisfied yet full of desire. When he lifted his lips from hers, he stared down at her dreamily, studying the expression in her half-closed eyes. "You don't know how long I've been wanting to do that," Walker said hoarsely.

"Just do it again," Miranda replied softly, her lips still warm and moist from his kiss. This time, standing on tiptoe, she raised her mouth to his. Parting her lips as they touched, feeling the magic he had promised, her whole body was set on fire. While the nine crewmen hooted and whooped and popped the tops off the bottles of champagne, Miranda felt the passion that had simmered inside her build and bubble and spill over into more kisses. Exciting, joyful, carefree kisses. Just kisses. Miranda let the waves of jubilation carry her along, knowing that the festive atmosphere and the playful attitude of the crew meant kissing was as far as it would go right there, right then. The on-deck abandon offered just enough freedom, just enough limitation to make those kisses beautiful and tantalizing—and safe.

"Oh, Miranda." Walker shook his head and smiled down at her, his gray eyes gleaming with a fire of sensual discovery. "You make me forget to breathe." She could feel his body trembling as he maintained control, easing them apart reluctantly. Brassy and tough as Walker could be, he was exhausted from the trip, but it was her nearness that had shaken him. Miranda knew nothing he could be feeling was more overwhelming than his power over her, a feeling more compelling and complete than sexual desire, but the realization that she affected him so strongly pleased her.

"Come on," Dennis called to them. "Celebrate." He thrust the champagne bottle out over Walker's head and let it pour. From then on, the madness continued with Jack Davis leading a conga line and only Lloyd, with close-cropped hair, calmly keeping *Persistence* heading for her marina destination. Reporters were already on the docks when *Persistence* sidled into her mooring. Even though the times and the class and fleet wins were unofficial, the newsmen wanted first shot at Walker Hall.

"I think I'll duck out now," Miranda said, still flushed with emotion. "This is your show."

"I want to see you when things settle down," Walker said, catching her arm and delaying her exit. "This is not the place. . ." He didn't have the opportunity to finish. Armed with an ice chest of cold beer, several crewmen from the next boat slip climbed aboard and the popping tops and spilling foam began again.

"Later," Miranda promised, anxious to get away before she was among those doused with beer or dumped into the marina. Neither possibility appealed to her. Like an explorer with a newfound treasure, she wanted to prolong the awe of discovery a little longer and enjoy the surge of emotions that had swept her away. What was happening between her and Walker was too new, too intimate to share with a crowd of strangers. Later—away from here—she would become logical and reasonable and sort it all out. But for now, while the throng around *Persistence* grew larger and noisier, she would go about her business, savoring the sensations she held inside, enjoying what had happened unexpectedly at sea.

The rest of the afternoon, Miranda kept up with the results as the remainder of the fleet continued trailing in. Weary crews spread the used, crumpled sails over any open surface, folding and repacking their inventory in numbered bags. Then the crewmen either collapsed or began to party.

"There's a protest against Hall," Howard Vaughn said grimly when Miranda met the incoming officials' boat.

"Not because he picked me up...?" Miranda asked, horrified that he might have his victory challenged because of her.

"Something else. A tacking violation. Someone says during the night he forced them to drop off when he didn't have the right of way. It has nothing to do with you."

"Who is making the protest?" Miranda questioned her father. From what she'd seen of Walker Hall he stayed within the rules.

"One of the class-B boats, *Double Play*." Vaughn kept his voice low as he walked with her toward the yacht club.

"That's one of Mason Porter's boats," Miranda remembered. "Who's the captain?" When Vaughn frowned and avoided looking her directly in the eyes, Miranda felt something about the protest wasn't quite right.

"Bobby Austin," Vaughn replied.

"Porter's son-in-law. How cosy," Miranda sniffed. "*Persistence* beats the pants off Mason Porter's *Elan*, and the only one who gripes is Porter's son-in-law."

"Don't go jumping to conclusions, Miranda," Vaughn cautioned her. "We handle this like any other protest. Just let things settle until the jury gets together tomorrow." His tanned face, creased more deeply after the tiring hours watching and recording the finish, became tight and expressionless as they moved indoors.

"Howard..." He was summoned left and right by others who'd been waiting to see him. "What's this about a protest?"

When she saw the uncharacteristic sag of Vaughn's shoulders, Miranda became protective, wishing to spare him another explanation, another interruption. "Excuse us, gentlemen, but we need to get some dinner," she said brightly, taking his arm and steering him right past the men who'd come to meet him. "You'll just have to wait in line, fellows," Miranda insisted. "My dad has been promising me food all day," she gushed, smiling in the bewildered faces of men unaccustomed to viewing impressive white-haired Howard Vaughn as anyone's "dad."

For his part, Vaughn remained silent, shrugging accommodatingly and letting her guide him on a straight path to the dining room. "Couldn't have done it better myself," he chuckled once they were alone. Then his smug smile faded and a new softness filled his eyes. "Thank you for the rescue, Miranda. I am tired. And I'm fed up with the noise." It was an uncharacteristic admission, a reward Miranda didn't anticipate.

"Me too." She didn't relinquish her hold on him. "My father and I would like a quiet seat by the window," she told the maître d'. "And we don't want anyone interrupting our dinner. So if you get any inquiries, please pass on that information." She said it with such gentleness that the maître d' nodded sympathetically.

"That I couldn't have done," Vaughn commended her. "I haven't had a meal in peace since I got here."

"You can have one now," Miranda said softly. "Although I do have one official question to ask. Don't worry," she added, seeing the wariness in his expression. "I want to crew on a boat next race."

"Not this *Persistence*?" Vaughn almost winced.

"No. I can go on Vinnie's boat, *Prophecy*. I'll get in ahead of most of the fleet, and I won't have to wait two days for any action. I don't like just observing, dad."

Vaughn nodded, both in understanding and relief. "Crewing on *Prophecy* is all right. But I have a feeling that regardless how this protest against Hall's boat turns out, he's in the hot spot from now on. I'd prefer your not being on that boat—especially since I'm heading the protest jury."

"I doubt if anyone thinks I could influence your ruling," Miranda said, stiffening indignantly. "I wouldn't try it even if I thought I could. You taught me to be a better sport than that."

"I don't know, Miranda," Vaughn said carefully. "I'm beginning to wonder what I did teach you over the years." Again a fleeting tenderness softened his blue eyes. "What you did in there was very thoughtful. You didn't learn that kind of thoughtfulness from me."

"You didn't think I was being particularly thoughtful when I took Jeff to Tortola," Miranda countered. "I was trying to keep everyone from destroying him, and you thought I made him a quitter. He needed more than a peaceful meal," she noted. "All the probing and poking and testing oppressed him."

Vaughn was watching her, his eyelids lowered slightly, lips pursed, regarding her with solemn interest. "I wanted him to get better."

"You wanted a miracle." Miranda reached out and

rested her hand on her father's arm. "You'll see, dad. You got one. Wait till Lauderdale."

Miranda pretended not to see the tears in Howard Vaughn's eyes. "Maybe I got two miracles," Vaughn said throatily. "You're one of them. You're tough, but not in the ways I realized." He cleared his throat, picking up the menu to curtail any further sentiment. "I intend to win you both over with the Florida branch of the company." He resumed his more formal distance. "You'd make an old man very happy," he told her.

"Don't pull that old man routine on me," Miranda shot back with a disbelieving grin. "Sneaking you away to dinner is a time-out, not a retirement."

"It was worth a try." Vaughn chuckled. Then he smiled softly as if he'd needed to be reassured he wasn't really so old at all. "I have to attend the awards party tomorrow night. Would you go with me?"

Miranda arched her brows thoughtfully. "I may hold out for another offer." She evaded a direct response. Captains were allowed to take "their ladies" to the award ceremonies after each of the six races of the S.O.R.C. Miranda wasn't sure she qualified as Walker's lady—or if she wanted to be, but until they had a chance to talk in private, she wanted to leave her options open.

"If the protest is discounted and Hall wins, I hope you're not thinking of going with him. Lord knows what kind of publicity stunt he's got planned." Vaughn had obviously been keeping track of Walker's media escapades. "I'm surprised you find his flamboyance attractive," he added deliberately.

"It's not his flamboyance, it's his body I'm after,"

Miranda joked. Then her face slowly began to turn deep red. The words were close enough to the truth to make her whole body blush.

"I noticed the kissing," Vaughn conceded. "There's no need to go into further detail. I'm not sure we know each other well enough yet."

Miranda looked up to see the glint of mischief in her father's otherwise expressionless face. "I didn't know you had a sense of humor," she observed delightedly.

"And I didn't know my daughter carried on in public with scruffy-looking boat builders." Vaughn's mouth twitched as he subdued a smile. Miranda had seen that same twitch hundreds of times on Jeff.

"A trophy-winning scruffy-looking boat builder," Miranda corrected him.

"Don't push it, my dear. Someone may think you're trying to influence a judge. We'll see about the trophy-winning part tomorrow."

"You may be seeing it more than once," Miranda added smugly, then followed her father's lead, ducking behind the menu, feeling closer to Howard Vaughn than she ever had.

After dinner, Vaughn took a stack of official-looking papers from a committee member they met in the corridor. "Back to work," he apologized for abandoning Miranda. "Tell Vinnie I said it's fine for you to crew for him Tuesday, but I expect to see it in writing, in advance, when he submits his crew list. No exceptions, not even for you."

"I'll tell him," Miranda agreed, then she pressed a daughterly kiss on his cheek. "See you later." She proceeded on, leaving Vaughn more flustered than he let show.

"While you're passing out kisses, I'll take a few." Phil Pittman saw her coming as he paused at the lounge entrance. "You and that Hall guy were all over the six-o'clock sports news. Getting pretty friendly, huh?" he taunted her, his breath already heavy with the smell of bourbon. Phil was smiling, but his eyes were cold and distant.

Miranda overlooked his attempt to embarrass her. "I saw *Hambone* coming across the line this morning, seventh in class A. Congratulations, Phil." Instead of a kiss, she offered him her hand.

"You have to be kidding." Phil rocked back, staring aghast at the hand. "I want a kiss." When he started to reach for her, Miranda put that hand on his chest, blocking him from pulling her close. "Before I lose all remaining respect for you, let me warn you that I'll put you on your rear end in front of everyone if you don't stop now. Imagine what an impression you'll make as a falling-down drunk," she whispered between clenched teeth. "Of course, I'll look alarmed and ask someone to help you up." She didn't believe for a minute that she'd go through with it, but she wouldn't have to. She knew image was Phil's Achilles' heel. He couldn't take looking like a fool. What Miranda was proposing would knock his perfect smile out of alignment.

"You really don't like me, do you?" He let his hands drop at his sides.

"I'm trying to find something to like," Miranda answered, matching his solemn look with her own. "Frankly, you're not giving me much to work with."

"Can I buy you a drink? A nice friendly, no-messing-around drink?" His halfhearted smile was little more than a face-saving device, intended to ward off the curiosity of the people going in and out of the lounge. Miranda was about to accept when she saw Walker Hall stroll through the doorway at the end of the hall.

"I think I'll pass." Miranda declined without taking her eyes off Hall. In a tweed jacket, open-collared shirt and faded jeans, he didn't look like a celebrity at all. Once he spotted her, his eyes never left her face.

"You still haven't made it aboard *Hambone*," Phil persisted. "One of my crew is coming down with a cold. I hoped you might be interested in riding second watch on the Lauderdale run. I remember how you love to sail at night." His voice dropped low, as if he hoped the memory would keep her from drifting too far. "Remember the night we made the Chesapeake Bay run. . . ."

"Phil." Miranda turned and stared at him. "Stop. Now. The end." She didn't want him going through their memories. Miranda suspected that allowing him to offer his rendition would be as repugnant as having a stranger rifle through her lingerie drawer. Her memories were intimate things, no longer accessible to him.

"Sorry." He looked genuinely dejected.

"Am I interrupting something?" Walker paused a few steps away. This was the first time Miranda had seen him wearing his metal-rimmed glasses, but they didn't hide the cautious expression he'd assumed. His gray eyes, flat and emotionless as stone, were leveled at her.

"Just a couple of old friends talking about the race today," Miranda responded promptly, watching the look in Walker's eyes immediately soften. He was relieved. She almost grinned at the change she'd caused. "Phil suggested I have a drink with him, but it's been a long day. I'd rather just walk back to the boat." She did everything but wave signal flags to get Walker to take over.

"I'll walk with you." He made the offer without sounding too anxious, but the devilish gleam in his eye had returned. "You never know what might grab you out there."

"Well, I guess I'll see you tomorrow," Phil commented, trying to sound as pleasant as possible. "Nice race today, Hall," he noted. "You've got an excellent boat in light weather." It was a limited compliment at best.

"She's excellent in any weather," Walker assured him, refusing to allow the least slight on *Persistence*'s performance. "I hope I get a chance to prove it. She's a good all-around design."

"And will you be producing more like her?" Phil asked what several of his boat builder cronies had been wondering.

"I'm not sure. I have a couple of other projects on the drawing board, and the Phantom will be my major production piece. I expect to have training fleets of Phantoms at yacht-club sailing centers on both coasts by this summer." Miranda watched his unwavering eyes, and she recognized the Walker Hall smoke screen was up again. "What happens with *Persistence* is all a matter of supply and demand."

"Yes. Well, good luck. And good night to both of you." Phil backed away.

Miranda and Walker didn't speak as they proceeded to the exit. Both needed the silence to think. Miranda resented the way the discussion with Phil had invaded her pleasant reverie. Bringing up talk of what Walker had planned after the S.O.R.C. made her few blissful moments aboard *Persistence* today seem short-lived. She hadn't been ready to consider all the very real yesterdays or the tomorrows wherein these moments might get lost.

"Is that true? You've got fleets of Phantoms ordered for sailing centers on both coasts?" Miranda finally asked.

"If you were listening carefully, you'd have heard only expectations, not orders. But I bet Phil will spread the word that fleets have already been bought. I'm hoping for word of mouth to start a stampede." Walker strolled beside her, watching her profile. "All it takes is for one yacht club to hear another club has decided to train on Phantoms. They start the ball rolling and order six or eight as a starter fleet. Other clubs who want to train competitive sailors will follow suit. After that, the boats will sell themselves."

"You haven't sold any Phantoms? Is that what you're saying?" Miranda turned to look at him incredulously. She realized that she knew little about Walker's boat-building enterprise, but she assumed it was a stable operation.

"I don't want to talk business. Not tonight," Walker replied wearily. "I've got a protest hearing in the morning. It's a put-up job, but I'm lining up some witnesses just in case I need them. Then one of my crewmen slipped on the deck and dislocated his kneecap. I've got to fill his place for the Lauderdale race. I was hoping you might consider crewing with us." They stopped under an overhanging banyan tree that blocked out all light from the pale moon.

"I can't. I've already said I'd crew on another boat," Miranda replied, feeling trapped by her earlier commitment. Especially in series races, there was a constant shifting of deck hands because of accidents and illness. Often fill-in crew members switched from one competitor to the next between races. She'd already told Sibyl she would sail on *Prophecy*. She didn't want any controversy now.

"You're not sailing with Mr. Perfect?" Even without being able to see him clearly in the dark, Miranda knew that Walker's eyes would have narrowed slightly.

"I'm riding on *Prophecy* with sweet potbellied Vinnie Albrecht, and I think my honor is safe with sixteen crewmen coming and going on a rotating shift."

"I wasn't worried about your honor." Walker stepped so close that she could feel his breath on her face. "I want some time with you. I want to watch you and listen to you." Walker lowered his lips to brush hers as he spoke. "I want you watching me." Walker slid his arms around her, drawing her gently against him. Miranda slid her arms beneath his tweed jacket, encircling his waist as the warmth of two bodies became one. Unlike the kisses that celebrated *Persistence*'s victory, there was nothing frantic or exuberant about the next kiss. This one began slowly and thoughtfully, with soft lips parting in dreamy intimacy, touching, caressing without any urgency at all.

Miranda took pleasure in the tenderness, the intoxicating sweetness of Walker's kiss, making her warm and shivery at the same time.

"I feel like a kid in high school," Walker confessed, his breathing unsteady, and the firm pressure of his body against hers clearly conveying his virile response. "Here we are standing in the shadows, with no place to go. I could invite you below deck in *Persistence* but she's stripped for action and she's neither comfortable nor private, especially not now with everyone trying to get a look at her. My place is an hour from here, across the bridge in Tampa. In forty minutes I've got to meet Ross to go over the protest information."

Miranda felt an emptiness, an aching need for another kiss and pulled his lips to hers again with breathless anticipation. His hands slipped down over the curve of her derriere and he lifted her against him, swaying as she clung to him. Miranda wanted more. She wanted all of him next to her, covering her, satisfying her. She wanted to feel that tremble when he left the world behind and lost himself in her. But not under a banyan tree in a park in downtown St. Pete.

"Walker..." She gasped for air, realizing that the sensuous movements she made so naturally with him were inviting an intimacy with very real implications.

She wasn't teasing, but she wasn't willing to run off to a hotel with him. "I think we'd better stop now."

Walker slackened his hold on her and took a deep breath, then he let out a slow stream of air. "I know, bad timing. Maybe you should change your mind and take to the high seas with me?" He was teasing, but his voice rumbled with desire.

"Surely this isn't your customary crew-recruiting technique?" Miranda countered breathlessly. "You put Dennis and Lloyd through this?"

"Hardly." Walker laughed, but the teasing put the emotional distance they needed between them. "Come on. I'll still walk you to your boat." He kept his arm around her as they fell in step, moving toward the marina again. There was something warm and very comfortable in his closeness, something that quieted the uncertain emotions Miranda felt.

"I'd like to make love with you, Miranda. I'd like it very much." Abruptly he had shifted from companionable silence to a soft-spoken, tender message that made her breath catch.

"You sure aren't one to tiptoe around a subject." Miranda glanced up at him.

"Tiptoeing implies someone needs to be coaxed. I won't talk you into anything. I may set up an opportunity, but the choice is yours. That includes a post crewing on *Persistence*," he added casually. "Not only do you kiss good, you're a darn good sailor."

"So are you. Kisser and sailor."

"Maybe we do have something in common after all." He was looking straight ahead as he talked, and the trace of defensiveness in his voice caught her by surprise. Walker had always sounded so confident and acted so sure of himself. Miranda wondered how much of that was merely a smoke screen, too.

"Surely you don't think you have to prove anything to me?" Miranda understood that until his victory in the race today, Walker's predictions could have seemed like mere bragging. Now he'd backed it up with a performance that was impressive. Even the protest didn't diminish the indisputable excellence of the boat he'd built. He'd established his credentials, apart from Porter Marine. What intrigued Miranda was how the change in his professional status and the victory in the race had prompted a transition in their personal relationship as well. Whatever they'd been keeping beneath the surface was going public.

"You and I will never be on equal ground," Walker said bluntly. "I've been the hired hand in this business for years; you grew up in the executive suite. When it comes to being on my own, I don't mind being the outsider. But I can't be that with you. In one way or another, I guess I do have things to prove."

"I feel I have things to prove, too," Miranda admitted. She wouldn't tell him now that she heard the song and questioned its meaning. But she would make Walker see her more realistically. That meant revealing more of herself to him, being vulnerable again. This time there were no convenient happy endings just around the bend and no tightly knit social set to make it all fit together nicely. They were on their own, without rules or direction.

"The odds are against us, Miranda Calvert Vaughn," Walker said quietly, stopping at the side of the Albrechts' cruiser. There were voices and laughter coming from the interior, but Walker wasn't going in. "I don't know what either of us can expect out of this." His openness in the cool, still night was without guile, without any of Walker's customary bravado.

"Maybe we just should see what happens next," Miranda replied. "No expectations."

"I didn't think you were that daring." Walker's expression mingled tenderness with a touch of his irascible teasing.

Right then Miranda made up her mind that she would chance it again. She wanted this man for whatever time, under whatever conditions, and with whatever risks that entailed. She just had to convince him that she could handle it. Then she'd try to convince herself. "I'm not daring," she said, pressing a light good-night kiss on his lips. "But a little magic can last forever."

Walker didn't make a move to stop her. He just stood there looking after her as she went aboard. "A little magic for m'lady?" he said, smiling, making a farewell bow like a courtier. "I'll see what I can do."

CHAPTER SEVEN

"RAY CALLED. The bottom dropped out."

The cryptic message Walker received aboard *Persistence* early the next morning didn't need further explanation. Ray Gibbs, the sail maker who had laser-cut the sails for *Persistence* and the first series of Phantoms, had not demanded payment until Walker could get on his feet financially. That meant carrying on his books the fifty-thousand-dollar cost of *Persistence*'s sixteen sails. Gibbs had been planning to hold the debt for a year if necessary, as long as his other contracts kept him afloat financially. "The bottom dropped out" meant one of his production contracts fell through. His financial security net had developed a gaping hole.

Returning the call to Gibbs during a recess in the protest hearing, Walker asked, "How long can you hold out?"

"I've got some itchy creditors," Gibbs replied apologetically. "Maybe a month. Six weeks. I'll stall as long as I can. I need twenty thousand."

Walker let out a slow breath. That killed every contingency plan he had made.

"Sorry, Walker. I didn't want to tell you, but I'm up against a wall. Or I will be in a few weeks. I figured maybe we can come up with a new strategy." His voice wavered with checked emotion. "I was so sure I could handle it, but these guys had a fire, and they won't be back in business for months. If they're not working, neither am I."

"Easy now, Ray." Walker soothed his old friend, knowing the pain it caused Gibbs to call that morning. Ray had been his mentor, offering advice and support throughout Walker's career. Retired from boat building because of a lung condition that was aggravated by all the chemicals, Ray had turned to sail making. In that past two years, he'd put in hours of expert consultation on both *Persistence*'s and the Phantoms' rigging. He'd also tracked down specific pieces of equipment without letting anyone know Walker had a boat in production. Ray Gibbs had been Walker's front man and his sounding board. And when it came to sails for *Persistence*, Gibbs had juggled his other projects and created an inventory on credit. Now he was the one in trouble.

"I'll get the money," Walker promised, sounding far more confident than he felt. "Stasch will just have to push a little harder and so will we. If one win isn't enough, we'll go for another one. Just don't worry. And don't believe anything unless you hear it from me."

"Just what have you got up your sleeve, fella?" Ray asked, feeling better now that Walker was being a smart aleck again.

"Wait and see," Walker shot back. "I love you, old buddy. I won't let you down." Walker's voice threatened to crack with emotion.

"You never have, Walker. I feel I'm the one that let you down."

"You kept me on my feet, Ray. Now it's up to me to stay there. Hang in there. I'll get back to you." Walker stood there staring at the phone for several seconds after he'd put it back on the hook, feeling the energy drain from his limbs. Somebody pulled the plug, and everything that seemed within his grasp was slipping away.

"Walker. . . ?" The salt-and-pepper-haired captain of *Razzle-Dazzle* stopped a few steps behind him. "Any word on the protest yet?" Throughout the entire Boca Grande Race, *Persistence* and *Razzle-Dazzle* had stayed within a few boat lengths of each other, one edging ahead, then the other. Even though *Razzle-Dazzle* finished second in both class and fleet honors after Walker's boat and would advance to first if Hall was penalized, the skipper Ted Irwin, a boat builder himself, had come in to testify on Hall's behalf. He'd followed on the controversial close maneuver Hall made overtaking the class-B boats during the night.

"None yet, Ted. Thanks for showing up," Walker replied. From his bandy-legged chum, Stasch, Walker had heard Mason Porter and his cronies had tried to convince Irwin not to come forward. The disputed maneuver had been made in pitch-dark. The boats only had running lights on, and no one could fault Irwin if he "couldn't quite be sure" who should have yielded. Walker had been sailing on the edge all night, coaxing a few additional inches—a few more seconds—out of every move. The protest was a matter of one man's testimony against another. Walker was uneasy as he waited in the hallway while his old boss Mason Porter, Porter's son-in-law, Bobby Austin, and two members of the protesting crew stood in a huddle drinking coffee.

"Protest disallowed. The official winner stands. It's *Persistence*." The notice posted on the bulletin board drew a crowd and sent a few crewmen scurrying off to pass the word. Walker took a long look at it, trying not to show his relief. It was settled. He had something now that could not be taken from him. Grimly he started out to the marina. Provisions for the long race had to be checked and rechecked. Once they set out the next day, there was no turning back for 370 miles.

"No hard feelings, Walker." Porter's son-in-law, Austin, came after him sheepishly and offered his hand. "From where I stood, you looked out of line."

Walker stopped and stared at the extended hand, but he didn't take it. "The only ones out of line were you and Mason. You never had a case and you both know it. I race by the rules, and I don't make mistakes. With my boat, I don't have to cheat to win." He kept his voice low, but in the crowded foyer of the club, everything halted. "Maybe your father-in-law can make you dance like a puppet in his boardroom, but you shouldn't do his dirty work in public where you come out looking like a fool." In a controlled voice laced with indignation, Walker berated the man. "Tell Porter that my attorney is keeping a file on this in case he pulls something again. You don't bad-mouth a fleet winner or its builder unless you're willing to go to court." Hall bit the words off with rapid precision knowing that the cowed son-in-law would run back to Porter with his response. It was a bluff. There was no attorney and no file, but Porter wouldn't know that. "See you at the awards banquet tonight," Hall called after him.

Walker continued out toward the docks, knowing full well that every eye in the place was on him. He hadn't done the gentlemanly thing. He hadn't shaken hands, dismissing the dubious protest under the guise of good sportsmanship. He hadn't accepted the protest or the hearing as no more than a difference in opinion and let it drop at that. He couldn't. They had pressured him when he least needed it. They had kept him dangling for a day. Now the win was official, and he intended to capitalize on a victory that both he and Porter knew should not have been controversial at all.

"What the heck are these?" Walker saw several boxes he hadn't ordered stacked up with the other dockside gear.

"Black-market goods," Ross Cornelius quipped without looking up from his clipboard. He was busy checking the inventory of food being taken on board. The items Walker had authorized—packages of instant soups and oatmeal, heat-and-serve sandwiches, liters of soft drinks, grocery bags of fruit were all disappearing below. But these flat boxes were obviously not foodstuff.

"Your friend Miranda came by to check if we had polypropylene long underwear," Ross said, placing a mark on the columns so he'd know where he left off. "We didn't. We have foul-weather gear to keep us dry, but no space-age long johns like she had. Word is that another cold front has slipped in right behind the one that fizzled, and tomorrow is going to be really bad out there. There's been a run in all the shops on this weird thermal underwear, and they're out. However, her friend Albrecht had ordered more than he needed. She grabbed them and brought them by. Said to try them. If we want them, she'll get us a good deal on them." Ross added the last part with a deliberately veiled look. He hadn't heard the outcome of the conversation with Ray Gibbs, but he imagined the news was bad.

Walker opened one of the flat boxes and looked at the wafflelike underwear that would breathe but still insulate the body from the dampness and the cold. Then he looked at the price tags still on the garments. The ten sets, top and bottom, were top-of-the-line arctic-weight garments with a cumulative cost of almost fifteen hundred dollars. Solemnly he stuffed them back in the box, then grabbed the others. "Take these back to *Prophecy* and return them. They're too rich for our blood." He handed them to Ross. "Thanks, but no thanks."

While Ross dutifully headed toward the dock where the class-A boats were moored, Walker took over the loading supervision. He was on his hands and knees, passing a case of soft drinks down to Dennis, when he heard her voice.

"What's the matter? Don't any of them fit?" Miranda leaped onto the deck beside him with a very concerned look on her face. "Surely some of the sizes will do for somebody." She stopped once she saw the stonelike expression on Walker's face.

"It's not the size; it's the price. I can't take these," Walker said gruffly. "Can't afford them."

"You what?" Miranda braced her hands on her hips, staring at him in disbelief. "Ross said you guys didn't have any gear like this and the stores have been cleaned out. You'll need them. It's going to get really cold."

"I appreciate that, but this is expensive stuff." Walker avoided meeting her eyes directly. "No matter how good a deal you're offering, I can't afford to buy it from your friend Albrecht, so we'll do with what we can put together." He had finally reached the point where he had to draw the line.

"How about a thousand for all of it?" Miranda knew the deal she was offering was a bargain.

"Miranda, I can't afford it." Walker stood and faced her. "Financially I'm strapped. I've got debts up to my ears and now I've a friend who's had to call in a loan. I can't owe anyone else. I'm not using your influence with Albrecht to get me equipment that I can't afford. It's as simple as that."

His countenance told her that he was determined. This was an encounter he'd wanted to avoid. He braced himself waiting for the light in her eyes to change when the truth of his situation sank in. When *Persistence* won, Walker had felt like he was riding high, high enough to pursue a princess. Admitting the cold facts of his financial limitations stripped away any illusions she might have had. And it stripped away his last defense, the impression that he was as invincible as he liked to pretend. Walker hoped his finances would hold out a few more weeks, but any setback now, any expensive repairs, could ruin his chances of coming out of the S.O.R.C. with his business intact. The thousand dollars she wanted him to spend for underwear could be crucial. Hall Marine's financial state had gone from precarious to critical.

"You can't afford not to take them," Miranda insisted, seeing the pained look that lingered in Walker's gray eyes.

"I've already got myself and my friends out on a limb..." Walker countered. Miranda didn't give him time to finish.

"Then make room on that limb for one more. Don't pull this noble act on me just because you're strapped for money." Miranda kept her voice low as she moved closer to him. "So you're not as solvent as you'd like to be," she conceded. "The weather doesn't care. Your pride won't keep you or your crew's fannies from freezing off aboard *Persistence*. We're talking bone-chilling breezes, fella—thirty-knot winds and subfreezing temperatures. If you don't take these suits," Miranda said firmly, "you'll lose the race. You can't get a top performance out of a frozen crew. Dammit, Walker," she said earnestly, "*Persistence* is worth it. If you can't pay Vinnie for the long johns, I'll loan you the money. I'll take one of your Phantoms as collateral. Just take the suits and get on with your packing."

"I don't want your money," Walker replied, wishing this discussion was taking place somewhere more private. Ross was hanging back on the dock, pretending not to listen, and all the movement below deck had ceased.

"If you don't want a mutiny, then you'll change your mind," Miranda persisted. "I'm not being generous or philanthropic, Walker," she assured him. "I just want to see a fair race, and it won't be if you deprive the men of protection. If someone beats you, you don't want to spend the rest of your days wondering if some underwear could have made the difference. You want to prove something to me?" She had moved in almost nose to nose with him, her voice no more than a whisper. "Prove that all your investors don't have to be men. Take the underwear. Take my check. Give me an I.O.U. or a Phantom, whichever you prefer. Just don't lose the edge you have," she said quickly, with a crackle of exasperation in her voice. "Please."

"Did I hear someone say mutiny...?" Dennis crept out of the hatch with a galley knife clasped between his teeth. With his long hair tied back in a kerchief and a maniacal gleam in his eyes, he looked like a pirate about to scuttle the ship.

"Well, is it mutiny or underwear, Walker?" Miranda challenged him.

Now Jack Davis's head popped up into view, and Lloyd's voice came from below deck. "Did she say what I think she said?"

"You don't know how difficult this is for me," Walker muttered.

"I think I do," Miranda replied, meeting his eyes steadily but keeping her words soft enough so only he could hear. "I know it must be tough taking off the Superman cape." Her voice wavered slightly, hinting that her uncompromising attitude wasn't completely natural. Instantly Walker knew how difficult this conversation was for her, too. She'd stood up to him, in public no less. There was no triumph in her manner. Her victory wouldn't be a defeat for him. It was a compromise, something Walker rarely made.

"Okay. We'll take the underwear," Walker agreed, realizing that the balance in their relationship was shifting. "But you may have to take a used Phantom if I don't get my business rolling." He managed a good-natured smile.

"I could live with that, but I'd rather see you win," Miranda countered. "Get back to work. I'll see you later." She stuffed the boxes of thermal underwear back into his arms. For a moment, his hands fumbled over hers as he steadied the load. In that brief contact, he felt that her hands were cold—a sure sign she had not been as sure of the outcome as she had seemed.

"Miranda..." He didn't quite know what to say next.

"I don't want to talk any more," Miranda replied softly, retaining what little she had left of her composure. So far they had kept the spirited discussion objective and rational. To an outsider, the underwear controversy would seem to be more comedy than anything else. Making it personal now, when they both felt vulnerable, would be a violation of an intimate sort. Regardless how nice it would be to let him comfort her, Miranda wouldn't make a spectacle out of a very delicate transaction. "I've got to go and help Vinnie. I've got a race, too, you know."

Walker stood watching her as she strode away, her dark hair flipping from side to side with each step. No one except him suspected she was not as confident as she looked. She was right about the polypropylene long underwear. Cold men couldn't sail competitively. He had over a hundred thousand dollars invested in *Persistence* already. In frigid conditions, a thousand more could make the difference between placing high in her class or not even finishing at all. This next race, the longest in the series, counted more points than any other race of the six S.O.R.C. events. He couldn't afford to lose.

"Take these below, open 'em up and pick the ones that fit you," Walker said, dropping the boxes in Dennis's arms. "And don't say a word," he warned Jack Davis and Lloyd who'd started up onto the deck.

"I'll see they get assigned." Quietly Ross Cornelius stepped behind Walker and discreetly sent everyone below.

Walker shot him a grateful look for a few minutes of peace while Ross took care of the details. Unglamorous underwear ranked right up there with boat design and sail inventory. Miranda had made her point, and she had risked disrupting the delicate new feelings they were discovering by refusing to let his pride—or her aversion to confrontations—get in the way. He respected her for that. With her quiet courage, she was becoming quite a match for him. He liked the way she stood up to him even though her hands were ice-cold. He liked the fact she'd met him head on aboard his boat, disregarding the people who could be watching. Yet she'd kept the private parts very hushed, very exclusive. She wasn't so intimidated by him, not like before. But she was vulnerable. What had shaken him the most was the concern in her eyes, showing him how easily he could hurt her yet clearly wanting to believe that he would not.

This was no passing-through lady. Walker frowned, knowing that she'd made him bend but didn't try to break him. There was something nice about having her look out for him, for his men, for his dream, but her concern triggered a confusion of emotions. Whether or not Walker thought he could fit a woman into his very unpredictable and solitary life, this one was making a place for herself. Whether he wanted her help or not, she was giving it. And whether he wanted to care or not, he couldn't help himself.

He was gambling now for higher stakes than ever, and he couldn't make his moves and worry about their impact on her at the same time. But she was willing to settle for a little magic, a memory that could last forever. She deserved better. She deserved someone with the time and means to care for her suitably, someone she could respect, someone who could look out for her. Someone with more than magic. Walker had felt all along he didn't measure up, not unless he made some changes. So he'd started by changing her, and she had met every challenge he'd thrown at her. Now it was his turn, and changing himself was a risk he couldn't take. He needed to be the same old Walker Hall he'd always been to pull off his plan.

"THERE'S YOUR FRIEND." Howard Vaughn leaned over and whispered in Miranda's ear as Walker arrived late that night. He took a seat among several other skippers and crewmen at an all-male table. The awards banquet had been under way almost an hour before Walker made his entrance. Clad in a navy blazer and gray slacks, and wearing his wire-rimmed glasses, Walker looked more subdued than Miranda expected. The familiar mask was in place once again; his unsmiling face had that aloof, arrogant expression that clearly acknowledged he was the man of the evening. All the speculation over his whereabouts had kept his name in every conversation. Being late was no accident.

"I see Mr. Humility has arrived," Phil Pittman commented to Miranda, directing an ever-so-polite smile across the room at Walker. "There are rumors flying that Hall has been offered a hefty sum for his boat and he might be willing to sell, but I can't get a line on what the figures are. You don't happen to know, do you?" He bent toward Miranda graciously as if their conversation was more social than business.

"No, I wouldn't know," Miranda replied indifferently. She had already been chafing over the fact that her father had stationed her between him and Phil, making it appear that she somehow belonged with both of them. Vaughn's dinner-table conversation had looped back repeatedly to Annapolis and the changes Miranda needed to see in her old hometown. Then Sibyl and Vinnie had joined them, sitting across from her, and the "old home" talk increased. Through it all, Miranda had tried to enjoy the dinner and remain detached. She'd been wondering why Walker hadn't arrived, half dreading he'd show up in foul-weather gear and deck shoes, just to be perverse. But now he was here, impeccably dressed and refined, and she kept watching him, waiting for something to happen. When his gray eyes met hers, for an instant, they registered something indefinable, then he was drawn back into the conversation at his table. He was up to something. Miranda could feel it.

When Walker stood to accept the two trophies, first for class E and first with highest fleet points, the entire gathering was waiting for his comments, anticipating some backlash over the protest incident. Walker was enough of a showman not to disappoint them.

"I'd like to thank my crew, my sail maker and myself for putting together such a magnificent boat," Walker said seriously. "And I'd like to thank Mason Porter for giving me the impetus to go off on my own boat-building enterprise. Making one's own shadow is far more exhilarating than standing in someone else's," Hall said, holding the trophy aloft so it caught the light and cast its shadow on his chest. "I wish us all a safe passage tomorrow. On to Lauderdale!"

Miranda almost winced when he mentioned Porter's name. Like everyone else, she'd heard about the post-protest handshake incident in the hallway, and she braced herself for the worst. But Walker's clever wording of his acceptance comments left the listeners agreeing with him. And the wish for safe passage touched a chord of apprehension everyone had been feeling. The cold wave had claimed the Suncoast. All day long the February skies were ominous, gray with occasional patches of bright blue—so similar to the eyes of Walker Hall.

"Surprised you, didn't I?" Walker said afterward, easing away from the throng that had crowded around him. Miranda had been noticing that now he was suddenly acceptable. The same men who had passed by *Persistence* without so much as a glance now surrounded Walker, bobbing their heads like pilgrims honoring a prelate.

"As a matter of fact, you did surprise me," Miranda answered with apparent relief. "You surprised all of us. I think we were expecting more sparks."

"No sparks. I'm sticking to a slow and smoldering approach," Walker joked. "One that simmers awhile, then bursts into a real conflagration on cue." He was watching the others in attendance, milling around as the gathering broke up. Then his glance settled on a face moving purposefully through the crowd toward him. The headhunter, Benjamin, tall and handsome, was making straight for Walker.

"Don't bother to tell me," Miranda said, sighing. "Act two. Am I right?" She suspected the entrance was too dramatic to be coincidental.

"You're right," Walker replied, grinning.

"I had hoped to talk to you privately," Miranda informed him, refusing to show her disappointment over not having any time with him alone. His earlier openness about his tight finances had upset her enough that she was ready to talk serious business. If he needed help, she had funds of her own and family connections she could call on. But knowing how proud Walker was, she wanted to bring it up carefully, as a business deal, not a personal commitment. Apparently there were other business deals in the offing tonight, and everyone in the room was trying not to appear too curious.

"Walker," Benjamin greeted him. "We need to talk. Sorry to interrupt your evening, but I have some feedback for you."

"I've got to go," Walker told Miranda. "Maybe we can get together later," he suggested as he gestured for Benjamin to wait just a moment. "This is important, Miranda," he said apologetically. "I really have to go." He smiled politely, still playing to the audience, but Miranda could see the tension in his smoky eyes.

"I'm going back to the Albrechts' boat to get a good night's sleep," she answered, resisting the temptation to ask him to come by later. "You could use some sleep, too. Don't stretch yourself too thin, Walker," she added, resting her hand on his arm momentarily. "You'll be up almost fifty hours straight. If I don't see you before the race tomorrow, have a good safe one."

Hastily she left him before her resolve melted away. Then Walker and the headhunter made their way out into the foyer, prompting another ripple of interest throughout the room.

"I'd like you to put in a good word for me." Phil cornered her once more before Miranda left the yacht club. "I just heard that Hall is being wooed by some Australian boat company. If he's going down under, I sure would like to have him for a contact there."

"Then you tell him that," Miranda snapped at him, finding it too tedious to keep being polite after all.

"Really, Mandy, you don't have to get so upset," Phil said, backing off. "Friends do look out for each other's interests."

"Hello you two. Let's duck in the lounge for a nightcap." Howard Vaughn stepped between the twosome, diplomatically smoothing over the situation. "I've been talking to Phil about my idea of starting a Florida division and having you head it," he said, taking Miranda's arm and guiding her toward the hallway while Phil Pittman fell in step with them. "Phil has a condo in Palm Beach and he's familiar with the boating situation there. He has some excellent suggestions about picking a location on the east coast." Vaughn continued talking, ignoring the fact that Miranda had politely declined further discussion of the offer he'd made concerning a Florida office.

"Unless we're talking the east coast of Tortola, you're on the wrong subject," Miranda replied, stopping abruptly at the entrance of the lounge. She was feeling once again that the two men were boxing her in. "You two go ahead without me. I really don't feel like having a drink." She could see Walker Hall and the headhunter Benjamin had already found a table inside. They were seated there with two other men. Vaughn and Phil had noticed the conference under way.

"Maybe you could slip right in and join them," Miranda suggested bitingly. "Or sit at the next table and eavesdrop." Both her companions looked with interest at the gathering. "Have a good time," Miranda bade them. Then, disengaging her arm from her father's, she proceeded out the doorway into the cold night. But when she passed beneath the old banyan tree where she and Walker had kissed, she slowed her pace slightly, glancing up at the few stars peering through the overhanging branches. "Business..." she murmured glumly, feeling colder than she had in years.

TUESDAY MORNING, crewmen layered in warm clothing slapped gloved hands together, staring at the gray skies. From the north-northwest the gusts of wind up to twenty miles an hour made temperatures in the low forties feel like arctic blasts. Tampa Bay's waters were choppy and small-craft warnings were out, but the second race of the S.O.R.C. would start regardless.

Hundreds of observers in lawn chairs, huddled beneath blankets, lined St. Petersburg's waterfront and municipal pier, waiting for the traditional parade of yachts to begin. Beginning at nine-thirty, loudspeakers carried the announcer's voice, introducing each competing yacht by size, hailing ports, skippers and owners as the magnificent boats motored out of the marina. Miranda stood on the foredeck of *Prophecy*, clad in red foul-weather gear like her crew mates as the red maxi moved out with the other class-A boats.

Walker was struck by a sense of unreality as he watched her through his binoculars aboard *Persistence*, who was still moored and waiting for her turn to leave the marina with the smaller boats. He knew this prerace pageant, so orderly and serene, was to be a short-lived illusion. Already reports of seven- to ten-foot waves in the Gulf of Mexico had crew members scrambling below deck, getting braced for a rough passage. In the few seconds he'd had to talk to Miranda before her early departure, Walker had teased her about her looking like a red snowman, then he'd hugged her and wished her a safe journey. But there had been an awkwardness between them, an uneasiness that was more than prerace jitters. There was undeniable danger ahead. The ruthless cold, the white-peaked waves and the erratic winds would conspire in a grueling test of equipment and crew. Now as Miranda and her crew mates moved south toward the starting point, Walker felt torn. A part of him wanted her to go and demonstrate her independence on the rough seas; part of him wanted her with him as they had been on the Phantom, in natural harmony again, where he would know she was unharmed.

"Time to move out." Ross Cornelius, serving as tactician, issued the first of his directives for the race. "Everyone on deck." The remaining eight crewmen led by Lloyd, Jack Davis and Dennis migrated to their assigned positions while the engine warmed up. *Persistence* trembled like a racehorse at the starting post. *Prophecy* and Miranda completely disappeared from view behind the far larger black-and-white *Shadow*.

As he lowered his binoculars, Walker knew that in one way or another, he would continue to watch for her and worry about her all through the race. He wouldn't feel right until he saw her face once more. He just wished he'd said something to her, something to assure her that he hadn't forgotten the magic. Instead, he had accommodated a news team who wanted footage of his crew just in case *Persistence* placed high at the finish. By the time the picture taking was over, Miranda was gone.

MIRANDA TRIED TO BE PHILOSOPHICAL about all the interest in Walker. There was already speculation that if *Persistence* could keep near the top of her class in another race, she'd be Admiral's Cup material. That meant racing off the coast of England in the summer, getting the feel of the winds there before the Admiral's Cup. Then there'd be another race, Miranda knew, and another. She just wasn't sure how far Walker intended to go with the racing part; he was a boat builder. He still had a business to run. But fame had a way of changing things, and Walker was certainly attracting a lot of attention. She could understand how sailing the circuit could be more appealing than trying to hold together a faltering business, and there were backers who would finance an Admiral's Cup or America's Cup challenger. Australia was another possibility she'd heard mentioned, especially after the previous night's meeting with the headhunter. Everyone was talking about Walker Hall—except Walker. And all the places they were mentioning were far from Tortola.

"It's like riding a giant surfboard." One of the crewmen came and sat next to Miranda, defying the chilling wind and occasional sprays of salty water. They'd made an easy jibe into the Gulf of Mexico and headed south, and for a while, there was nothing to do but ride. With the wind coming from behind them, *Prophecy* and the other boats were on a straight run, slicing through the waves, heading downwind. For the next 180 miles, until they reached the turning point off Key West, Rebecca Shoals, the course was uncomplicated. Riding high and kept warm by their gear, most of the crew on second watch stayed on deck while the first-watch crew worked their positions. Cheered by the sunshine and the breathtaking speed, crew members relaxed and the party spirit began to chase away the cold.

"Vinnie said you're some kind of writer. What kind of

writing do you do?" The voice from Miranda's other side belonged to another young man, a marine-electronics specialist named Bernie, who had been shadowing Miranda since the race began. For the next two days, she'd be the only female in sight, and the men were unashamedly vying for her interest.

"How about some hot chocolate, Miranda?" Still another crewman moved in, crouching behind her while he balanced a Styrofoam cup of steaming liquid.

"I think you guys had better ease off," Miranda suggested to all of them. "First of all, I'm not used to this kind of attention. And secondly, I'm here to follow the race, not to grab a little shipboard romance between sail changes. But I will take the chocolate," she said sportingly. "Then next round, I'll get some for you."

"I'd still like to hear about your writing," Bernie persisted, even though he'd lost the eagerness he'd shown before. There were lots of miles ahead and they still needed good company to pass the time.

"I'm just writing about the S.O.R.C.," Miranda replied obligingly. "I'm covering the overall summary—winners, losers, favorites, breakdowns, whatever." She shrugged. "I am curious how you guys manage to take off six weeks from whatever job it is you have somewhere else and then come here to race." She was deftly turning the focus back on them. "What is it you do out there in the real world?" She looked at Bernie expectantly.

"Are you going to use it for your writing?" He seemed eager to be immortalized in print.

"You talk, I'll listen. If you don't mind, I may use

some of your information. Or if you prefer, I'll guarantee not to use your name." She didn't want any of the men to feel uncomfortable.

"Use my name. I'd love it if you use my name," Bernie insisted enthusiastically. "I could flash it around and prove that I was really here. Man, my friends back home would get a kick out of it."

"Yeah, use my name, too. Danny Harris," the next fellow urged her. "You can write about us unsung heroes who crew these monsters. Then my wife won't think I'm such a jerk for taking off like I do."

"You have a wife...any kids?" Miranda looked at Danny's youthful face and wondered why he'd been one of the first to start putting moves on her. But it was part of the vagabond life, a part she didn't like to think about.

"One wife, two kids," Danny replied sheepishly. "They're back in Annapolis. This is off-season in boating up there, and I can pick up good money crewing. Plus I make some connections for other races and for business. Bernie and I have a little company." He gestured to the bearded fellow on her left. "We specialize in boating electronics. You can even use the name of our company if you want. Every little bit helps." Again Miranda felt boxed in, but this time the two enterprising young men were so earnest, Miranda couldn't resent their bid for free publicity.

"I'm not married," the one who'd brought the hot chocolate assured her. "My ex-wife put up with three seasons of me crewing, then she told me not to come back. Can't blame her. She wanted a normal life, and I just couldn't give it to her."

"Yeah, I'm staying home after this year," Danny said grimly. "My wife isn't too thrilled about all this, either."

"He said that last year," Bernie teased. But no one smiled.

Later while Miranda sprawled against the deck out of the cold wind, she kept recalling snatches of the conversation with the men. Always there was a trace of wanderlust in their eyes as they talked about crewing on boats and traveling to exotic ports for training and competition. Even with the loneliness that she'd detected in them, a loneliness they would try to ease with the boisterous camaraderie of their shipmates or the company of a convenient and accommodating woman, they still returned to the yachting circuit, year after year. Compelled by finances, boredom, the excitement of racing, the opportunity to promote their business, many of them left wives or girlfriends, children, homes and businesses behind. Waiting.

Miranda didn't want that. Time and again she'd tried to think of what was possible, what kind of relationship she could have with Walker Hall. She kept reaching the same conclusion. The perfect boy-meets-girl romance wasn't for them. Like the S.O.R.C. itself, they could have a few weeks of excitement and high emotion. Then the fantasy ended and everyone went home. Or in Walker's case, he would go wherever his fortune led.

There was more separating their tomorrows than mere geography. There was a difference in basic needs. Miranda had left the yacht-manufacturing realm and found her nest, a snug cove in Tortola where the island breezes always blew. What she'd found there was a home, a sense of her own identity. In Tortola she'd acquired stability, an unsophisticated, unhurried quality that had become part of her nature, and as essential as breathing. So far Walker Hall was not essential. And "nesting" didn't seem part of his vision at all.

Staring at the passing clouds, Miranda let her fantasies run free, imagining the moment when she and Walker would make love. Touches, sighs, soft laughter and the incredible joy of being immersed in a world of sensations. Pulling herself back into the real world, she knew she had to settle for the here and now. Walker wasn't the kind of man to promise more, but she'd spend her life regretting it if she didn't take what he could give, if she couldn't share what she felt. It was an unfair but realistic exchange, with neither one dependent on the other. Like images in clouds, all the other half-formed dreams, ones that lingered in her heart—of someone to share her life, of years together, of children—those dreams would have to drift by, like the clouds, until the time—and the man—was right. And if they never came true, nevertheless, she would have loved a remarkable man.

BY NIGHTFALL THE WINDS WERE GUSTING eighteen to twenty-five knots, and the cold temperatures had forced all but the skeletal watch crew below deck. With his face wrapped in an old flannel shirt, Walker stood in the cockpit alone while Lloyd grabbed a hot meal and a few hours of sleep. Ross Cornelius, bundled in so many layers of clothing that his thin form was barely recognizable, brought the latest reports.

"Two class-A boats have broken down—*Sorcery* and *Hambone*." Ross recited the growing list of crippled boats that had lost either steering or rigging under the extreme conditions of heavy seas, wind and brutal cold.

"What happened to *Hambone*?" Walker asked, curious to know the problem that had disabled Phil Pittman's boat.

"Broke a rudder."

"One of those experimental carbon-fiber rudders," Walker recalled. "These new lightweight systems fool everyone. Designers overestimate the capabilities. Where's *Prophecy*?" He wanted some reassurance that Miranda was well ahead of the bad weather that had hovered, like a malevolent presence, over the later starters and had dogged them down the coast.

"*Prophecy* is fine," Ross answered. "She's ahead of the bad weather and is right up there with the front-runners. No problem." He couldn't see Walker's expression behind the flannel face warmer, but the gray eyes shifted momentarily from the running lights of the boat ahead to a dark space to the east. They were cruising fifty miles away from land, but hours ahead, *Prophecy* was off in that direction.

"A shroud failed and the rig went over on two class B's," Ross noted. "No one was hurt and the coast guard is standing by while they motor in." The erratic winds had reportedly blown out several sails during the night with ominous cracks like shotgun blasts. Thousands of dollars worth of sail were left flapping like shredded rags from the rigging. Shrouds, the narrow cables that helped keep the mast erect and stable under stress, broke with a twang like a slingshot. Then the strain on the mast could cause the entire upper rigging—sail, mast, boom—to surrender to the force of the wind like trees felled in a forest. What could be salvaged would still take days to repair, and both Walker and Ross knew that they had to be careful. They had neither the days nor the money to recover.

Awaiting them ahead was the dangerous turn eastward when the boats would round the Keys. Then came a second crucial turn north off Plantation Key to try to catch the Gulf Stream off Florida's coast and ride it toward Fort Lauderdale. Each course change would put the boats still under sail through another ordeal, where helmsmanship and equipment would be tested to the breaking point.

Walker fixed his course following *Razzle-Dazzle*, the only other class-E boat in range. As before, the two of them had surfed through the field, holding the lead. But *Razzle-Dazzle* had the edge, and Walker wouldn't let her slip out of sight. He had beaten her before. Somewhere in the remaining two hundred miles, he would try to do it again, if his luck and his equipment could withstand the pounding of the wind and the frigid inky water.

By daylight, more boats had succumbed to the elements, but *Persistence* held on intact. A mile from the shift around the Keys, *Razzle-Dazzle*, running barely within sight of Walker's boat, lost her rudder.

"You need help?" Walker radioed to *Razzle-Dazzle*'s skipper Ted Irwin, who had backed him in the Boca Grande protest. "We'll give assistance if you need it,"

Walker offered, knowing that he wouldn't leave Irwin stranded.

"Just get on with your run," Irwin responded. "If I can't take you this race, I sure don't want you holding back. When I do beat the pants off you, I want to look real good, so go on. We'll motor in. See you in Lauderdale—eventually. Good luck."

By the time they were witnessing their second sunset at sea, Walker was exhausted from countless hours on deck. When he wasn't on deck, he'd go below and dutifully crawl into a berth to sleep, without success. Sometimes, on the dreamy borderline of sleep, he pictured Miranda riding high on the *Prophecy* and he'd awaken, then check the radio reports.

"She's off the Keys; no problems," Ross informed him without having to be asked. Then Walker would head back to lie down for a little while longer, chiding himself for worrying about her. He had to concentrate on his own boat, his own course, his need to sleep. But she was there, in his head, like a second self, and he'd never had anyone intrude like that. He'd never had anyone whose presence was so crucial and whose absence was so compelling. His thoughts tracked her like radar.

At five that night, Miranda and *Prophecy* had almost reached the north turn, 110 miles from the finish. A twin-engine plane tracking the fleet leaders reported winds of twenty-five miles an hour and ten-foot waves crashing over the bows of all the boats. *Prophecy* and the maxiboats were into the homestretch, faring well, while Walker and the rest of the fleet still had to face that turn. Already, *Persistence* was rolling with the wind, her decks wet and slick when Walker went up before the crew change.

"When you see Miranda," Dennis said on one of Walker's trips to the foredeck, "tell her she was right. If it wasn't for these funny long johns, you would have had a mutiny on board. And I'd be leading it. Man, it's cold." His damp mustache hung dismally down either side of his mouth.

"I'll tell her," Walker assured him. But thanking Miranda wasn't what was on his mind. Seeing her safe, holding her, feeling the passion that she concealed from everyone but him, finding a place for the two of them just for a while, had obsessed him all day. Like a hunger, his need for her had been constant. At night, when he was on the helm alone, it would only be worse.

CHAPTER EIGHT

AT DAWN THURSDAY MORNING, Miranda stood on the foredeck of *Prophecy*, anxiously waiting to get into port. The shoreline hotels of Fort Lauderdale stood like gleaming armored sentinels, windows reflecting the light of the morning sun. Ahead a cruiser with an orange flag and a round orange international Styrofoam float marked the end of the race course. Crossing it now seemed anticlimactic. The course of *Prophecy* had been relatively uncomplicated the entire two days since they left St. Pete. The two venerable maxiboats, *The Shadow* and *Kialoa*, had sailed across the Fort Lauderdale finish line at 3:19 that morning, setting a new race record of thirty-nine hours. Now at 8:20 A.M. *Prophecy* was claiming the sixth place in class A.

But it was the boats still coming up the coastline that held Miranda's interest.

"I really didn't think you were missing anything." Vinnie Albrecht apologized once more for letting Miranda sleep through the night without coming on deck for her watch. "What could you have done but worry?" At breakfast Miranda had heard snatches of reports on the conditions behind them—boats disabled, skippers slacking the pace to ride out the rough conditions. She had slept peacefully through it all while Walker had dropped out of sight. Even in the latest fly-over by the Fort Lauderdale Yacht Club commodore, Walker and *Persistence* hadn't been sighted and no distress call had come in.

"We located him...." Vinnie's second-watch navigator came loping toward Miranda and her companion. "Hall and a couple of others must have headed out for the Gulf Stream earlier than some of the bigger boats. He's in radio contact again and looks like he's running about fourth or fifth in class E."

The news about *Persistence* eased part of Miranda's tension, but until she got a look at all of them, Walker, his crew and his boat, she knew she couldn't calm down. She'd been imagining disasters since dawn. Too many grim stories had been circulated about damage to the smaller boats and injuries to crewmen. So far none were life threatening or irreparable, but Miranda wanted to see the conditions aboard *Persistence* for herself.

"How far back is Walker?" she asked, trying to estimate the wait she'd have. From the location the navigator gave her, she guessed it would be six or seven hours before *Persistence* made it into port.

When the first class-E boats finished, Miranda was on the dock with Ted Birmingham and Phil Pittman. Both of them were still chafing that their boat *Hambone* had to be towed into port. Already the docks were filled with repair teams working on engines, booms and rudders. A steady caravan of sail makers' vans carried off damaged sails for repairs. The next race was three days off, and the frantic activity to get boats and crews in shape wouldn't cease until that Sunday race start.

Among boat owners and boat manufacturers from the American yacht clubs gathered on the lawn to drink Bloody Marys and watch the competitors come in, an uneasy attitude persisted. Two American-owned boats that had done poorly in the first race came in first and second in this long race. But American performance was erratic. The German-crewed, French-designed one-tonner, *Divine*, took a respectable third place just as it had before. In combined total points from both races, she moved ahead of the fleet. All she had to do was continue to be consistent, to place—not necessarily win—and her total point score would entitle her to take the S.O.R.C. trophy home.

"Where the heck is Hall?" Ted Birmingham muttered. Even though *Persistence* couldn't win top honors in this round, Walker Hall's boat had been reported closing in on fourth place, high enough to accumulate a good point score. With his first in the Boca Grande Race, on combined overall points, *Persistence* was the only American-designed-and-owned boat in the fleet that could take the lead. Whether they liked Hall's brashness or not, his boat could keep the United States yacht clubs in contention for the S.O.R.C. title.

"Ted and I were talking about making Hall an offer on building us an Admiral's Cup entry," Phil commented. He sounded as if he was making casual conversation, but Miranda knew he was testing her. "If *Persistence* keeps up a steady show, Walker Hall may take the S.O.R.C. trophy," Phil continued. "Hall may even be willing to sell *Persistence* if we get together a syndicate with an impressive enough offer. Our yacht club is ready to back a winner. He could work on her right here in Florida." He glanced at Miranda to gauge her reaction.

"I doubt that he'd sell *Persistence*," she said casually. "He's put too much hard work into her, and she's one-of-a-kind. But taking her design and coming up with a brand-new boat—" she nodded thoughtfully "—that might interest him." Miranda didn't react to the mention of Florida, but she suspected Phil had added that as an enticement to her. Rumors were rampant that Walker had foreign investors trying to lure him away—to Australia, Japan and even Brazil.

More than patriotism was at stake. Keeping Walker in Florida would mean he would be more accessible to Miranda since there were regular flights to and from the Virgin Islands. But she could decrease the distance even more if she accepted her father's offer to set up business in Fort Lauderdale. Phil was using every tempting angle he could think of, but Miranda's instincts told her Phil could not have come up with that idea alone. Somewhere in the scheme, Howard Vaughn was at work.

"Here she comes," a crewman bellowed as *Persistence* appeared, gliding along under motor power through the canal toward the dock of the Lauderdale Yacht Club. Miranda held back as the crowd of onlookers jostled and sidestepped one another, moving in to see how *Persistence* had fared during her forty-nine-hour voyage. Miranda's eyes were riveted on the face of Walker Hall. Though his eyes were hidden by sunglasses, she could see that he was smiling—however forced. But he was all right. And suddenly she found it easier to draw a breath.

Before anyone else reached Hall, Stasch, the Portuguese crewman, leaped aboard and handed him a note. Dennis and Lloyd and the others wearily accepted the accolades and cold beers being handed them, but Walker only spoke briefly to Ross. Then he stepped off the boat, cutting through the dockside gathering, heading straight for Miranda.

"I had other plans for you and me," he began grimly. "But I've got to get across the state and pick up a trailer load of Phantoms," he explained, sounding totally exhausted. "They were supposed to be here already, but something went wrong." Walker's shoulders sagged as he glanced at his watch. It was three in the afternoon. Miranda had been waiting on shore for nearly eight hours. "Even if I could drive straight through, I can't get back here until tomorrow."

Miranda reached up, lifting his sunglasses and staring at his face. "Did you get any sleep at all the last two days?" she asked softly, trying not to burst into tears of relief. He was so close, safe at last, but so tired.

"Not much," Walker admitted. His puffy, bloodshot eyes were the giveaway. "It was pretty tense out there," he said with a shrug. "And I worried a lot about you." It was an admission he hadn't intended to make.

Miranda put his mirrored glasses back in place, disguising the extent of Walker's weariness. "Get your bag, superman," she directed him, with more gentleness than teasing in her voice. "I'm going with you to Tampa. You sleep; I'll drive. Then coming back, we'll take turns. I've driven a trailer with boats on it before. Let's go."

"You'll get no argument from me." Walker squeezed her hand affectionately, the only intimate gesture he'd made in front of all the members watching from the sprawling green lawn of the Lauderdale Yacht Club. "Be with you in about ten minutes, then we'll call for a rental car."

Miranda kept her smile from disappearing totally as Walker turned back to his boat to collect his belongings. Then she sought out Phil Pittman. "You said you had your company's private jet in St. Pete. Is it here now?" she asked bluntly. For an instant, a peculiar hopeful light gleamed in Pittman's eyes.

"Sure. You want to go somewhere?"

"Walker Hall does. If you want to ingratiate yourself to Walker and possibly put him in your debt," Miranda began, "have your pilot fly us to Tampa. Walker has to get there immediately, and he's too exhausted to drive." Miranda felt a little guilty taking advantage of Phil's self-serving, ambitious nature, but the plane could reduce an eight-hour drive into less than an hour of air time. It would give Walker a little time to unwind.

"You said *us*." Phil bit off thc words. "You're going with him?"

"I'm going along to help him drive a boat trailer back. In return for my passage, I'll also make a strong pitch for your syndicate offer," she promised, "and if you agree to fly us, Walker will have a good reason to listen. Just hurry up and make the flight arrangements."

"When will you be back?" Phil narrowed his eyes,

obviously wondering what else would be going on besides driving.

"That depends how soon you can get us over there. The quicker the better." Miranda could tell Phil was calculating his professional gains against his personal losses.

"Okay, you got a plane. You just soften Hall up for our offer. I'll get some folks together and have something to talk to him about when you get back."

"I'll soften him up all right," Miranda promised, thinking more of massaging Walker's tense muscles than setting up business strategy. She wanted to get him somewhere where he could drop the conquering-hero role and be himself. By arranging for the jet, she had saved him hours, and that was all that mattered to her now.

WALKER HESITATED before opening the door to the Hall Marine factory in Tampa that evening. "It isn't fancy. It's set up to be efficient," he said, anticipating the look of dismay Miranda would have when she saw the interior of the warehouse. Before he could apologize further, someone inside rolled open the sliding doors.

Limping and obviously embarrassed by the cast on his foot, Harry stepped around to meet them, his dark eyes somber and uncertain. "Sorry, Walker. One of the Phantoms started to slip, and I tried to keep it from chipping."

"By stopping it with your foot?" Walker said, shaking his head. "I'm not about to let you work the clutch on the truck with that thing." Walker had told Miranda about the accident on the flight over, but now as she looked at the silent older fellow, she realized how earnestly the man had wanted to make the trip in spite of the cast and his obvious pain.

"Miranda, this is my right-hand man and good friend, Harry." Walker introduced them. "He's Lloyd's father, and the best fiberglass-laminating expert in the area."

"If the Phantom is an example of your work, I'm impressed. Nice to meet you, Harry." Miranda shook his hand.

"Lloyd told me about you," Harry said as he took a good look at her. "He said you weren't too amused by that Rasta-wig business or those beads and dreadlocks." He smiled shyly. "Neither was I. Lloyd's a business major at the university here. He thought he had to do something different to keep up with Dennis."

"The only difference is that Dennis wasn't wearing any costume," Walker interjected. "He always looks that way. What you see is what you get."

"Your son is an excellent helmsman," Miranda complimented the man. "And he's quite a good musician." The comment came out so naturally that Miranda didn't realize she'd never mentioned the music show in front of Walker until now. "I heard him singing the other night," she added a bit self-consciously.

"Yes, yes he's good," Harry responded proudly. "But he promised to get a degree before he has any funny ideas about becoming a performer. And if he wants to stay in college, he'd better keep his old man in work," Harry insisted good-naturedly. "I'll give you folks a hand finishing loading this trailer, then you can be on your way back to Lauderdale. We want everyone clamoring for these Phantoms so we can get back into production."

Only now did Miranda look around the warehouse and see that no work was under way. There were no laminators or craftsmen of any sort; no boats were in progress. Apparently Walker's staff had finished the four Phantoms already loaded on the trailer and the one left to be loaded. These were his demonstrators; the future of his production plant hinged on their generating purchase orders.

"I told you I was stretched a bit thin," Walker said, reading the expression on her face. Then he looked away hastily, taking Harry by the arm. "You go home, get off that foot, and don't worry. We'll take over from here. Just take care of yourself now." He guided the older fellow toward a parked car.

"But you and the lady can't load these by yourselves..." Harry protested, stoically denying his discomfort.

"The lady and I can handle anything," Walker assured him, not stopping until Harry was securely belted behind the wheel. "Go home. Get a good night's sleep, and don't forget to read the sports page. We're hanging in there, buddy. One solid win in any of the next four races, and we'll have ourselves a reputation."

"I've been reading the papers. You've already got a reputation," Harry said, chuckling. "What we need is business. You just sell some boats and let's get back into production before the smell of resin fades entirely. Good luck," he wished him, then drove away.

Miranda was still inside the factory, moving from one work station to another, examining the equipment in a production plant ready for action, but strangely silent. Rolls of fiberglass mat hung like shimmering gauze from mounted brackets, and wooden tables stood vacant with power tools neatly stowed in cubbyholes. "Is this the entire extent of your company?" she asked, wondering what products other than the yet-unsold Phantom Hall manufactured.

"This is it. All the men crewing for me on *Persistence* work here—Dennis, Ross, Jack Davis, even Lloyd sometimes." Miranda nodded thoughtfully, realizing how many futures rested on Walker's shoulders and on the success of his dreams.

"What about the rumors that you have another business, a whole other division where you do some kind of secret industrial work in fiberglass?" Miranda had heard that information several times during the S.O.R.C. gatherings.

She turned to see him leaning against the doorway, studying her. "I have to admit it. I started those rumors, or at least I saw to it they got started. Those rumors spread and kept everyone in the boat business from wondering what I was actually concentrating on. I do have some industrial contracts," he admitted. "We all had to eat, and putting the Phantom into production and redesigning and equipping *Persistence* was expensive. I guess I'm something of an inventor at heart, so I manage to keep some money coming in by making safety guards, satellite disks, cable equipment and half a dozen other pieces of unique equipment. I've even put together some artificial beaks for injured pelicans. But that 'other division' you've heard about is that series of cabinets over there," he said, pointing to some wall-mounted cupboards and shelves containing a variety of molds set off in one corner of the rectangular building. "We want to build boats. We've all made certain sacrifices to get this far."

"What is your connection to that headhunter Benjamin?" Miranda asked, wanting to confirm or deny all the gossip she'd heard over the past few weeks. Now that she had him alone, on his own ground, he didn't have to play a role.

A half smile softened Walker's ragged features. "I don't want you in the middle of anything, Miranda," he replied. "Ken Benjamin is just helping keep things on edge."

"What things?"

"I can't tell you." He said it simply, without defiance or arrogance.

"Will you tell me about that little man Stasch from the Portuguese boat? What's his connection to you?" She pressed him with determination.

"You've heard of a red herring," Walker quipped. "Well, Stasch is really red. He's a Russian. He was loaned out of Russia as a technical advisor to a South American country, then he discreetly jumped ship and defected. I met him at a boat show. He speaks eight languages, and he's one heck of a sailor."

"But what is his connection with you?" Miranda

couldn't seem to penetrate the wall of mystery Walker insisted on keeping between them.

"Stasch and I have a business gamble in the offing. That's all I'm free to tell you right now." He brushed one hand through his tousled hair wearily. "I'm not used to confiding in anyone, Miranda. I keep pretty much to myself. I don't know what kind of offers I'm going to end up with after the S.O.R.C., so I've got to keep several irons in the fire. But they have nothing to do with you." Sheer fatigue made his voice sound hollow.

"But I feel so uninformed, so cut off from what is really important in your life. I want to feel like I fit in somewhere." She walked toward him, stopping an arm's length away. "Let me know you, Walker. Please."

"You know me," he said softly, moving close to her, touching her cheek in a wistful, tender gesture. "You know me better than I know myself at times. Your eyes look right into my soul. I've never felt such peace or such sublime peril as when I'm with you. And when I'm not with you, I want to be." His hands clasped her shoulders, pulling her to him easily as his mouth lowered, meeting and caressing hers, melting any uncertainty in a smoldering, dreamy kiss that seemed to draw the warmth he needed from her.

Miranda slipped her arms around him, feeling the tension in his body as he held her to him, caught between desire and exhaustion. Hungrily his mouth moved over hers, devouring the softness and the warmth she offered him. Miranda stroked his back, rubbing the taut muscles of his shoulders. As her massage became more sensual, more stimulating, Walker pressed his hips against hers, and Miranda forgot her ministrations. Clinging to him, she molded her body against his, feeling his response and knowing that neither of them had any defenses left.

"I want to make love with you, Miranda," Walker breathed against her lips, then claimed them again with a ferocity that thrilled her. The pure and explosive need in his kiss brought a tremor of warmth from deep within her, a building fire that made her more bold. "Miranda, take it all away," he moaned. "Make everything become just you."

Miranda let her kiss, soft and sensual, answer for her. This was to be the time, the place and the man to free her passion again and to flood her being with sensations that only he could reach. Yet it was his need to have the pressures he'd been enduring disappear, to make the troubles that had dogged him fade for just this moment—his need that overwhelmed her. Only she could take it all away. His refuge was in making love with her.

When he drew his lips from hers this time, he shuddered with barely controlled emotion, releasing her from his embrace and lightly covering her eyes, her face and then her neck with feathery kisses. "Come home with me." He took her hand, leading her to the heavy factory doors. Then he slid them shut, with him and Miranda enclosed inside. "Be it ever so humble, this is it, Miranda." He led her through the darkened interior of the factory, past empty boat molds and sealed containers faintly smelling of resin and chemicals, to the wood stairway that led up to his office and the living quarters there.

Inside the loft entrance, behind the glass windows overlooking the factory, was the administrative headquarters of Hall Marine. It consisted of his desk, files and a design table covered with boat plans on rolls of milky-colored mylar. Beyond that was a living area. The deep-plum carpet and indigo furniture suggested an elegance, an affluence and a time before Hall Marine.

"I wasn't always this hard-pressed for money," Walker confided. "I did well with Porter Yachts. It's starting over on my own that has depleted my resources. When I say 'This is it,' I mean business, home, plans, future...all in this building." Miranda followed him wordlessly, feeling as if he was opening a part of himself to her that he shared with no one else.

Beyond the sofa, the introduction to his bedroom was simply a massive watercolor painting suspended from the ceiling rafters with slender chains. Pale purple, mauve and aubergine captured an exotic array of shadowy chess pieces on a surreal checkered board.

"I can't afford walls," Walker said, watching her expression for any sign of disapproval. But Miranda gazed with wonder at the opulent colors and the enigmatic painting of chess pieces. On the open shelves along one side of the bedroom were more chess sets—onyx, marble, pewter and jade in various shapes and sizes. Some of them had games in progress.

"I keep several games going at a time, and I play both sides," Walker explained. "Each time I think up some new tactic, then I try to get around it. Either way, I win."

"Makes sense to me," Miranda said softly, feeling more aware of the solitude that seemed essential to Walker's existence. Here, alone, before they ever met, he challenged himself just as he'd been challenging her, to test his ability, his cleverness, his own imaginative resources. These private skirmishes somehow equipped him to deal with bigger battles and more powerful adversaries in the world beyond this warehouse.

"I've already made love to you a hundred times," Walker said, taking her into his arms again and kissing her lightly on the lips. "You were with me every time I tried to sleep during the race. I'd close my eyes and imagine I was holding you. I didn't want to lose consciousness because I knew if I woke up, you wouldn't really be there."

"I'm here now. If you drop off to sleep, I'll be here when you wake up," Miranda promised. "Just tell me when to wake you so we'll get to Lauderdale in time."

Walker shook his head reproachfully. "No more Miss Efficiency here," he kidded her. "Lauderdale can wait for us until tomorrow," he whispered. "We've waited for each other long enough. I've got you now, Miranda. I don't want to have to hurry." Walker's mouth lowered again to meet hers. He touched his tongue lightly to her lips, testing, tantalizing, inviting her to return the intimacy, denying the world the power to interfere. Miranda declared her independence from that outside world, claiming for herself what instinctively she felt was right and more essential than she had ever admitted. Parting her lips slightly she welcomed him at last.

When his hands moved down her body, feeling

curves, pressing her close, holding her tightly, Walker murmured her name while his body communicated its praise of hers. Miranda felt suspended. His kisses, like his whispering, summoned from secret parts of her hidden feelings that had been safe in the shadows. Like a ritual of blossoming, soft and languid, petal by petal, they undressed each other slowly, touching and caressing as time slowed to a standstill. He lifted her sweater over her head and let it drop onto the carpet. She touched his lips with her fingertips, then with his moist kiss upon them, she unbuttoned his shirt so their bare skin could touch.

Miranda let herself nestle against him, her breasts tingling against his chest as Walker moved with her, letting her curves naturally fit with his. His hands moved down over her rib cage, then to her waist, trembling slightly as he fumbled with the waistband of her slacks. "Let me..." Miranda said, knowing that he was fumbling from fatigue. First she finished undressing herself, then Walker.

"I should have guessed it would be a water bed," she murmured, holding back the covers and sliding beneath cool magenta sheets. After sleeping in a cramped cabin berth on rolling seas, the huge bed gave her a luxurious, wanton feeling. It was like skinny-dipping in the ocean with nothing but endless ripples surrounding her. And when Walker slipped in next to her, the sudden full-length contact with his naked body added a sense of harmony, a communion with a kindred spirit, that made her gasp with delight. "Walker..." She whispered his name again and again as he touched her, taking time to savor the exploration, to arouse and give pleasure.

Sliding lower down her body, he trailed soft kisses from her throat to the curves of her breasts. When his lips lingered there, content for now to taste their sweetness, Miranda cradled his head, entwining her fingers in the cluster of curling hair that still held the salty scent of his voyage. His hands glided over her hips and thighs, and Miranda floated on a golden wave of passion, keeping nothing from the arousing movement of his hands, inviting a deeper touch, a promise of an inevitable intimacy.

Her senses smoldered, delighting in the press of his lips, hands, fingertips. Miranda needed to touch him, to give him the total sense of being vitally alive that he was giving her. With cool strong hands, she reached down, trailing her fingers over the taut muscles of his neck as his lips caressed the darkened sensitive peaks of her breasts. Then he lay with his cheek pillowed by her curving body while she kneaded his shoulders, back and arms, easing away the dull aches the long race had left here.

"Your hands on my body feel wonderful," Walker said, sighing. "But if I get too relaxed and go to sleep now, I'll never forgive myself," Walker said huskily, rolling her onto her back and pulling his body over to cover hers. "Want me, Miranda. Want me now," he breathed raggedly, his voice vibrating with a near-savage desire that defied restraint.

"Yes. . . Walker. . . now." She gasped with wonder at the amazing sense of completeness she felt when he entered her. All feeling, long subdued and dulled by memory, found new expression. Once again Miranda was in communion with herself totally, denying herself nothing. She was aware of every aspect of her body, straining, receiving, reciprocating. Eyes wide and gleaming, she watched the glorious abandon in Walker's expression, part joyous, part almost agonized as his body moved in primal harmony with hers, trying to prolong the mystery yet compelled to seek fulfillment. Every part of her consciousness was in intimate communion with him. Watching, feeling, surrendering, taking, then becoming one, they held each other tightly, finally reaching a pulsing moment of release and possession, of freedom and submission, contradictory yet perfectly clear.

As the undulations of the water bed subsided they lay together, arms and legs entwined. Gradually the tremors of pleasure dissolved into a contented closeness that only confirmed that it was more than a physical attraction they felt. When he could finally move, Walker drew his rough hands over her bare body, tracing what little of her was exposed.

"I knew I wanted you," he said, gently lifting her hair at her temple and letting it trail between his fingers. "I never really comprehended how much you wanted me. The way you look at me totally unhinges me. You open my mind to possibilities, Miranda, ones I never thought were for me." Dreamy-eyed and very exhausted, he contemplated her serene countenance. "I'm sorry but I'm about to collapse. You wiped out what was left of me," he groaned, trying not to be too clumsy as he twisted to the side so his head rested on the pillow next to hers. Neither of them wanted to let any movement break the closeness. "I promise, if you'll stay here, I'll be better company after a few hours' sleep. Don't go anywhere," he murmured, succumbing at last to fatigue.

Miranda lay still, savoring the sensation of being totally surrounded by him. His hand still cupped her breast, his leg lay crossed over hers and his breathing became softer and more steady, rippling through her tousled hair. "You're definitely extraordinary company as it is." Miranda carried on the conversation, doubting that he even heard what she said. "And you open my mind to possibilities, ones I don't think I can ever have with you." More than ever, she understood what discipline he had used to channel all his energies into all the projects he needed just to make *Persistence* and the Phantoms exist. His unique vision, his ambitions, made no accommodations for her, and Walker didn't need another person, another responsibility. Not now. Perhaps not ever.

She stroked his mass of curly hair, tumbling over his forehead, and looked into a face now totally at ease and free from care. Walker was asleep, half on top of her, holding her to him ever so softly. "You wipe me out, too," she added. "Don't leave me, not for a while." She knew it would come to that when the S.O.R.C. ended. He would have offers that he couldn't turn down. So Miranda fought off the temptation to weave fantasies with happy endings. Instead, she simply watched him, memorizing every detail so this moment would linger in her memory forever. It was worth any future hurt just to have discovered herself through loving him. And it was undeniable; she loved him. Like the physical attraction that had turned into something breathtakingly exquisite, loving him seemed so natural, not really a surprise at all.

Sometime in the dark of night, he woke again. And she was there, looking like a kid with one hand tucked under her cheek and her silky black hair fanned out over the pillow. His pillow. The strange possessiveness he felt toward her set off all the warning signals. She had said she'd settle for a little magic. She hadn't asked for more. And Walker knew, especially now that she'd seen how much of him was merely showmanship, she was smart enough to avoid getting tangled up with him. But she was tangled up, he admitted, feeling her silky leg beneath his and gently pulling the covers up over her bare shoulder. But when his hand brushed against her and she stirred in her sleep, he stopped thinking about how far apart they seemed, and knew only that her nearness fired him with a passion he could not deny. Only this time he wouldn't be satisfied until he had pleased her more, until she exulted in her own sensuality. He would seductively and masterfully make love to her again.

But it didn't work that way. Walker began by stroking her bare body lightly, then with his lips and tongue he teased her from dreams, arousing and caressing her, hearing her soft breath turning to sighs. He was totally in control, absorbed in orchestrating a symphony of sensation, until she wriggled down next to him suddenly and slid her arms around his waist. Then she nibbled the taut tips of his breasts, and his thoughts flew into a thousand fragments.

But at the center of his thoughts were a pair of dark eyes that met his steadily, asking nothing but to have him near, reading his mind so each part of him that ached to be aroused by her special touch was touched. Excitingly, unhesitatingly. They sailed on the lusty wind of passion, intuitively balancing and heeling on the edge of ecstasy. Without needing any distinction between her being and his own, Walker let loving her take him out of the world again.

MIRANDA AND WALKER finished loading the last Phantom on the boat trailer and left Tampa at dawn, before the Friday-morning commuter traffic clogged the highways. Fortified with a fast-food breakfast of sausage biscuits and coffee, they stopped along the way only briefly for Miranda to call the West Palm-Fort Lauderdale Airport and confirm the arrival time of her brother's flight in from the British Virgin Islands.

"You can drop me off at the terminal, and Jeff and I can take the limo in to the hotel," Miranda said graciously, trying not to cause Walker any unnecessary inconvenience. Lying next to him in the night, she had reminded herself that he had not bargained for any lasting entanglement. She was determined to keep him from thinking she had any intentions of letting her other responsibilities interfere with his commitments. She would continue to be the independent lady and take care of her unique family reunion herself.

"I can swing into the airport and pick up your brother," Walker assured her as they passed through the toll booth of the Everglades Parkway and headed east. "I'm not in that big of a hurry. Besides, I'd like to meet Jeff." The two-lane road, nicknamed Alligator Alley, straight, flat and gray, spread ahead through the wet grasslands of south-central Florida in an unbroken, monotonous line toward Lauderdale.

"It really isn't necessary, Walker," she insisted. "Jeff and I have managed on our own for five years."

"Don't you want him to know we ran off together and performed various graphic and intimate acts upon each other's body?" Walker shot back testily. "If I'm an awkward encumbrance, Miranda, I'll make myself scarce." In spite of his flippant delivery, there was genuine pain in his voice, a pain that caught her off guard.

"Oh, Walker, I'm sorry if I made you think that," Miranda apologized, stunned that he thought somehow he was an embarrassment to her. "I'd like Jeff to meet you. Really." She turned in the seat facing him, uncertain of whether she should touch him or sit there clutching her empty Styrofoam coffee cup. "I'm not used to the morning-after rituals, and I simply don't want to make anything awkward. I know you've got a lot on your mind. I just didn't want what I have to do to put you off schedule."

"Move over here and sit close to me," he said evenly, without taking his eyes from the road. "And quit being so damn considerate. It makes me nervous," he admitted with just the faintest trace of a smile. He glanced out over the vast expanse of grass, scruffy pines and twisted bushes of the Everglades. "You've been so polite, I thought I'd done something wrong."

"You did buy coffee with real sugar instead of that fake stuff," she joked, feeling more like herself than she had since they awoke.

"That's it? The sausage biscuits were all right?" He was teasing, too, but the air suddenly felt clearer and purer than it had since they'd left Tampa.

"I have no other complaints," Miranda replied, snuggling close to him. But when her hand settled naturally on his thigh, both of them became immediately silent. The discussion of breakfast was suddenly irrelevant.

On the drive across the state back to Fort Lauderdale, Miranda had deliberately kept the conversation channeled toward safe issues, ones that involved no reassessment after the night of lovemaking they had shared. So they had talked about Tortola, and the abandoned rum factory Miranda was considering converting into a boat-supply store, and being a debutante in Annapolis, and sailing the Chesapeake Bay—anything—except them. Reality would claim them soon enough.

"Maybe we should talk about us," Walker suggested, his voice soft and low and apprehensive.

"Maybe not," Miranda answered, not willing to translate into words the complexity of emotions and obligations in which both of them were caught. "Don't spoil it," she said softly, unable to stop herself. "Just let things stay as they are a little longer."

Walker didn't object. For now, he simply held her next to him, wishing he had answers instead of questions.

CHAPTER NINE

"JEFF CAN MANAGE pretty well in his wheelchair, but he's never had to negotiate an airport by himself," Miranda breathlessly commented as she and Walker hurried across the airport parking lot. Because of the boat trailer they were towing behind Walker's truck, they had to park far across the lot, well away from the terminal. Jeff's flight was already on the ground before they arrived. "I hope he doesn't think I forgot him," Miranda added, glancing up at the video monitor to confirm the gate number where they were to meet.

"Relax, Miranda," Walker said, catching her arm and slowing her down. "If he's as independent as you are, he'll have everything under control. Just don't worry. We're only five minutes late."

"It's just that I want everything to go smoothly for him. It's his first flight since we left the States...." She spoke nervously, unable to conceal her concern. Then she stopped abruptly and stared at the procession coming her way.

"I guess he hasn't been anguishing over your tardiness," Walker cracked, seeing the two female flight attendants who were escorting the smiling sandy-haired young man toward the baggage claim area. One strolled on either side of his wheelchair as Jeff laughed and talked with them, propelling himself along by hand, with his carryon bag on his lap. The taller attendant, a curly-haired redhead, had Jeff's guitar case.

"I'll say..." Miranda replied softly. She let out a sigh of relief that the disembarkation had not been the least bit traumatic, but she felt an inexplicable twinge of disappointment that after all her haste and worry Jeff didn't seem to need her there at all.

"Susie and Laura...this is my sister, Miranda." Jeff made the introductions smoothly, then reached out his hand to greet Walker. "I already know who you are. Walker Hall. Saw you on the news. I can't wait to get a look at your boat."

"You won't have to wait long," Walker answered. "We've got five of them sitting out there in the parking lot."

"You're kidding." Jeff's grin widened and his eyes glinted with a curiosity that Walker had seen before—in Miranda's eyes. Immediately Walker could see the family resemblance—traces of both Miranda and of Howard Vaughn in this muscular young man.

"Okay, ladies, time for me to roll out of here." Jeff bade his pleasant companions farewell. "It was real nice to meet you gals. If you're ever in Tortola, look me up. There's nothing better for a holiday than a nice leisurely cruise. Calvert Charters," he reminded them good-naturedly. "Here, take a card so you don't forget." He handed them each his business card, with a whimsical cartoon sailor stretched horizontally, clinging desperately to the mast of a boat. The caption read, "In the Caribbean there's always a steady wind."

"I doubt if they'll forget you," Miranda declared after both girls had said goodbye by planting a kiss on his mouth. "But the business card was overdoing it a bit, don't you think?"

"Hey, they can get cheap flights. They take vacations." Jeff shrugged, his casual invitation clearly not a sales pitch. "I wouldn't mind showing them around the islands. They were very nice folks."

"Not to mention good-looking and female," Walker teased. "Or did you notice that?"

"Just a coincidence," Jeff answered, chuckling. "They all look good to me. It's tough when the best-looking woman I see most days is my sister. I get off that island and suddenly it's like being in a candy store. Goodies everywhere." He and Walker laughed again while Miranda went off to get Jeff's suitcase. By the time she'd caught it as it passed along the conveyor belt, Jeff and Walker had come after her. Chatting like old college chums, they were now discussing the S.O.R.C. fleet and individual boats that had done well.

"If you guys don't mind moving this conversation outside, we should be getting on to Lauderdale," she interrupted them, handing Walker the suitcase while she took the guitar.

"Pushy broad." Jeff winked at Walker. "If she thinks she's right, there's no sense in arguing with her."

"I've noticed that," Walker responded, remembering the dispute over the expensive polypropylene underwear that had literally kept *Persistence* in contention during the last race.

"You can stop talking about me as if I'm not even here," Miranda muttered testily, disliking the feeling that the two of them were having fun at her expense. "I just want to remind you that since the weather is so gorgeous today and there's a cocktail reception at the yacht club, everyone will be out sunning on the patio and the lawn until the sun sets. It may be a very good idea for a particular ambitious boat maker to sail around there this afternoon and flaunt his stuff." She aimed the reminder at Walker knowing that for the rest of the afternoon and into early evening, an audience for his Phantoms would already be assured. Tomorrow, Saturday, the third race of the series, the Lipton Cup would be held, but after that brisk four- or five-hour race, there would be four days of socializing. Having the Phantoms available now would pique the interest of potential buyers before everyone scattered.

"These are the ones Miranda sailed in St. Pete, aren't they? She said when she called that they were really slick." Jeff wheeled ahead of them straight up to the trailer load of Phantoms. "I want a crack at playing with one of these," he declared enthusiastically. "I like the looks of this thing."

"You'll like her even better when you're at the helm," Walker assured him. Then giving a running commentary about rigging and design features, he helped Jeff pull himself into the front seat of the truck. Walker folded the wheelchair, plopped it in the back and kept answering Jeff's questions as Miranda stood by, amazed at the ease with which the two men had cooperated in making the transfer. No one asked for assistance or offered it, they simply got the job done. To her relief, there was not an awkward second between them.

"Have you been around paraplegics before?" Miranda asked Walker quietly once they reached the Lauderdale Yacht Club and Jeff had proceeded in ahead of them.

"No. Why?" Walker looked for a minute as if he expected to hear he'd done something wrong.

"You acted so comfortable with Jeff. Generally there's a peculiar in-between stage when we have to figure out how to shift him without anyone feeling helpless. Cars, he can handle on his own, but I was worried that the high seat of the truck would be a problem."

"It is a problem," Walker agreed. "Sometimes I bump my head climbing in." He said it with his typical dry humor, turning the subject totally inside out.

"I still want to thank you, Walker." Miranda wouldn't let him brush it off so lightly. "You made it easy for Jeff and for me."

"So now I'm a saint." Walker shrugged amiably. "Get the lines and help me put a couple of these boats in the water." That was the extent of the sentiment he allowed, but Miranda could tell that behind his braggadocio, he was as touched as she was—and relieved that he had done well.

"I SUPPOSE YOU HEARD. There's a For Sale sign on *Persistence*," Phil Pittman said as soon as he saw Miranda alone in the yacht-club foyer. "I had hoped you could get him to hold off until we had that conference you promised to set up."

Miranda had just finished a late lunch with Jeff in the informal lounge while Walker had gone to the dock area to round up his men. All five Phantoms were rigged and ready to be shown off, but Miranda had no idea that among the "few details" Walker had left to attend to, putting a For Sale sign on *Persistence* was included. She tried not to look as astounded as she felt.

"Walker has a mind of his own," Miranda replied, substantially understating the case. The sign on *Persistence* would immediately start the rumors flying. Miranda wasn't sure whether Walker's move was simply a device to draw even more attention to him, his boat business, and therefore the Phantoms—or if it was even true. Something inside made her desperately hope the For Sale sign was gamesmanship. She didn't like the implications of Walker selling off a boat into which he'd put so much of his energy and imagination—and love.

There was no doubt he loved that boat. It showed in the polished teak and the caringly mended leather hand-grip, and in a hundred other details. If he could blithely put *Persistence* on the market, then apparently nothing he cared about had any lasting hold, or earned a lasting commitment. Easy come—easy go. Miranda had returned to reality with more of a thump than she had been prepared for.

"The least you could have done was to give Ted and me a chance to act as his brokers. Really," Phil sniffed, "this do-it-yourself sale of a boat is amateurish, shows no class at all. We could get him the price he wants and get our commission without any of the auction-block atmosphere Hall is creating. It isn't the type of professional conduct one would expect of a serious yachtsman."

"Perhaps nothing is serious to Walker," Miranda conceded, her face frozen into a noncommittal mask to hide the conflict she felt inside. Miranda had felt so close to Walker throughout the trip to Tampa and back, yet he hadn't even mentioned selling *Persistence* to her. Now it seemed as if he'd deliberately avoided telling her, since it was one topic that would have triggered a serious controversy between them. He obviously was good at keeping everything separate and neatly compartmentalized, but she was not. She knew that she had to get away by herself before she let her own romantic instincts betray her. Here, with Phil studying her closely, she had to act like a realist, just like Walker, even if that meant helping him hustle his wares.

"I suggest if you're really interested in representing Walker, you might talk to him now, before he does anything else amateurish," Miranda said sensibly. "He's out back with his Phantom crew. I've heard that two yacht clubs are trying to equip their sailing centers with fleets of Phantoms. I know they're a little small for your taste, but when you're talking six or eight of them..." She left the rest unsaid. She had whetted Phil's appetite with the kind of rumor Walker would have approved, and she'd sent Phil off salivating over a potential deal with Walker Hall. As far as she was concerned, they deserved each other.

"Miranda!" Howard Vaughn called to her just as she was trying to escape out the back door of the club. He was carrying a stack of manila folders, some from the protest hearings earlier that day and others containing the official race results. "I'd heard you'd gone off with Walker Hall," he said quietly, once he'd caught up with her. "I thought we had an understanding about keeping a low profile when it came to him." He was trying to maintain a pleasant expression, but his disapproval seeped into every word.

"You suggested that I don't crew for him. I haven't. But it was not an all-inclusive agreement." She wasn't in the mood to be treated like an errant daughter after spending years away from Vaughn. "I went with him to Tampa to pick up some boats. If I thought you were going to worry about me, I'd have left a note."

"Well, I wasn't exactly worried. I did think your absence was a bit indiscreet. Walker's sudden departure with you did generate a bit of speculation. I don't want to interfere with your private affairs..." He faltered a moment, uncomfortable with his unfortunate choice of words.

"Then don't interfere." Miranda smiled a cool, polite, public smile.

"Yes. I suppose you're right." Vaughn backed off the subject tactfully. "I also heard that Jeff is here. Have you seen him?"

"Walker and I picked him up at the airport. Jeff and I had lunch, and he took off toward the dock to look over the boats. I think he was planning to sail in one of Walker's Phantoms." Miranda considered going out there with her father, tracking down Jeff and making it easier for the two men to get reacquainted, but she knew Walker would be there. So would Phil, oozing charm and talking bids on *Persistence* and the fleet of smaller boats. She couldn't take it. Not the For Sale sign and the hype and the feeling of being caught in the middle of too many exchanges.

"If you don't mind parting with your files, I'd like to look over the race results before the awards dinner," Miranda said, seizing an opportunity to become a recluse. All she needed was a little time to stabilize, to quietly remind herself that she couldn't change any of this—not Walker, not the hustling, not her father's sense of family propriety, none of it.

"I have a meeting scheduled regarding the next two races," Vaughn noted, glancing at his watch. It was a gesture Miranda had seen him make throughout her life in Annapolis—there was always somewhere he had to go, someone to meet, and no time for her or Jeff unless it was on deck during a regatta or across a conference desk. Even now, he didn't have time to stroll out and greet his son. "You can take these files into the office upstairs," Vaughn suggested. "When I get out of my meeting, I'll come to get you. Then you and Jeff and I can get together."

"Fine," Miranda agreed, suspecting that her father's meeting might not be as pressing as he indicated. Perhaps he wanted her there—the mediator—when he met his son again, and if she wasn't eager to go now, he'd wait. And for once, she wasn't going to drop everything to accommodate him; he could wait until she was ready to face the world and Walker Hall.

By the time Miranda had analyzed the computer printouts listing the make, rating, finishing time, elapsed time and place each boat had ranked in the fleet, in its class and in the combined races so far, she could see how the long race had put *Persistence* in a position to hold the overall S.O.R.C. lead. It was also clear why Walker had chosen this time to start a bidding war on the sailboat. With her points from the two races so far and her ability to sail in both light and heavy conditions, if she had no breakdowns, *Persistence* would be the boat to beat. And if someone wanted to own a winner, she would also be the boat to buy. Her price would only escalate if she continued to perform well, so the longer Walker could hold out, the more potential buyers would come forward, and the more excitement would build. What bothered Miranda was her own very sentimental attachment to the boat, a kind of affection that Walker apparently found it expedient to forget.

"How about a break?" Howard Vaughn came into the office to get her forty minutes later, just as he had promised. "Let's find Jeff."

Finding her brother wasn't difficult. He was sprawled out across the stern of one chocolate-colored Phantom, neatly tacking back and forth across the channel that ran on three sides of the peninsular grounds of the Lauderdale Yacht Club. His mate on board was a very small sandy-haired boy who sat straddling the centerboard, shifting the orange-and-gold jib from one side to another as Jeff directed.

"They've been going back and forth for ages," Charlie Birmingham told her as soon as Miranda joined her amid the lawn-party crowd watching the boats. Lloyd and Dennis had each taken out passengers; two foreign crewmen who were trying their hand at sailing a small craft. There were more eager volunteers sitting cross-legged on the seawall, waiting their turn. But the most picturesque of the Phantom crews was the one with Jeff as skipper and the sandy-haired lad, enough like Jeff to be his son. "That's Josh...." Charlie beamed, but Miranda had already guessed. This was Charlie and Phil's son—the kid whose stuffed frog she'd carried around the St. Pete waterfront.

"I see Josh has overcome his inhibitions about sailing," Miranda observed as the duo made a quick turn and Josh handled the lines neatly. He was sitting tall, smiling smugly and trying not to be too obvious when he glanced over at his mother to make sure she wasn't missing any of it.

"What inhibitions?" Charlie laughed delightedly. "When your brother came out in his wheelchair and then shifted right into that boat, Josh hung back a bit. In fact, everybody did. But after Jeff zipped across the channel and actually got the boat back to the dock where he started from, Josh was so impressed and so curious, he dragged me down to check Jeff out. He started asking some rather blunt questions," Charlie admitted. "But apparently Jeff has fielded a few of them before. They moved past the discussion about Jeff's legs right into the problems he had trying to work the jib from the back of the boat." Charlie paused momentarily as her smile wavered just a bit.

"You know what Jeff said?" She went on without waiting for Miranda to guess. "He said he needed someone really small to wriggle up front and pull the blue ropes. Blue ropes." She repeated the words as if they contained some mysterious formula. "Phil always insisted Josh use absolutely correct terminology. With Jeff he just has to grab the blue ropes, and for the first time being small is an advantage. Next thing I knew, Jeff handed Josh a life vest, and they took off."

"Sounds like Jeff," Miranda said, nodding. "Not one for a lot of preliminaries."

"You missed the part when Josh got to steer," Charlie continued eagerly, her blue eyes sparkling as she kept her gaze riveted on the little boy. "They went straight across the canal, missed the turn and drifted smack into the dock on the other side."

"Apparently they survived," Howard Vaughn spoke from behind Miranda where he'd been standing, listening. Like Charlie, he'd been watching his sandy-haired son, sailing free and easy, as Jeff had been doing since he was a lad.

"They not only survived," Charlie affirmed, "they lay there laughing. I was expecting to hear yelling and maybe some cursing, but all they did was giggle. I'm not complaining, mind you. But you sure missed a show." Now that she finally had someone to share her delight in the afternoon's proceedings, Charlie kept on adding tidbits, not the least of which was the fact that Ted

Birmingham had agreed to buy a Phantom for his grandson.

"I don't see Walker out here anywhere." Howard Vaughn craned his neck and peered over the crowd.

"Phil and my dad took him off to the lounge to talk about a boat deal of some sort," Charlie said, unwilling to let anything detract from the blissful sight of her son having fun. "Phil was too preoccupied with Walker to pay any attention to Josh. You'd think that since this is the only afternoon to socialize before the race tomorrow, they could let up a bit. But no..."

"If you two will excuse me," Howard Vaughn began, already distracted by Mason Porter and several other old friends who had stationed themselves prominently under a striped umbrella near the patio. "I'll be back when Jeff comes in," he promised. "I just want to visit for a while."

"I've heard that before...." Charlie sighed after he left. "Sounds like a tape recording of my father. Just visit, my foot. There's been more buzzing and scheming going on here all afternoon than I care to discuss. Is it true you and Hall went off together to celebrate yesterday's race?" Charlie's pale halo of curls didn't match the devilish grin on her face.

Miranda wished she could say it was all as exciting and romantic as Charlie inferred. For a while it had been. But since the night together, a new day had definitely dawned—one in which something as beloved as *Persistence* became expendable. Next could be she. "We went to Tampa and drove back in a truck pulling five boats." She didn't supply the missing details.

"Frankly, I liked the gossip better." Charlie frowned in displeasure. "I had visions of pounding surf, caviar and champagne, and wild acts of sexual abandon."

Charlie had part of it right, Miranda thought to herself. But to Charlie all she said was "No such luck."

"Well, let's hope our luck improves over the weekend," Charlie said sportingly. "There's going to be a band and dancing after the banquet tonight. You should come, listen to the music and see what happens. How about it, Miranda? If Walker Hall doesn't know a good thing when he sees it, you can always look elsewhere."

"I'll think about it," Miranda said halfheartedly. She was envisioning the wooden dock behind her marina at Tortola. In the evening it was a tranquil spot where she would carry out a mug of coffee and put her feet up while Jeff strummed away on his guitar. Sometimes she just sat there alone, watching the silent flight of birds returning home for the night. Here it was seawall-to-seawall people. The S.O.R.C. boats moored next to the club were packed in tightly together with crewmen still making last-minute repairs. All the congestion was making her claustrophobic, and Miranda wished for open spaces, unspoiled nature—Tortola and home.

"If you want to go to the awards banquet and stay to hear the band afterward," Miranda volunteered, "I'll keep Josh back at the hotel with me. We'll eat in one of the restaurants, maybe take a walk on the beach, then I'll put him to bed." When Jeff and Josh finished their sailing spree, Miranda could see the little fellow was worn out. There had also been something very warm and comfortable in the conversation between Jeff and

Charlie, a certain gentle quality that Miranda didn't want cut short by the necessity of taking care of a hungry, grumpy four-year-old. Besides, she felt a lot like Josh, worn out, a little disagreeable and wanting to be left pretty much alone.

"Good idea," Jeff agreed, speaking for both Charlie and himself. Then he glanced over Miranda's shoulder and straightened up. "Here's dad," he whispered. Then he wheeled back, making room for Vaughn at the patio table where they'd gathered, and adeptly he became the host. "You're looking good, dad. Nice to see you," he said, reaching out and clasping Howard Vaughn's hand.

"Good to see you, son. I was watching you handle that boat. Seeing you in a sixteen-footer really takes me back," Vaughn answered.

"Yeah," Jeff recalled. "I flipped mine over into the Chesapeake more times than I can count. But this Phantom is a honey, isn't it, partner?" Jeff praised the sailboat while he lifted Josh onto his lap and let the shy little boy settle comfortably against his shoulder.

Miranda sat listening as the talk shifted from the sailboat to the S.O.R.C. highlights and finally to the evening agenda. Occasionally she or Charlie made a comment, but the feeling-out process between father and son was typically polite, superficial and painfully slow. Miranda could see the restraint in Jeff's expression as the conversation stayed essentially impersonal and Vaughn avoided any reference to Jeff's condition. She had been going through the same process with her father herself, and had only broken through to something vital once or twice. Mending required patience, something Jeff had acquired in abundance in the years since the accident.

"I'm hungry." Josh's comment called for more immediate action.

"Then let's get you some food," Jeff said, chuckling, hugging the boy. "I don't know about you guys, but I need a shower and a change of clothes if I'm going to be presentable tonight. How do we get from here to the hotel?" Jeff said, eager to get the evening activities under way. "Who's got wheels, besides Josh and me?" he joked.

"I've got a car," Vaughn offered. "Shall we get started?" He slid his chair back, and Miranda could see from his expression that he didn't quite know what to do next. In the months after Jeff's injuries, there had always been a nurse or an attendant to handle moving Jeff around. Obviously Jeff didn't need that kind of solicitous care now, but Vaughn didn't quite know what was acceptable. When his eyes met Miranda's she pretended not to see the uneasiness there.

"I'll stay behind you." Miranda moved next to Jeff, ready to push if he lost traction on the way.

"Are you folks leaving already?" Walker Hall cut through the crowd and joined them. "I just got through talking to some guys," he said apologetically to Miranda. "I don't mean to impose, but what's the plan here?" In spite of all the other things she was feeling toward him, Miranda was relieved he could help smooth over the next few minutes.

"The plan is to get out of here. Everyone has to change for the dinner," Miranda said to explain their mass departure. Charlie, Josh, Miranda and her father were all inching around the table, ready to make a wedge through the crowd between them and the yacht club. Now Walker was here, a more direct route was possible. "If you'd give Jeff a hand getting across that grassy stretch, I'll go with my dad to get the car. We'll meet you out by the entrance."

"You can stay where you are, kid," Jeff told his sandy-haired passenger. "You navigate, Walker can steer and I'll be the power."

The look of relief on Vaughn's face was immediate. Miranda linked her arm through his and led him along, realizing he needed a little more time, and a less public occasion, to learn how little or how much help to offer his son.

"The problem is the darn grass," Miranda explained easily without making Vaughn ask anything at all. "On any firm surface, Jeff goes it alone. On sand or grass or even a thick carpet, you simply grab on and push but only when he needs it."

"What about getting into the car?" Vaughn cleared his throat nervously. They had reached the vehicle he'd rented, and suddenly he was looking at it as if it were an adversary, a mechanical obstacle that his son would have to battle.

"Cars are a cinch," Miranda assured him. "Just stand there and let him do it himself. At home, Jeff drives his own car all over the place. It's just a regular car except it has hand controls, not foot pedals. But he just grabs the wheel, balances one hand on the chair and swings himself in. Then he folds the chair, sticks it in the back seat and takes off." She didn't mention the countless unsuccessful attempts when Jeff was getting the maneuver down pat. Howard Vaughn had missed the grumbling and the wisecracks and the occasional frustrated collapses that came with mastering the transfer. But the victories had been superb. Vaughn had missed them, too, and Miranda ached inside for all the highs and lows her father would never share.

"He doesn't need a hydraulic lift or anything?"

"Nope. The break was low. His upper body and arms are well developed enough to let him do almost anything under his own steam. He isn't fragile, dad," Miranda added gently. "He's a tough, hardheaded, independent, proud individual. A lot like his father," she teased.

"A lot like his sister," Vaughn countered with the first trace of a real smile Miranda had seen from him all afternoon. He pulled the car into the curved driveway in front of the yacht-club entrance where Walker and the others were waiting. Before the others got in, Howard Vaughn tried to change her mind. "Are you sure you won't come back to the dinner with us? It seems a shame to miss an evening with your family." In spite of the confidence she'd tried to give him, he was not above pulling the old strings, trying to keep her standing by just in case he needed her.

"You'll both manage without me," Miranda assured her father, refusing to attend the function simply out of duty. "Charlie will be there. Walker will be around. Jeff will let you know what to do, if anything. I need some time to myself."

"You're skipping the dinner?" Walker looked bewildered when she told him she was staying with Josh at the hotel. "Look, I'm sorry I was tied up all afternoon," he said earnestly. "But I figured you'd understand. I'd hoped tonight you'd be with me."

"I'm already committed," Miranda said carefully. Everyone else was already in the car, ready to leave. "See you tomorrow, Walker. And good luck on the race."

"If there's something wrong, we should talk." Walker kept his voice low, and the urgency in his gray eyes almost made her change her mind.

"No time to talk now. Good night, Walker." Miranda stood on tiptoe and brushed a light kiss on his cheek. She hadn't intended to do anything so public. But he had that effect on her—some things with him just happened naturally.

SHE'D NEVER ONCE MENTIONED the For Sale sign. So that had to be the problem, Walker concluded. He sat staring pensively out the windows of the lounge, watching the crowd outside laughing, dancing and standing about in groups on the lantern-lit patio of the yacht club. He should have been feeling terrific. Everything was going his way, even more successfully than he'd hoped. *Persistence* had made it through the two tough races without any structural failures. Stasch had been busy spreading carefully phrased rumors suggesting that foreign investors would woo Hall away from the States. And suddenly, everyone, even Mason Porter's chums, was very charming. At least, to his face. Groups of investors had been courting his favor, talking about forming an American syndicate to back him for future America's Cup and Admiral's Cup competition. The St. Pete Sailing Center had been the first to order six Phantoms for their training program. The bandwagon effect would soon gain momentum.

Even Phil Pittman, with dollar signs in his eyes, hovered around, trying to associate himself with Walker so that anyone interested in inconspicuously making a bid on *Persistence* could use Pittman as the middleman. The fact that Walker blatantly refused to put a set price on the boat and was in no apparent hurry to accept a bid had everyone buzzing. He was making them try to outguess and outbid their anonymous opposition. The tactic was effective. Eventually the early bidders would come back and raise that bid until Walker accepted someone's offer.

Walker was finally in the position to call the shots. And he should have been enjoying himself. But he felt as if he was caught up in a bad joke. He was getting what he'd worked for, what he'd wanted for the past two years, but none of it would wash with Miranda. He could take the money, pay off his debts and run. He could expand his boat factory in Tampa or sign with a syndicate in the States or travel from one Cup race to another—but not if he wanted her. He had all the keys to the doors he'd wished he could walk right through, but now they all opened to the wrong places. None was in the British Virgin Isles.

What he hated to admit was that he'd underestimated Miranda. She was really serious about Tortola, about going back there and gutting an old Moorish-style factory that had once housed a thriving business in rum. She would refurbish the building with ferns and stained-glass windows reminiscent of its Spanish heritage, then turn the interior into a modern marine-hardware operation that would supply parts to boat owners, repair shops, marinas and sailing schools throughout the Caribbean.

Ironically Miranda was the one who could walk away from all this status and power. She was the one separating herself now, quietly choosing to stay away, but not insisting he change at all. She made no demands, gave no censure. He was ready to be chewed out by her for putting *Persistence* up for sale, but she surprised him. She said nothing. But she made a date with a four-year-old instead of him. He had to admit, as he gazed glumly into his glass of Scotch, she might have made the right choice. Tonight he'd been the center of attention, and if she'd been with him, every glance they shared would be scrutinized, every gesture observed. And what she meant to him was nobody's business. He hadn't figured it out himself. He just knew he couldn't get her out of his head.

"Walker," Phil Pittman's voice broke through his dark cloud of contemplation. "I've got a proposal I'd like to run by you. It's very tentative and quite flexible—" Walker stopped him before he went any further.

"It will have to wait until tomorrow," Walker insisted, signaling for the barmaid to bring him a refill. "I'm going back to the boat. I've got to get some sleep."

"But this could be important," Phil persisted. "It's about a package deal on some Phantoms. It doesn't hurt to listen."

"I'm listened out. I'm tired of words. I want to take my drink, crawl into my bunk and listen to the water slapping against the hull. That's all." Walker took his refill and strolled toward the exit, leaving Phil standing by the windows, staring after him.

Dennis, Jack Davis and Lloyd were still on deck when Walker boarded *Persistence*. The rest of the crew had either holed up below or had opted for the more comfortable hotel rooms in a complex of modern buildings a shuttle ride away. That was where the action would continue until dawn. That was where Miranda and all the owners had rooms. But Walker was staying aboard *Persistence* with the guys, keeping an eye on his boat, just in case.

For a few minutes, Walker sprawled out on the deck, staring up at the endless dark expanse of the night sky whose tiny bright stars had guided seafarers home for centuries. But tonight they offered no direction, no answers for him. Jack Davis played his dulcimer until Dennis fell asleep and Lloyd started to nod, then he nudged his friends and they all climbed below. Finally Walker followed down the companionway, stepped into his quarters and collapsed on his bunk. He lay there listening to the water, hearing in its whispers echoes of her voice. In the dark, his body recalled her hands and her touch, and he ached to have her near. Closing his eyes, he was immediately assailed by images of her—dark intelligent eyes, an incandescent smile, a warm melodic voice, skin like velvet—and he surrendered to the temptation to breathe her name and seek release in fantasy.

"Miranda," he sighed, swept away by memories of the night they shared. He had taken her to the place where he felt most in control, and she had shaken him to the very center of his soul. In that loft apartment, surrounded by his possessions, he had never felt so vulnerable in his life. And he knew she understood. But she used her power only to love him, not to make demands. Then she'd been so sure not to ensnare him in her tomorrows, not to encumber him at all. And he understood how dearly she valued her hard-won independence—so much that she wouldn't infringe on his.

"Damn it," Walker muttered in frustration, wanting to know what she'd been thinking when she avoided seeing him this night. On the eve of another race, one *Persistence* was favored to win, all he could think of was how to juggle it all—his affairs, the money he owed, the people depending on him, the plans to expand, the chance to build an America's Cup entry—and Miranda. She'd shattered his priorities, leaving them like scattered glass from a broken kaleidoscope—without form, without design, without meaning.

"Who's up there?" Jack Davis's voice shot through the night. For a few seconds, there was only silence, then the soft sound of footsteps above signaled a retreat. Walker and Davis both bounded toward the hatchway, jostling each other as they hurried on deck. Outside, no one stirred.

"Maybe it was just some guy going back to his boat,"

Jack Davis suggested, turning slowly in a semicircle looking over the adjacent sailboats. They were all packed into the yacht-club moorings like sardines in a can. Whoever had cut across *Persistence*'s deck had apparently ducked into one of the nearby boats.

Razzle-Dazzle. Divine. Walker looked intently at each of them. Unless the visitor had been up to mischief, there was no reason for him to hide. Passing through was no offense. Then he narrowed his eyes, peering at *Elan*, his former boss's boat, just the other side of *Razzle-Dazzle*. It was impossible to detect any movement in her shadows, but Walker waited just the same. *Elan* had been repaired after her damage in the race around the Keys. She was ready to race again. Walker had the uneasy feeling that if someone had been tampering, trying to improve her chances against *Persistence*, Mason Porter could be behind the scheme. Any structural failure in *Persistence* would make Porter look like less of a fool.

"Let's take a look around," Walker suggested. "Get a flashlight."

"How about waiting till morning?" Jack replied, just as uneasy as Walker. "You go and get some shut-eye, and I'll just grab a sleeping bag and camp out here the rest of the night. I'm just a good old country boy anyhow. Won't bother me a bit," he insisted.

"It is too dark to see much," Walker agreed. "Okay, you get the bag. I'll wait here until you get back." Even while Jack went below, Walker never shifted his gaze from *Elan*'s deck. And when he finally saw a shadowy form duck down the hatch, he knew he'd be rising early.

Persistence would need a thorough going-over before he took her out for the race at eleven the next morning.

"Good night, Walker," Jack said as soon as he returned. "Sleep."

"Sure, good night," Walker replied, knowing Jack was right. But this time, as Walker lay there thinking of Miranda, he tried not to replay those muffled footsteps in his mind. Finally, she came to him, out of the darkness of his mind.

MIRANDA PADDED TO THE HOTEL DOOR and cracked it open. Then she took the glass of warm milk and the roast-beef sandwich that she'd ordered from room service and snuggled back on the sofa next to the sleeping boy. She didn't even turn the light on. The glow from the colored lanterns around the hotel swimming pool outside spilled in across the room and that was enough to see by. She didn't want anything to disturb the loveliness of the moment. She just sat there, munching thoughtfully on her sandwich as she watched Josh. His long lashes, a deep tawny shade, far darker than his hair, formed miniature fans against his sun-kissed cheeks. Like his father, he would tan beautifully. A few more days in the Florida sun and he'd be golden all over.

They'd started off walking barefoot on the beach, eating hot dogs from the snack shop in the hotel. Then they'd ridden the elevator to the top floor where the circular bar revolved, giving them a complete view of Fort Lauderdale's oceanfront. They didn't talk much. They just looked at what Josh called "neat stuff." Then they went back to Miranda's hotel room, kicked off their shoes and sat there eating oranges and nuts, watching a movie. They both fell asleep before it ended.

Miranda had awakened during a commercial break, a bit embarrassed that she'd omitted a few steps from her baby-sitting procedure. So she gently tugged off Josh's play clothes, slipped his droopy arms and legs into his pajamas and steered him to the bathroom. Then she carried him back with her, enjoying the clean scent of toothpaste on his breath, the silky texture of his hair against her cheek and the cuddly warmth of his little body. It was very nice to hold the sleepy child while he drifted off to sleep again.

But now Miranda tried to suppress the maternal yearnings that had slowly crept up on her throughout the evening. Being with Josh was another reminder of what might have been if she had married Phil. The wish to one day be a mother was another half-formed dream that seemed to be slipping farther and farther away. Miranda studied Josh's features wondering how different a child of hers would have been. But it wasn't Phil Pittman's child she was imagining. Nor could she see Phil being the kind of father that a kid like Josh really needed. Another face kept taunting her, a curly-haired boyish face with a lopsided smile.

"Whoa..." Miranda pressed her fingertips to her temples, trying to block the flow of thoughts besieging her. There had been a rightness between her and Walker, and perhaps it had summoned up those deep-rooted desires to be fulfilled in many ways. But Miranda was realistic enough to know what she felt simply wasn't practical. Walker was well on his way to becoming world famous—the boat builder extraordinaire, always traveling, always competing, always preoccupied. Settling down anywhere with anyone wasn't on his mind. She wanted a husband and a family bound by love and commitment, not an absentee lover and a child to fill a need.

Being with Josh reinforced the sadness she felt—for her father and all he'd missed out on, for Phil Pittman, using his marriage as a means to success and disregarding his only son, and for Charlie, who tried so hard to play by the rules when the rules changed arbitrarily. There had been such potential for love in all the relationships—such potential for caring. But people kept letting go, allowing what was important to slip away. And when it was time to be let go, you were supposed to slip away gracefully, without making waves.

"Persistence..." Miranda sighed, trying to imagine the boat without Lloyd or Walker at the helm. It wouldn't be the same. Not without long, lanky Dennis and his little buddy Jack working the foredeck sails. Not without slender, solemn Ross Cornelius carefully planning her tactics. Even the second-watch men were not the typical sailors. They were all Walker's craftsmen or a few of Lloyd's fellow students, temporary seafarers, temporary caretakers.

"It won't be the same without me..." Miranda warned a lover too distant to hear. She knew she and Walker had wandered into something special, something unique enough not to be temporary at all. But it took two to hold on, and even then there were no guarantees. When he loved her in the night he hadn't held back anything, neither had she. And in the exchange of passion, they had given far more to each other than mere sensual pleasure. If he went on without her, he would never find that balance, that harmony, that instinctive flow with anyone else. Like Phil Pittman, if Walker changed his mind later on, it would be too late. She'd already learned that letting go was an irreversible act.

"You'll miss me, buddy." She sniffed as tears welled up in her eyes and slowly trickled down the sides of her nose. She'd miss him, too, every day of her life. But like *Persistence*, she could sail away—and make no waves, no scenes, no trouble—nothing that would last, except the memories.

CHAPTER TEN

SATURDAY DAWNED GRAY AND HUMID, not at all uplifting for the hundreds of sailors about to face another ocean race. Clumps of clouds hung over the choppy Atlantic and gusty winds hinted at storms hidden within their rumbling depths. But the Lipton Cup starts would proceed as scheduled, with class A beginning at 10:00 A.M. and the other five classes departing every ten minutes after that. The thirty-seven-mile race was an irregular diamond-shaped loop around the Lauderdale Sea Buoy, south to round the Miami Sea Buoy, then back to the starting point. Miranda would ride the course in a powerboat with Sibyl Albrecht, Charlie Birmingham, Josh and several other owners while Jeff crewed aboard *Prophecy*. With binoculars and radio, she would see the entire fleet starting and finishing, and this time she wouldn't miss a thing. The only drawback was that she had to leave from the hotel dock at eight o'clock, without a chance to speak to Walker before the event began.

Several miles south at the yacht-club marina, Walker was determined not to miss anything, either. "I've checked her over. You've checked her," Ross Cornelius noted with his soft-spoken logical delivery. "I think she's ready to sail. I don't think anyone harmed her."

Walker took one more look at the deck hardware and agreed. "Maybe it was just some guy passing across the boat," he said hopefully. Whoever had been on deck *Persistence* in the night had left no trace of any tampering. Now Walker wondered if someone from *Elan* had merely been trying to psych him out, disrupt his concentration by making him suspicious, and waste his time by prompting him into an unnecessary spot check. Already that morning Walker and his men had put hours of energy into testing and retesting equipment, energy they needed to give a peak performance on the short course under these threatening weather conditions. But no one could spot anything out of the ordinary. Now it was time to get out there with the other class-E boats, and he could only hope that he and his crew had been thorough enough in their safety check.

"HERE COME THE CLASS-E BOATS." Someone standing behind Miranda made the announcement, but like Josh and the others, she was already staring through the binoculars at them, watching *Persistence* hold back, delaying an obvious choice of position before the start. When the blue starting flag was dropped signaling one minute until the start, Walker and his crew pulled a fast tacking maneuver, timing it so the boat would cross the starting line just at the starting gun. Almost simultaneously *Razzle-Dazzle* and the German-crewed *Divine* duplicated the tactics, with the three of them abreast, cutting ahead of the class right from the start.

"We'll stick with 'em a while," the captain of the powerboat called out. He kept a safe distance from the leaders but equaled their speed. All three E-class boats stayed together on an identical course, perfectly matched until they closed in on the first sea buoy, an obligatory turning point that required a skillfully timed change in direction and sails.

At the buoy with *Persistence* edging ahead, the crew ready to switch sails, and Walker directing the change in tack, an ominous twanging sound reverberated through the heavy air. Instantly it was clear that the noise wasn't a blast starting the final class of boats elsewhere on the course. It was the loud report of a support line snapping; *Persistence*'s shroud, the support to keep the mast from excessive side-to-side flexing, had snapped under the stress of the change in direction. With a burst of shouting and desperate shift in direction, Walker made *Persistence* fall off the wind. Dipping and drifting with the current, she lost all power. Her windless sails flapped listlessly, loose and helpless, as the two pieces of her severed side shroud coiled and danced like whips in the air. *Razzle-Dazzle* and *Divine* stayed clear and continued on course.

"Get the sails down," Walker yelled. "Get all the pressure off the rigging, now before we lose the mast." All hands on deck leaped into motion, lowering the sails before the gusty wind could catch them. Even then he couldn't be sure that the mast hadn't already sustained enough damage to topple sideways into the water, dragging lines and boom overboard.

Watching from the cruiser, Miranda was on her feet

like the others, openmouthed and horrified, dreading to see the broken support cable damage the rigging or snare one of the crew. Worse yet, she was listening for the snap of the mast if it collapsed, ripping everything with it. But Walker kept the boat facing into the wind, so the force was on the front of the mast, not the side where the broken shroud was dangling. The cablelike stays in front of the mast were intact and holding, but *Persistence* was off course, crippled and unable to go on. Even before risking turning back, a maneuver that would expose her to the erratic force of the winds, she'd have to be patched up.

"Pull up next to her," Miranda urged the cruise skipper. He was already circling about to lend assistance, but Miranda's only thought was getting on board, helping in any way she could to keep *Persistence* from sustaining further damage. With clenched fists, she waited anxiously, wishing she was on familiar waters with her own toolbox on hand.

"Get the heck out of here or you might get hurt," Walker barked at her when he saw Miranda standing on the cruiser deck ready to jump aboard *Persistence*. With a jacket wrapped around one hand, he was holding the upper portion of the severed shroud cable, keeping it from thrashing about wildly, while Dennis retrieved what was left of the lower portion. One of the other crewmen was rummaging through the toolbox.

"Give me a hand." Miranda ignored Walker's warning and called to Lloyd to reach out and help get her aboard. Seeing she was going to try the leap, with or without his assistance, Lloyd tossed her a rope so she wouldn't slip and end up crushed between the two boats.

By now the boats trailing in E class were making the turn around the buoy, while *Persistence* moved farther off course, bobbing in the choppy waters. Then the first rumble of thunder rolled out of the dark, oppressive storm clouds hanging over the ocean and a gray drizzle swept toward the land. Miranda knew they had to get *Persistence* back into a sheltered harbor before the deluge began and storm conditions jostled the weakened rigging of the sailboat. Grabbing a pair of pliers from the toolbox, Miranda clamped them on the wire just above Walker's fist.

"I can hold this. You go after the parts to fix her." She took his position and freed him for the emergency repairs.

"If you see the mast start to go, get clear," he ordered her.

"I've been through a demasting before," Miranda countered. "I know which way to jump. Just worry about the repairs, not me."

"Easy for you to say," Walker snapped back at her. But there was concern for her safety, not anger in his tone. Stripping the jacket from his hand, he began rifling through the toolbox, laying out clamps and cable pieces. Then Miranda saw the angry red stripes across his palm, deep slashes cut by the wire before he'd used the jacket wrapping for protection. The blood that the jacket had stopped began to trickle down his fingers.

"Stop handling those grimy tools and put something on that hand," Miranda insisted. "Stop the bleeding.

And don't get anything in the wounds. Please, Walker." She could tell by the lack of color in his face that the pain had to be extreme.

"Yeah, get out of the way." Dennis backed her up, seeing the gashes for the first time. He took the clamps and extensions away from Walker. "You can supervise. I'll patch her up. Hey, someone bring out the first-aid kit."

With the spare parts they had, Dennis was able to loop both ends of the broken shroud and put in an extra piece to bridge the gap and hold it all together. While he did that, Jack Davis poured peroxide over Walker's palm and bound it in sterile gauze.

The makeshift repairs on *Persistence* weren't reliable enough to permit them to go on under sail, but the mend would keep the mast from any sideways flexing on the trip back to port. But even after the reconnection was made, Walker stationed the crew all around the deck, watching the remaining shrouds and stays as they negotiated the turn across the wind before heading in. "Someone must have crimped partway through the cable, then covered the cut with wax or something, so it wouldn't be conspicuous," Walker told Miranda how the shroud was sabotaged. "It was strong enough to hold until we hit a sudden change, but it sure wasn't a normal break. If he got to one support, he may have gotten to another," he said grimly.

Rocking with the motion of the waves *Persistence* limped under motor power back toward the Fort Lauderdale waterway, with Miranda, Walker and the rest of the crew standing like sodden sentinels in the depressing drizzle, anxiously watching the rigging.

While the other boats finished the course in the storm and gradually returned to port, *Persistence* was secured in her mooring and her depressed crewmen lumbered off to the lounge for hot coffee and a few hours of grumbling. Miranda borrowed her father's rented car and drove Walker to the emergency ward. Twenty-three stitches later, since neither one was eager to go back to the yacht club, they went to her hotel nearby to eat lunch and wait out the storm.

"What now?" she asked, sitting across from him in a warmly lit alcove of the hotel restaurant.

"Personally or professionally?" Walker quipped, trying to appear less dejected than he felt. The waitress came and deposited the cups of coffee they had ordered and left them to contemplate the menu.

"What are you going to do about the sabotage? Are you going to report it?" she asked quietly. Walker had already told her that there were no witnesses and no evidence other than a trace of a silvery substance on one end of the severed shroud. He hadn't actually seen anyone on *Persistence*. He'd only seen someone move aboard *Elan*; that was not enough to implicate Mason Porter or anyone else. But an investigation would be good press. A broken mast could have permanently damaged *Persistence* and in its fall could have killed or injured the crew. The publicity would keep *Persistence* in the limelight in a more spectacular way than mentioning her nonfinish in this race. Nevertheless, rumored sabotage would be a blow to the sporting reputation of the Southern Ocean Racing Conference.

"I'll decide what to do about an investigation after I look at the rest of the shrouds and stays," Walker answered. Until the rainstorm ended, no one would be able to climb the rigging to see if any other wires had been partially cut. "We've got five days before the Ocean Triangle," he noted. The break before this race and the next one was the longest in the series. "We have time enough to totally redo the rigging and test her out. But if we try to make a case out of this, we may get hung up with red tape and lose time getting her in shape to race. It's not worth it if we end up without enough proof to convict anyone. Whatever evidence might have been left after our scrambling all over this morning will sure be washed away right now," he muttered, staring out at the unrelenting rain. "Maybe we'll just pass it off as an unfortunate equipment failure," he offered sullenly, weighing the situation carefully.

"*Persistence* has three more races to recoup the lead." Miranda stressed the positive prospects. "All we have to do is take a front-running position in any of them, then hold on. We'll just improve the in-port security to stop any other mishaps. *Persistence* can win the S.O.R.C.," Miranda declared confidently. She'd seen the figures and she knew how many points each race counted. Walker's boat still had a very good record. No other competitor had been equally consistent, and since the next two races were traditionally tricky, anyone could come out ahead or succumb to problems. The 135-mile Ocean Triangle required a sweep out near the island of Bimini, and the longer Miami-Nassau Race had both distance and demanding currents to negotiate. In either case, more points would be awarded for them than for the race Walker and *Persistence* hadn't completed.

"I thought I heard a *we* in there...." Walker looked at her cautiously. Their encounter so far had been dominated by the necessities of handling an emergency of one kind or another, and there had been too much action and tension to allow time for anything personal. But now both *Persistence*'s shroud and Walker's hand had been treated. "Was it merely a slip of the tongue?"

"You won't be much good on deck with that hand," Miranda went on, a bit flustered when she realized she had spontaneously included herself in *Persistence*'s team effort. "You said I'm a good crewperson," she reminded him. "So...I'm offering my able-bodied assistance."

"We are talking about on-deck activity?" The provocative glint in Walker's gray eyes was the first sign of the indomitable streak Miranda loved about him. "Is there any way we could turn this into a more inclusive arrangement?" he proposed, lowering his voice and reaching across the tabletop to graze her hand with his bandaged fist. "I don't know about you, but I don't sleep too well alone. Not since I slept with you. And my days aren't too great, either. As long as you're offering your indisputably able body..." He fell silent, looking at her pensively for a long, still moment. "Miranda," he breathed the word almost reluctantly. "Right now my life is more fouled up than I ever imagined it could be. And here I am looking at you, seeing my goofy face reflected in your eyes and feeling like king of the universe. Granted, it's a very small universe,'' he joked, his voice warm and soft with tender sentiment. ''It's not your body I want. I want everything there is to you,'' he stressed, his smile faltering as he spoke. ''The body just holds it all together. And you hold me together. When this is over, can't we discuss this reasonably and logically and see if there isn't some way we can make something out of it. . . out of us?''

Miranda watched the uncertainty in his face, recognizing there a familiar combination of hopefulness and caution, a kind of wistful desperation she'd felt herself. There was nothing wrong with wanting to be loved and valued, to be irreplaceable. Only she'd been determined not to ask him for more than she thought he wished to give her.

''I know how you feel about going back to the islands, and I know that you're really steamed I put *Persistence* up for sale,'' he continued, his eyes anxiously locked onto hers as he spilled out all the concerns that had been plaguing him, ''and I understand that I'm pushy and I don't have a lot of class and I put you on the spot a lot. . . .'' He ran the fingers of his uninjured hand through his mass of curly hair as if he was impatient to get all the problems into the open. ''I've never really wanted someone else in my life. . . . I mean, a woman has a right to expect certain things.''

''Walker. . .'' Miranda tried to stop him. In spite of the downpour outdoors, inside, with just the two of them, the sun was breaking through clouds of confusion and caution, and she didn't need to hurry the process along. Just that it was happening was enough for now. Walker's distress was so like her own, his terrible need for her was as compelling as her need for him. All she wanted to do was to hold him, to comfort him, and to feel a reaffirmation of her own unique womanliness in his arms.

"Now let me get some of this off my chest," he cautioned her. "I'm not much for talking about really emotional things. It isn't often I get on a roll...." He saw the waitress heading their way, and signaled her off with an impatient wave of his injured hand. Then he winced.

"Walker, please," Miranda tried again, taking his bandage-wrapped hand and pressing it against her cheek. But he was still talking, trying to pull the threads of his thoughts together into a complete whole. But they were coming out unevenly, more special because he was trying so hard. Miranda sighed. The man had sincerity. And his earnest efforts excited her in a way more titillating than soft murmurings and glib compliments. This was pure outrageous Walker trying to say what she had felt and hoped but feared was too fragile to believe.

"Look, we haven't had much time to talk about real basic things like money. I don't know much about your finances, but mine are pending somewhere between flush and bankrupt. Nothing is stable."

This time, she didn't try to interrupt. While he went on about his friend who needed twenty thousand dollars advanced in sail inventory to keep his sail-making company in business, Miranda opened her purse, took out the key to her hotel room and dangled it in front of his nose. Walker stopped in midsentence, stared at it, then looked at her, obviously startled by the implicit invitation.

"They have excellent room service here," she assured him as the familiar devilish grin spread across his face. "We could order some food and coffee and discuss all this. . .later."

"What if someone. . .? Your father or brother. . .?" But the grin was getting brighter.

"The hotel takes phone messages and I have a Do Not Disturb sign," Miranda assured him.

"You don't even want me to get to the good part?" Walker hesitated. "I mean, I really love you. I really do. I thought you might like to know."

"Oh, I want to know, all right," Miranda acknowledged, sliding out of her chair and coming around to him. "I just think I'd rather be closer to you when you tell me."

"You're right," Walker said, nodding. "And I'm not supposed to argue with you when you're right. Oh man, are you right," he moaned playfully, wrapping one arm around her shoulders and accompanying her toward the door.

"Oh, I'm sorry I didn't get back to you two," the waitress apologized. "Are you sure you wouldn't like to change your mind and order now?" She looked mortified that she'd inadvertently neglected her customers.

"The coffee was excellent, but I think we'll wait a while on lunch." Walker shrugged, handing her several bills that more than covered their debt. "We have pressing business,'' he added, trying to sound official.

''What pressing business...?'' Miranda asked in a hushed voice as they headed for the elevator.

''If we can't come up with any business, then we'll think of something else to press...'' he said seductively. ''Starting here.'' He grabbed her hand and held it against his chest. ''This is embarrassing. My heart is thumping like a tom-tom,'' he said, laughing, undisguised joy sparkling in his eyes. ''I've never wanted to be understood more and been able to explain it less,'' he admitted. ''You don't read my mind, you don't even have to try,'' he said softly. ''You only have to touch me...''

''I plan to do a lot of that,'' Miranda promised, silencing him this time with a soft, discreet but not at all innocent kiss.

''And I thought you were too aloof to be my kind of guy,'' he replied with his characteristically boyish expression. Then he chuckled, making an erotic sound deep in his throat.

''And I thought you were a boat coolie.'' Miranda reminded him of their first encounter on the docks.

Walker arched his eyebrows thoughtfully. ''You were close to the truth.'' The doors opened to a vacant elevator.

''I plan to be closer,'' Miranda breathed against his ear when the doors closed behind them.

''Please be gentle with me. Remember, I'm injured,'' Walker kidded her. Once they were inside the lavender-and-rose hotel room, he drew the floral curtains to hide the dismal gray sky. The rain had muffled all sound and chased the usual poolside sunbathers inside, and the intimate silence was broken only intermittently by the distant thunder. But in each other's arms they found only warmth and the delicious pleasure of sharing. "You'll have to give me a hand," Walker said, holding his gauze-wrapped fist out helplessly.

"Anytime," she answered. "It's nice to be needed."

Their lazy-afternoon-in-bed playfulness turned to far more worshipful caresses as each stroke of fingers, each tracing of lips, produced pleasant jolts of arousal, encouraging them to seek more, to enjoy more, to ask more.

"I love the way your eyes turn soft, then clear and fiery," Walker whispered as his lean form pressed on top of hers, their bodies naked and flushed with building passion. "If I could see you every minute of the day, it still wouldn't satisfy me. I'd still wake up every morning wanting more. Nothing, no one, has ever gotten to me like you have." He moaned as her silky hands glided down his back and fit against the contours of his buttocks, and she rhythmically moved her hips beneath him, taunting him, inviting him, wanting him as he wanted her. Nothing, no one, was like Walker Hall.

"I love you, boat coolie," Miranda whispered, exciting him even more with the laughter in her voice. She was glowing, radiant, like the afternoon he'd seen her riding on the huge red maxiboat—a princess with her scarlet guard and the word *Prophecy* beneath her toes. Then, in spite of his uncertainties, he'd wanted to reach out and hold her, at least for a while. Then he thought he could let her go. Now he didn't even have to reach at all, and he wanted her forever. Passion thundered in his heart, his chest, his ears as he made love with her, finding his destiny in her arms, a destiny he never dreamed possible. Without wanting to be found, he'd been discovered; without searching, he'd made the discovery of his life.

Miranda exalted in the sheer beauty of their bodies moving in harmony, seeking a tempo that carried them along on winds of sighs. He knew she belonged with him. Walker balanced and complemented her in so many ways, and he needed her counterpoint. He understood the terrible incompleteness that they both would be condemned to bear if somehow their separate existences couldn't become one. Like her, he hadn't come up with any answers, but he was sure he loved her enough to try. At his factory, he'd told Harry "the lady and I can handle anything." Miranda began to believe it now.

Afterward she lay next to him, her skin still prickling with the heat of his touch, listening to him as he talked, seeing the pieces of his scheme click together. Everything was bankrolled by *Persistence*, but she was built to be sold. Creating her was an act of passion, too, a sweet form of revenge. *Persistence* proved to the boatbuilding community that the lad who worked his way from laminating to decking to inspection and purchasing to an executive post at Porter Yachts was more talented than anyone realized. His eye for design and his knowledge of his building craft put him in a category by himself, just as his Phantoms would be in a class by themselves. Unique. Not quite classifiable.

"I have to sell her," Walker explained. That was why he'd had Stasch and the headhunter Benjamin, and several others planting rumors of foreign investors, to keep the attention on his work and intensify the competition. The higher her selling price, the more flexibility Walker would have to operate in the future. "This shroud problem will slow down the sale. And unless we do win another race, the price will never be as high as it should be. I don't want her to be a bargain," he said solemnly. "She's a great boat. Waiting for a staggering price will guarantee that she'll be treated right." But Miranda could see the darkness in Walker's eyes. He was bracing himself for the inevitable separation, knowing no boat would ever mean as much to him. "I just don't want to be forced into taking a lesser bid."

"I might be able to come up with the twenty thousand you need to repay your friend," Miranda offered. "I know—" she stopped him before he could object "—you already owe me a thousand for the underwear. But this isn't my money. Not exactly," she said, intending to clarify her plan. "I've got an emergency account with money my dad sent Jeff and me over the past five years. Dad kept thinking Jeff needed a lot for medical expenses and hydraulic lifts and all kinds of contraptions. He didn't, so we banked it. I'm sure Jeff would consider this an emergency. I'll give you a check. You give me an I.O.U."

"You'd be buying me some negotiating time," Walker conceded.

"I'm buying *us* negotiating time," she corrected him. "We have problems beyond money. Problems of logistics—like how to sustain a long-distance relationship after the S.O.R.C. ends. Loving each other is going to involve a very complicated and unorthodox life-style."

Walker watched her thoughtful expression as she lay back against his arm, knowing neither one of them expected to reconcile their professional commitments simply or swiftly. Compromises and negotiations would be necessary. Regardless, he knew he wouldn't let Miranda be uprooted. "I'm going to try to make it as uncomplicated as possible," he promised, easing down next to her, gliding his bandaged fist lightly over the rise of her breasts, then downward over her silky skin. "I can't do much about the unorthodox part, though," he admitted. "That sort of comes with the territory."

"I'm trying to get used to that," Miranda replied, unable to disguise her body's eager response to his touch. And once again, holding each other, they chased the rainy day away.

That night the postrace partying at the yacht club had been relocated to the multiple downstairs lounges of the adjacent three hotels where everyone was staying. In the Admiral's Inn, Ted Birmingham was hosting a celebration for *Hambone*'s third-place finish in its class. Phil Pittman left six messages inviting Miranda downstairs to join them. The weather had caused a variety of upsets, and even Vinnie Albrecht's *Prophecy* had taken a third place with Jeff on board. The only consistent class performance was in class E, with *Persistence*'s rival *Razzle-Dazzle* recovering after her Keys disaster to place first, and the German-crewed *Divine* second. Walker would have to beat both of them in the next race. Any one of the three of them could take the S.O.R.C. trophy.

"I really don't feel like celebrating," Walker insisted before stepping into the shower. "But you should go down to the parties and congratulate your friends. Go ahead. I'll take the shuttle back to the boat and pick up a change of clothes. I'll look for you downstairs when I get back." She'd been getting dressed while he sat propped up in the bed, talking and watching her.

"Fine," Miranda replied, trying to sound perfectly calm about walking into the celebrations knowing everyone would be wondering where she'd been most of the day. "I put the check for the money on the dresser," Miranda called to him, as she applied a touch more lipstick. "Just sign an I.O.U. in blood, and I'll get it when I come back."

"Will you accept ink?" Walker countered, peering around the corner of the bathroom door. "I'm a wounded man, remember?" He dangled his pathetic bound fist out toward her.

"For a wounded man, you sure act very healthy," Miranda walked over and gave him a quick, light kiss, backing away in case he grabbed her. If he had, she knew she'd never get downstairs. "See ya later, Walker."

"You bet," he called after her. "Just don't smile like that, or they'll all know exactly what we've been doing." He tossed off the reminder just to unnerve her. But Miranda didn't even pause. She walked out grinning; the old Walker Hall was still alive and well—and apparently hers.

Miranda didn't need to worry about attracting attention. Among the hundreds of crewmen, guests and local fans, being anonymous was simple. With all the loud music, the boisterous laughter and the continuous flow of people from one celebration to the next, she was free to drift along, congratulating the winners and catching tidbits about the race. At the entrance of the Birmingham party, she was noticed.

"Too bad about *Persistence* not finishing." Phil Pittman mentioned the incident the first chance he could. "Mason Porter said he thought there would be some structural problems. I guess he was right." Behind Phil's glazed grin, Miranda detected a smugness that chilled her to the bone. If Mason Porter wasn't responsible for the weakening of *Persistence*'s shroud, Miranda had found another candidate.

"I can see that you're heartbroken," Miranda replied icily. "I certainly hope that in the next few races there aren't any other structural problems." She kept her voice low but filled with deliberate menace. "I'm working the midship on *Persistence*," she informed him. "If anything happens to endanger me, I'm sure my father would be relentless in determining those responsible."

"You're father is relentless all right," Phil sneered. "He had me convinced you were still pining away for me so I went out of my way to patch things up. He convinced Sibyl to dream up some excuse to get you back here. And all his relentless scheming got him was a daughter who sleeps around and a crippled son who's nothing more than an overgrown kid."

Miranda stood motionless, feeling the noise and heat

in the room close in around her. She stared at Phil's cold and vicious expression and was suddenly reminded of the crooked supplier on Tortola, Jack Flint. Flint had called her ugly names for exposing his inflated prices, and he even carried his hostility with him in his exodus to Nassau. Flint had thought he had good reason to bad-mouth Miranda, but she hadn't done anything to Phil, and his verbal assault disgusted her.

"Personally I have a certain respect for kids, overgrown or otherwise," Miranda replied shakily, determined not to lose control. "It's supposed adults who can't hold their liquor or their tongue who turn my stomach." She immediately walked away from him before he recovered enough from her comeback to launch into another round of abuse.

In the ladies' room she stood facing the mirror, pressing a cold towel to her face and trying not to cry. Phil had verbally hit her from more directions than she could handle, and her hands trembled from anger and utter frustration. She could handle the part about sleeping around. That was pure adolescent jealousy on his part. But the rest of it, picking on Jeff, lying about Sibyl and her father, that was sick. Then Miranda took a deep breath and steadied herself as a second wave of anger swept through her. Phil had too many drinks to dream it all up. She'd have to find Howard Vaughn to confirm any of it.

"I THINK WE'D BETTER HAVE A TALK," Miranda said, grasping her father's arm. She led him into the bathroom hallway leading from his suite full of officials and guests. "Your little confidant Phil has given me another version of our family reunion," she notified him. "Instead of having a loving father who would like to know his children again, his version stars a scheming manipulator who still wants to run our lives. Did you try to set me up with Phil? And was all this stuff about writing articles for Sibyl just fluff to lure me here? Who's really paying my expenses and Jeff's?" Miranda had her white-haired father backed into a corner and wouldn't let up. Nervously he opened the bathroom door and motioned her inside. She followed.

"Oh, Miranda," Vaughn groaned her name as the color drained from his face. "I didn't mean for you to find out any of that. Certainly not now."

"Then it is true. . . ." Miranda bit her lower lip and glared at him, shaking her head sadly as the knot in her chest tightened.

"It is partly true," Vaughn confessed, reaching out to catch her arm as she backed away. "Wait. Just listen. Please," he asked, looking pale and thin and miserable. "I wanted you here. And Phil's right, I am the one paying the expenses. But Sibyl didn't invent the articles. They're the real thing. And if there's nothing between you and Phil, then that's up to you. I didn't know what it would take, so I tried everything. I know you better now. I'm not really comfortable with you yet, but I'm catching on. Just don't let us lose it all because I did what I'm good at. I organized. But I got you here, and I'm not sorry about that." He scrutinized her with blue eyes etched in pain. "So I'm hardheaded. So are you. But I didn't mean to hurt you, baby."

Miranda softened at the word "baby" and the vague memories that it stirred. He had called her that when she was very little, before he became the marine-hardware king and she became his princess. Back then, he was just her dad, and the instinctive love that had been obscured through the years still survived. She'd been fighting to keep it alive for as long as she could remember.

"You're still telling me what to do..." Miranda struggled to say as the tears she'd held back finally spilled over, trailing down her cheeks.

"You're right. And I don't know if I can quit. But I'll try," Vaughn said, his own voice choked with emotion as he embraced her awkwardly, patting her shoulder as she sobbed. "I'm sorry, baby," he whispered. "Come on, now. Don't cry."

"You're doing it again. You never let me cry." Miranda looked him straight in the eye. "Not even when mother died. Now that I'm finally showing what I feel, will you please let me get it out of my system?" Her impassioned plea was more poignant than angry. And there was a glint of humor in her eyes, acknowledging the absurdity of chastising her father in the bathroom of a hotel suite.

"It's your face, your tears. Go to it," Vaughn responded with a dignified nod. Then he patted her once more, a little more confidently than the first time while he searched frantically for a handkerchief with his free hand. He settled for several squares of toilet tissue. And when he held them out to her, they both smiled at the absurdity of their surroundings. The confrontation that had been so long overdue had taken place in a washroom. Nevertheless, they were both relieved.

"Hey you in there, how about giving someone else a turn." A desperate partygoer needed access to the facilities.

"Just hold it a minute," Vaughn answered gruffly, instantly reddening over his phraseology. "I guess I should apologize to Jeff, as well," Vaughn proposed, ignoring the rattling doorknob and the impatient man testing it. "If you're ready, my dear, we can find him together."

Miranda patted her face quickly, then gave him a nod. "Just hope we don't run into Phil," she muttered. "I think now I could give him what he deserves."

"As one who has royally messed up my own activities," Vaughn said grandly as they exited, "I don't want to get what I deserve. So I can hardly wish it on another."

"Wait till I tell you what he said," Miranda stressed. "You might want a crack at him, but I'm first."

WALKER CHANGED HIS MIND about going all the way back to the club. Instead, he came down to the festivities, facing the teasing of the other entrants with as much humor as he could muster. Wandering from one roomful of socializing crew members to the next in search of Miranda, he and his injured hand provided a new topic of conversation.

"I had to give the rest of the fleet a chance," he joked. Behind his glasses, his steely gray eyes scrutinized everyone he met, checking for some evasive look that might reveal the culprit who crimped the metal shroud. But even Stasch reported nothing, not a whisper to suggest anyone suspected sabotage. Among the international boat owners, the only reaction to the shroud breakage on *Persistence* was a consensus that it was bad luck and relief that no one had been seriously hurt.

"Have you seen Miranda?" he asked Charlie Birmingham who passed him in an arcade between two of the hotels.

"Someone told Jeff that she was at our party a little while ago, but left after she and Phil had words. I don't know what the words were, but he's been drinking and he's really acting contemptible. Jeff went looking for her over at his father's suite. I was going to check her room." Charlie glanced about over the heads of the passersby, hoping to spot Miranda.

"She's not in the room. I just checked," Walker informed her. The faintest sign of a pleased smile softened Charlie's lips. "Maybe I should ask Phil what he said to upset her," Walker suggested, feeling very protective. But Charlie's expression now was apprehensive as she stared past Walker at someone nearby.

"I find it amusing that being disabled is some kind of a come-on these days." Phil spoke from behind Walker. "What with you and your bandages and that wheelchair Romeo running around, my ex-wife can't seem to get enough of cripples." He sneered at the stunned look on Charlie's face.

"I used to wonder, now I know," Charlie said. "You really are depraved."

Walker glanced at his bandaged right hand and

turned to Charlie, handing her his wire-rimmed glasses. "I know I promised Miranda not to behave like a caveman, but tell her just this one time..." He didn't bother to complete the sentence. He just turned and slammed his fist across Phil Pittman's jaw. They both yelped in pain, but it was Phil who leaned against the wall and slid slowly to the floor.

Charlie caught Walker's arm, supporting him before he joined Phil down on the walkway.

"I really didn't plan to do that," Walker groaned, doubling over and cradling his hand against his chest. "Tell Miranda I'm sorry," he requested shakily. The lanterns in the walkway gleamed brighter, grew beautifully luminous and then diminished into darkness.

"Do you want to try another hospital-emergency room, or were you pleased with the last one?" Miranda's voice broke through his consciousness. Walker cracked open one eye cautiously and peered up at her. The face he recognized; the suite was a place he didn't recall.

"I guess I made a fool of myself," he declared.

"Actually, you did pretty well," she said lightly. "But you won't be doing any sailing for a while. Not at the helm. We've all concluded that this is probably broken. If the doctor puts a cast on it, you're demoted to ballast," she informed him. "I'll take your job."

"Did I embarrass anyone?" he asked softly so her father and the others standing nearby couldn't hear. "Charlie will tell you he had it coming."

"You just beat me to him," Miranda said to calm him. "Your reflexes are obviously better than mine."

Both with Phil and the infamous Jack Flint, Miranda wished she had used more than words to defend herself.

"You've got great reflexes..." Walker mumbled, turning ashen as he tried to sit up.

"Let's get Rocky Four into the car." Miranda appealed to her father for help while Jeff backed up to open the door. "He's punchy but mobile," she declared. Supporting the arm in a sling Jeff had made from a pillowcase and a soft towel, Miranda and Howard Vaughn escorted Walker down the hallway and out into the covered entrance drive in front of the hotel. The rain had turned to little more than mist, almost iridescent under the Admiral's Inn neon sign.

"I guess I won't be climbing any rigging, either," Walker grumbled.

"We'll manage without you," Jeff attested, following behind. "Ross Cornelius decided to call in your friend Roy Gibbs the sailmaker. He asked him to come down and oversee the rerigging. Ted Birmingham is flying Gibbs in tomorrow."

"Does everyone have to get into the act?" Walker said before ducking into the car Charlie had driven around to meet them. But he was smiling in spite of himself. Gibbs was precisely the man who knew *Persistence*'s rigging top to bottom.

"There's a growing list of those who want to collect the money you owe us," Miranda answered, climbing in next to him. "Our interest in you is purely fiscal," she joked.

"Would you care to spell that?" Walker quizzed her.

"If it starts with phys. . . then Charlie had better keep her eyes on the road."

"Be quiet," Miranda warned him.

"Be gentle," Walker begged, reminding her of a more pleasant time.

Charlie giggled.

Miranda sighed. And with an idiotic grin on his face, Walker wisely rode the rest of the way in silence.

CHAPTER ELEVEN

When Miranda called the hospital the next morning, Walker was gone. He'd checked out on his own after he'd been specially fitted with a cast.

"Have you seen Walker?" She talked to Dennis on the phone after finally tracking *Persistence* to a Lauderdale boatyard where the rerigging was under way.

"Well, he was here for a little while. Then he talked to Gibbs and got the work plan straight, and he took off. He said he'd be back in a couple of days." To Dennis, Walker's departure seemed perfectly acceptable.

"Did he say where he was going?" Miranda asked bewilderedly. When she agreed to leave Walker at the hospital all night for X rays and observation, he hadn't mentioned any pending trip.

"He didn't say. He just said there was nothing he could do here, so he was going to take a few days off. He left an envelope for you. I guess it tells you more."

When Miranda got to the boatyard, the letter was a dismal disappointment. "We both know love is not enough. Not that I'm complaining. I needed to get away and look at things from another perspective. When I get back, we'll reassess. I love you, lady."

"Reassess..." Miranda stared at the enigmatic

correspondence, trying to still the uneasy feeling in the pit of her stomach. She'd finally found the courage to tell him she loved him. To her that meant a complete commitment, one without secrets or uncertainties. But Walker apparently could compartmentalize love as readily as he could the other aspects of his life, and reassessing sounded cold and calculating, not at all like the relationship she thought they shared. To make matters worse, he'd gone off with the check she'd given him, apparently without mentioning it to anyone. Miranda stared at the last part of the note, seeking reassurance in the words. "This is Walker. My Walker." Steeling herself against the old doubts, the thoughts of betrayal that had tormented her for years, she concentrated on Walker's signature and his words. "I love you, lady." She had to believe him. She had to trust him. She had to wait until he made sense of it all. Tucking the note in her shirt pocket, she headed for the toolbox aboard *Persistence*.

"Hi. I'm Miranda," she introduced herself to the balding, weathered seaman who was obviously Walker's friend Gibbs.

"So you're the one I've heard so much about." He winked as he greeted her. "'Bout time. Got a lot to do here." He put her straight to work on the foredeck helping Dennis pull and guide the slinglike seat containing Jack Davis clear to the top of the mast again and again.

Walker didn't show up in Fort Lauderdale in two days as he'd said. He called twice and left messages for Miranda saying that he was fine, but nothing more. Every evening Gibbs got a call from Walker checking on their progress and setting out the next day's agenda. He managed to miss connecting with Miranda in every instance. On the third morning when *Persistence* made a trial run with Miranda alternating on the helm with Lloyd, he had not returned.

"He says as long as we're doing all right, he's got other irons in the fire." Gibbs passed on the little news he had. "He always was a bit tight-lipped when it comes to letting anyone know what he's up to," he grumbled, tugging his faded hat over his thinning hair. Then he looked at Miranda warily. "When he gets back, I'm going to have a talk with him about his manners." He comforted her. "He's got no sense about how to treat a lady."

Miranda agreed. She tried not to fabricate possibilities, but the talk around the club had gotten back to her. She'd heard that the headhunter Benjamin was absent, too. The speculation was that he'd whisked Walker off for an important interview, perhaps including a tour of a boat-building plant that wanted his talent. No one knew where.

After the morning run in *Persistence*, Miranda met her father for lunch, but by the time she arrived at the hotel, the gathering had expanded to include Jeff and Charlie Birmingham and Josh. Seeing the cosy foursome across the room, Miranda hesitated. They looked like a real family. And that was exactly what she'd hoped to pull together when she came to the S.O.R.C. But without Walker, the part of the picture that was especially hers wasn't right.

"Nothing like group effort," Jeff gloated as he held up the newspaper for Miranda to see. Jeff and Josh had made the front page, a full color shot of them in one of their afternoon expeditions in the Phantom. "We even got Charlie out in one," he added. "She's getting pretty good."

"I have the bruises to show for it," Charlie noted proudly, sticking out one lightly tanned leg with her badges of honor. "This one I got tacking, and this one climbing over the thing that holds the green lines," she explained. "But we had fun, didn't we?" she said, nudging Josh.

"It's called the mainsheet, not the green lines," he corrected her, giggling mercilessly. "My mother is just learning," he excused her, patting her hand affectionately. "We're going out again this afternoon, just the two of us. Jeff says we're ready."

"I also said you've got to eat your salad like your mom asked," Jeff reminded him. The way he rested his hand on Charlie's arm as he spoke was a gesture so casual and caring that Miranda knew what she'd sensed and had been hearing about from Sibyl and others was true. Jeff and Charlie had something going, something beautiful. Regardless how the romance grated on Phil Pittman, Josh apparently approved.

"Right," Josh surrendered, dutifully stuffing a chunk of pineapple into his mouth. "Jeff said when we come down to visit you guys, I gotta eat like you do. He said they don't allow picky eaters in the Virgin Islands," he added for Miranda's information.

Miranda concentrated on the menu, trying not to laugh or feel envious of the loving exchange.

"Ross Cornelius says two other yacht clubs have contracted for Phantom fleets," Howard Vaughn noted. "Looks like I'll have to talk the Annapolis Club into getting in on the action."

"Since when did you get so chummy with Ross?" Miranda asked, wondering how her father had found time to chat with Walker's right-hand man.

"Doing business. Where do you think they got all the new rigging?" Vaughn countered, smugly. "I figured if you were sailing the thing, the least I could do was make sure you had the best shrouds and hardware."

"You donated it?" Miranda knew how uncharacteristic an act that was.

"Not quite. It's more of a sail now, pay later deal—at cost. I talked it over with Gibbs; Walker gave his okay by phone. It wouldn't hurt to have Vaughn Marine Hardware credited with outfitting an S.O.R.C. winner." Vaughn was making it sound more like a business than personal arrangement, but this time Miranda believed he'd made the offer to please and to protect her.

"That's very generous," Miranda noted cheerlessly, wondering how benevolent her father would feel if he knew that twenty thousand dollars of his money was already in Walker's hands. Vaughn was trying to be fatherly, and she wouldn't diminish his pleasure by telling him about the money, but she didn't want him exploited, either. This new family feeling that she'd helped revive was very precious to her, and she wished Walker had talked over the rigging deal with her before he'd dealt with her father.

By the next morning, Miranda was in no mood to be philosophical. She had spent the previous evening alone, compiling and editing the material she wanted to include in the S.O.R.C. article so far, but she kept finding herself staring at the telephone, willing it to ring. She'd asked Gibbs to relay the message to Walker that she'd be in her room. Please call. But he didn't.

All night she tossed restlessly. It wasn't fair. Everyone else who had pitched in to help Walker, at least got to talk to him on the phone. She needed to hear his voice. He had blithely wandered off to gain another perspective, but she was getting an insight she hadn't asked for and didn't like at all. This was just a preview of the existence she could expect with him coming and going, walking into her life for a time, then leaving again and again. That was the nature of his role in the boat business, and she had gone into a relationship with her eyes and her heart wide open. None of it was Walker's fault. But unless she could tolerate the in-between time, the lack of continuity, the highs and the lows, she was the one who needed to reassess.

By dawn, Miranda had passed through the morass of self-pity and moved into the realm of firm resolve. Before anything spoiled the moments they had, she'd take them as they were. The rest of it—the absence and the insecurity, she couldn't and wouldn't take at all. As an act of self-preservation, she was ending it now. Surrounded by friends and activity, she could make the break here instead of waiting till the last moment and facing the loneliness at home. They'd been attempting a windward passage, sailing against the tide and the wind and common sense. Walker would understand.

"YOU LOVE ME. But you don't want any involvement anymore." Walker sat across the table from Miranda, repeating what she told him. He could see the pain in her eyes and hear the tremor in her voice, but he couldn't penetrate her wall of self-control. He'd flown back and caught the limo straight to the yacht club where she was working with her father on the notes for the briefing for the next three races. There had been no welcoming kisses, no rapturous reunion, only a very polite, brief embrace while Howard Vaughn stood by. Then they'd moved outside to look over *Persistence*. Next came a constant stream of other people, Gibbs, Dennis, even Jeff, all reassuring him that everything was under control. But Miranda had avoided looking directly into his eyes. She had stayed on the fringe of the activity, and he knew that meant trouble. He just hadn't expected this.

"Won't you give me some time to explain where I've been and what I've been working on?" Walker asked her. When she insisted on talking in the yacht club's Cove Room, Miranda had eliminated any chance of intimacy. The nautical tables were crowded with S.O.R.C. participants, which guaranteed they would be under constant scrutiny. When she told him that she wanted the romance to end, he knew she'd chosen a public place so she could get it over quickly and wouldn't change her mind. In private, he would have made her listen, he would have held her and talked to her and made her understand. But he wouldn't do it here. No one had a right to see that part of their lives.

"I really don't want to get too wrapped up in what

your future plans are," Miranda replied. "I don't see any point in making this any more difficult for both of us than it is. I'm not suggesting we stop talking or avoid each other," she added hastily. "We're not children, and we're not angry with each other. The problem all along is that we care, but like you said, love is not enough. I still plan to race on *Persistence* and help to see that she wins. But I don't like the way I felt when you just took off," she said honestly, pausing to make sure she did not lose control. "I just want a more normal life. But I know my limitations, Walker. I can't take the extremes."

"But Miranda..."

"Please don't say anything, Walker. Please." She cleared her throat and looked at her watch while she desperately maintained her composure.

Rather than argue, rather than upset her more, Walker let her get it all out, admiring her remarkable courage, and wishing he could kick himself for having insisted on doing things his way. He had wanted her to stand up for her rights, and she was doing just that. Having a normal life wasn't an unreasonable expectation. But it required a lot of changes, ones he had tried to make on his own. He'd made her suffer, and for that, he'd never forgive himself. Now he would shut his mouth, stop trying for the grandstand play and feel his heart breaking for her.

THE TEARS CAME AFTER she closed the car door. Miranda had made it through the entire explanation without losing her dignity, and with very little interruption from Walker. She was right. His silence only confirmed it. He understood how futile it was. By not arguing, he made it easy on her. They'd both acted so civil and adult that no one watching would suspect anything was wrong. Then she had glanced at her watch, exactly as she planned, and excused herself, knowing he wouldn't follow. But once she pulled out of the yacht-club parking lot and started back to the hotel, she couldn't hold back any longer. Being right didn't make it less painful. The only real feeling Miranda had was a terrible sense of loneliness.

Miranda pulled off the road by the stretch of beach she and Josh had explored. Offshore she could see the sails of S.O.R.C. contenders, out on shakedown runs before the Saturday race. On the sandy beach were three small children with pails and shovels, digging in the sand, while two mothers sat and talked, watching their small architects. And Miranda didn't feel a part of either world. "Someday..." she whispered. "Someday it'll be my turn." She blew her nose and sniffed. "Someday..."

"We need to talk." Walker knew he was interrupting something when he saw that Charlie was in Jeff's room. But he couldn't go on with his plans without inside information, and Jeff was the only other person besides Miranda who could fill in the gaps.

"I would like to know what's going on," Jeff admitted, backing up to let Walker come in. "Miranda has been walking around being charming and cheerful to everyone. I love my sister, but I know she's a bit of a loner. There's something fishy when she finds crowds to hide inside. I guess you're the one she's hiding from."

"I think so," Walker admitted. He looked apologetically at Charlie who stood with arms crossed, studying him. "I messed up," he said, shrugging. "I wanted to make things work out for Miranda and me, but I was a bit late about including her in the plans. I wanted to see what was feasible before I sprang it on her—just in case I couldn't swing it."

"That sounds reasonable, very protective and dreadfully patronizing," Charlie spoke up. "Two out of three isn't bad," she noted with a disconcerting cynicism. "I'm not faulting your intentions, but I think you should look at it from her viewpoint. Her father was like a bulldozer, making decisions supposedly for her own good, and she finally worked up the courage to leave him. And Phil had the same technique, telling her what to think and what to feel and totally dominating her in another way. After being on her own all this time, I doubt if she wants to get back into that kind of a situation. Not even if she loves you. There is no such thing as a unilateral decision when it comes to planning a joint future."

"Give him a break," Jeff cut in sympathetically. "When it comes to dealing with women, two out of three is a darn good record. Besides, from the look on his face, Miranda has made a unilateral decision herself. Only she decided to dump the whole idea. I don't really think she wants to," he added. "She just knows what it's like to wait for a miracle, and not find one. But she helped make one for me, the least I can do is return the favor. What can we do to help?"

"I need some information about zoning ordinances and building permits on Tortola." Walker sat forward on the edge of the sofa as he spoke, with a note pad of minute figures and scribbles flipped open for consultation. "And I need to know something about the availability of labor and cost of construction. But to start with," he said, tilting the pad so Jeff could see the sketch he'd made, "I need to know how many square feet of space Miranda would need in the old rum factory to accommodate the marine-hardware business she's been talking about."

"I'd rather hoped you wanted her ring size..." Charlie kidded him, obviously pleased that his efforts showed his interest in Miranda was sincere and very serious.

"And I thought all you two had been doing was foolin' around," Jeff said, laughing. "You really talked about that place. Then you went down there and checked it all out." He shook his head approvingly. "What did you think of the marina? I assume the guys haven't lost all our boats?"

"Your setup there is really nice, and the fellows you left in charge have it running smoothly. I was impressed." Walker complimented him on Calvert Charters. "It's even nicer than I expected. I wanted to look over Tortola and see about setting up a factory there. I can build boats anywhere, but I had to see why Miranda loved it there. After sitting on your dock looking out over Brewer's Bay, now I know. It's beautiful there," he admitted. "I just don't want to crowd her by shifting the whole operation. If I could start up in that old building, then we'd see how it goes. Benjamin has been negotiating a deal for me to build a twenty-four-foot catamaran, an Australian design. I could work on it in Tortola and keep the Tampa factory running just doing Phantom orders alone."

"One foot in and one foot out," Charlie murmured. "Just like a man. Refusing to burn any bridges just in case you want to retreat."

"It's in case things don't work out."

"They'll work out if you make them work out, and not by leaving the escape hatch open," Charlie insisted. "It's either a for-real marriage, or simply grown-ups playing house. It takes two very honest people to decide which it's to be." She was sitting on the arm of Jeff's wheelchair with her arm around his shoulders. From the stiffness in Jeff's sudden smile, Walker knew that there had been a lot of honest talking going on in this room before he'd arrived. And they hadn't come up with any quick solutions, either.

"I sure can't help you on the square footage business," Jeff commented, focusing the attention back on Walker's notes. "I know something about the other things, but it's too bad Miranda isn't here. She knows all the technicalities."

"Funny how a woman can come in handy every now and then," Charlie quipped. "Sorry." She shrugged regretfully at the reproachful look both men aimed at her. "Truce? I'll order up some coffee as a peace offering," she volunteered. "I just wish there was someone I could tell."

"You wouldn't dare. . ." Jeff challenged her.

"I was going to wait until after the Ocean Triangle tomorrow," Walker explained. "I thought I'd wait until she was worn out and her resistance is low." He was trying to joke, but there was no real joy in his gray eyes.

"I won't tell Miranda. I promise," Charlie declared. "But that doesn't stop me from wishing I could."

"I have the strange feeling there is some logic there," Jeff commented, chuckling. "I just can't get a hold on it."

"You'd have to be a woman to understand," Charlie shot back at him.

"Thank you but I'm perfectly happy as I am," Jeff retaliated. Charlie didn't answer. She was already phoning down to room service for the peace offering.

THE 138-MILE OCEAN TRIANGLE had a reputation for being the nastiest of the S.O.R.C. races, next to the St. Pete-Lauderdale marathon in which *Persistence* had earned a fourth place. The Triangle required crossing the Gulf Stream twice, going to and from a key south of Bimini, then finishing with a leg from Lauderdale to Miami. The boat would dock for a day and a half before departing for the two Nassau races.

Miranda was on deck early Saturday, reviewing tactics with Ross Cornelius and Walker just as if she was one of the guys. She would take the helm for the first few hours, since Lloyd and Walker had spent the night on deck maintaining tight security. While they got under way, the men who had rotated on the all-night watch in the marina could rest or perhaps sleep while the others crewed. With a fifteen-knot easterly wind, clear skies and relatively smooth water, the class-A boats left at noon with Jeff riding *Prophecy*. *Persistence* and the rest of class E started at 2:02. If there were no surprises, the boats would sail all afternoon and most of the night, and would begin to arrive from two or three in the morning right up till midday Sunday. But Miranda knew she wouldn't be sleeping at all. Keeping her distance from Walker was difficult. But the ocean was her domain, her place of peace, and day or night she loved to sail its changing waters. She would savor every moment, in spite of the awkward circumstances.

Snuggled up in a waterproof sleeping bag, Walker stationed himself in the cockpit of the boat, smack in front of Miranda so she couldn't miss him no matter how hard she tried. Standing behind the wheel, she had to look past him to read the instruments and to discuss tactics with Ross who was stationed just below her with the navigator. Visor tugged down over his eyes, his cast cradled on his chest, and a satisfied smirk on his face, Walker lounged comfortably out of the wind, watching her. Eventually the movement of the boat and the warmth of the low afternoon sun conspired against him, easing away the prerace tension. When Walker looked up again, the person at the wheel was tall and black and handsome. Lloyd had taken over while Miranda ate dinner with the off-duty crew.

"She's kept us ahead of our class," Lloyd reported once he realized Walker was awake. "We're crowding through the C and D boats now. We're not the only E boat up here, but we're doin' good."

"Would you like me to bring you some food?" Miranda asked Walker. She was delivering a cup of coffee to Lloyd at the time, so her offer wasn't preferential. She deliberately made it sound as if any warm body occupying that space and coincidentally impeded by a cast would be given identical care. "Or coffee?"

"Coffee would be very nice." Walker matched her politeness with his own. "With a little cream, if it wouldn't be too much trouble." He struggled to an upright position, sleeping bag and all.

"Oh, no trouble," Miranda replied with maddening cheerfulness, and Walker wished he could reach out and grab her fanny as she passed him just to add a little reality to the scene.

Night sailing together was even more nerve-racking for Walker. Seeing her silhouetted in the moonlight, riding the rail, with her hair flowing in the wind, aroused him even from his post back at the helm with Lloyd. Here was a woman he could grow old with, and she wouldn't even look at him now. He could imagine being with her in the islands, finding a cove, undressing together. He could also picture her in that ugly pink stucco rum factory, transforming it into something beautiful, then running a marine-supply store with the streamlined efficiency that characterized Calvert Charters. He could imagine all kinds of possibilities with her, if she would only look at him and let her eyes go soft and believe in him again.

Just before midnight, with the moon spilling a billion shimmering diamonds over the ocean, Lloyd left the helm to Miranda and took up his position midship with Jack Davis and his dulcimer. With Dennis playing harmonica, they sent song after song floating on the night wind. But when they played "Daughter of the King," Walker watched her, both her hands clasping the destroyer wheel, her hooded jacket zipped up to her chin, and her face so beautiful and serene. She was so breathtaking, he had to keep himself from disturbing the moment by trying to tell her now.

All Charlie's words came back to him. After he was sure she loved him, he had become protective, even patronizing, just like her father. Howard Vaughn had nearly lost her by being so domineering; Walker—out of love—had made the same mistakes. And neither one of them had asked her help in designing her own future.

On the second cut through the Gulf Stream, they were passed by another class-E boat, *Outsider*. Nevertheless, when they began the final leg to Miami, they were already celebrating. Even with a second in her class, *Persistence* would lead the S.O.R.C. fleet in overall points. When she crossed the finish line at 7:55 Sunday morning, her red-eyed crew were on deck, cheering. They were riding the indisputable star of the series.

Walker never saw her leave. Sometime during the docking procedures, Miranda simply vanished into the crowd of dockside well-wishers. By the time Walker went through the technicalities of recording and filing their finishing time, he guessed she was already at the hotel, hiding again.

Walker was in no mood to be diplomatic.

"What the heck are you doing here...?" she blurted the second she opened the door and saw him standing there, windblown, unshaven and grinning as if nothing at all about his presence there was unusual.

"I've missed you, too." He laughed, then stepped in and swooped her into his arms, almost dragging her across the room and onto the bed. "How many square feet do you think it will take for your marine-hardware business?" The words he breathed against her throat and punctuated with hot eager kisses were hardly what she expected.

"My what...?" She wriggled in his arms, trying to escape.

"That's a great operation you and Jeff have going down there. I could see what you mean about having the kinks out and being ready to diversify."

"What are you talking about?" she asked as he pinned her down, thrusting his thigh between her legs to keep her from moving away. "Are you crazy?"

"Probably," Walker acknowledged, moving his hips so she couldn't ignore the hardness of his body brushing against hers. Miranda looked up into the gray eyes, sparking with flashes of blue, and knew she was lost. The involuntary warm flush of arousal was already beginning.

"I'm sorry how I handled everything," Walker said as simply as he could. "I know you dumped me because I took off and left you, and I admit it was a stupid thing for me to do. But don't stop loving me. Don't put up those damn walls again. Please." The struggle now was not physical.

"Damn you, Walker. Why did you leave me and why wouldn't you call?" She'd been miserable, and her chin trembled slightly as she looked up at him.

"If I'd tried to tell you face-to-face, we'd have ended up like this," he answered unashamedly. "If I'd heard your voice, I wouldn't have been able to concentrate. I had to take off while I had the courage and the money, most of which I've already passed on to Roy Gibbs," he assured her. "Besides, I thought everything was under control here."

"So where were you, and why are you asking about square footage?"

"I went to do a feasibility study in Tortola. I looked over your marina to see how you manage a business, then I went out and walked through that rum factory you were talking about."

"You went there—without me?"

"It would have been a little difficult carrying on business with you around. Especially there. There are a lot of very isolated beaches down there where people could run naked in the surf and stuff like that," he reminded her. "I kept imagining how it would be one day, with your long legs and your..."

"Okay, okay. Just stick to the subject," Miranda urged him. His wanderings into her tropical paradise had her very curious.

"Anyway, I got more done than I expected. That rum factory is bigger than I'd visualized. Since I've been back, I had Jeff check with someone in zoning there. I could adapt an outbuilding into a factory the size of the one in Tampa. With outside storage and office space in your building, we might be able to get into a joint venture, that is, if you're serious about you and me."

"You'd move to Tortola to be with me?"

"Now don't get cute on me, Miranda," Walker chided her. "I told you I'm not used to working my plans around someone else, but you're smart enough to know

I didn't take off to Tortola at a time like this just because I wanted to look at the natives. Of course I'd do it to be with you. Dennis and Jack will fit right in with all the off-beat flora and fauna I saw there," he added with a throaty laugh. "Ross and Harry can run the plant in Tampa. It is possible. . ." he said evenly, looking into her eyes and chasing her doubts away. "If we pool our resources."

"But first you have to sell *Persistence*." She guessed the remaining condition. Even she had come to accept that as an actuality. Walker wouldn't have the money or the time to maintain or race the sailboat. And if he were to have any resources to pool, they had to come from *Persistence*.

"I do have a bid that sounds reasonable," he informed her.

"I thought you were holding out for a spectacular offer," she questioned him.

"You haven't made me one yet," he said. "But I'll wait until you've had time to think one up."

"I want to hear your offer first," she insisted.

"I'm offering you a partner, someone who wants to stick with you forever," he said earnestly. "I want to love you, and work with you, and renovate a warehouse with you, and sail with you, and plant flowers, and all that normal stuff." His eyes glowed with a touching tenderness that sent waves of reassurance rippling over her. "I want my life from now on to be with you. I want to be needed by you. And I want to earn your respect. And if I mess up, like I did by taking off without discussing it with you, I want to have your patience. I'm not good at being a partner, but I want to be. I want to be yours." He lay propped on one elbow looking down at her, waiting for her response.

"Partners..." Miranda said the word thoughtfully, studying his solemn expression. "Just partners?" The faint trace of laughter in her voice set his heart racing.

"You know me. I'm very ambitious. As long as I'm taking on a challenge, I might as well go for broke," he added with a droll smile. "No sense in settling for less than everything. I love you. Miranda, marry me."

"What about a family? We've never talked about children. When you said everything, does that mean babies, orthodontist bills and drivers' licenses?"

"Not to be too puritanical, but I do think the marrying part should come first. A simple ceremony with a few friends will do just fine. And I'd like to hold off on the orthodontist, at least until we get the kids out of diapers." Walker leaned down and kissed her lightly on the nose. "With you I'd be content just to go through the motions," he said seductively, "but if those motions make babies, I'll give fatherhood a real try. I want it all, Miranda. But only with you."

"I want it all, too, Walker," she said, smiling up at him. "Just with you."

"You want to start now?" He chuckled that familiar, mischievous, passionate chortle as he lowered his mouth to caress hers. But when he raised his head, Miranda could see the bright tears in his eyes, tears of relief, of affirmation, of promise.

"You're really a fake, Mr. Hall," she declared lovingly, reaching up with her fingertips to softly brush over his cheeks.

"Not with you. Never with you," Walker promised, his lower lip quivering as he spoke. "I'll get better."

"Now don't overdo this changing business," Miranda said seriously. "I fell in love with you the way you are, not an edited version. Granted you could make a few improvements. So could I. But let's keep the old Walker around. Frankly, I found him rather appealing." Her eyes danced with humor, passion and love.

"How appealing?" Walker buried his face against her throat, pressing warm moist kisses in the hollows. "Be very specific," he urged her, again moving his body against her thighs so she could feel his response to her. "I could use a little positive reinforcement."

"I'll show you how appealing," Miranda replied pushing him back and rolling him onto his back. Then she unzipped his jacket, and unbuttoned his shirt, grazing his bare chest with the tip of her tongue as she undressed him. Her trailing dark hair made his skin tingle with anticipation.

"That's very positive." Walker groaned with pleasure beneath her touch. "Boy, am I glad we're going to make this legal."

WHEN MIRANDA PADDED TO THE DOORWAY wrapped in her bathrobe late that afternoon, she didn't expect to see Charlie Birmingham standing in the hallway with a blue-gripped pair of pliers. "I rather hoped I might find Walker here." Charlie smiled politely as she stood in the doorway, wriggling her eyebrows hopefully.

"He's here. . . ." Miranda let her friend come in, knowing her uncombed hair and the rosy flush on her cheeks gave away how intimate a reconciliation she and Walker had been having.

"I know I'm interrupting," Charlie whispered, keeping her voice low, thinking Walker was asleep in the bed. "I know it's a little late to do much now, but Jeff and Josh and I were wandering around looking at the boats after the race today. That little fellow named Stasch came up and asked Jeff if we knew where to find Walker. He gave me this." She held out the pair of heavy-duty wire strippers, sharp-edged pliers that could pierce through an outer layer and strip bare the inside wire. "He said one of his drinking buddies, a crewman from Mason Porter's *Elan*, developed a loose tongue and an urge for blackmail. He said he used these on the shroud, but Mason Porter put him up to it. Until Jeff told me, I didn't know the shroud had been tampered with."

"At least now I know I wasn't paranoid," Walker said, rolling over and tucking the covers around him. "Let me see what it was he used." He took the pliers and examined them. "This would have done it all right."

"Will it do you any good to have this now?" Miranda wondered.

"It will do me about forty thousand dollars worth of good," Walker estimated, holding the pliers in his left hand and tapping it lightly against his cast.

"I don't understand. . . ." Charlie looked at him blankly. "You're not going to sue him? All you've got is this crewman's word and he doesn't sound like a sterling character. His account may not stand up in court."

"Mason Porter will just deny everything. I doubt if you'd gain anything but enormous legal fees," Miranda concurred.

"I'm not going to sue anyone," Walker assured them. "But Porter doesn't know that. I have a feeling that there's a way to get precisely what I want. Pittman made me an offer for *Persistence*. He's acting as the middleman in a deal with an American syndicate that wants my boat very badly. That's the offer I was talking about," he reminded Miranda. "The not-quite-spectacular but reasonable one."

Miranda nodded, trying to comprehend the connection.

"I asked my friend Benjamin to do some snooping and find out who is involved in the deal. Phil insisted on making it a blind bid from what he called 'an association of businessmen.' It turns out that association is headed by Mason Porter and his son-in-law. Pittman, of course, is part of it, too," Walker explained. "Apparently Pittman wants to race *Persistence* and Porter intends to duplicate her design. He can't do that without my releasing her. I wouldn't doubt now if they got together and dreamed up the sabotage attempt in an effort to lower the selling price. Regardless, I think I might persuade Porter to ante up about forty thousand more, just to keep this quiet," he said confidently. "I'll have to tell Stasch he just came up with the most expensive hand tool on record."

"Why forty thousand?" Miranda narrowed her eyes

questioningly. The sum sounded too precise to be merely arbitrary.

"That's how much I need to pay back your father for the rigging and to settle the rest of the sail costs with Roy Gibbs. It all went into *Persistence*, so I think Pittman and Porter can raise an even two hundred thousand."

"I think it's a marvelous idea," Charlie declared. "Phil has always liked expensive playthings. Maybe we should frame the pliers and let Porter and him take turns hanging them on their office walls." Her innocent blue eyes sparkled as she talked. "We could even have a tiny plaque engraved. I wonder how 'underhanded cowardly sneaks' would look in Old English script?"

"Let's just settle for the money," Miranda suggested.

"Right, partner," Walker agreed from the bed. "We'll use whatever is left over for ferns and orthodontics."

Charlie caught the very personal look that passed between them. "Now that I've made the delivery, I guess I'd better be going," she said, blushing ferociously and trying not to grin. "I still think an engraved plaque would add a nice touch," she called out as she closed the door behind her, leaving the lovers alone.

"She might have a point," Walker noted. "But no self-respecting engraver would print the caption I'd want."

"Walker, enough is enough," Miranda insisted as she dropped her robe and climbed into bed with him.

"Never," he growled, and wrapped her in his blanket of warmth.

CHAPTER TWELVE

"WE'LL TALK NOW," Walker told Phil Pittman in the foyer of the Bahamian hotel on Paradise Island where the S.O.R.C. participants were settling in after the race from Miami to Nassau. While crewmen, officials and followers milled about the casino area, pumping the handles of slot machines, Walker had another gamble on his mind. In the fifth race, the 197-mile Miami-Nassau Race, with her spinnaker puffed out majestically, *Persistence* had placed second in her class after being edged out at the finish by only three seconds. But the boat that beat her didn't have the consistent record of *Persistence*; in the race for the S.O.R.C. trophy, *Persistence* was well ahead in overall points. Walker was confident that the one race of the series left, the twenty-seven-mile Nassau Cup, to be held the next day, would be a formality, her coronation run. All the momentum was in his favor, and he'd kept that "association of businessmen" dangling long enough.

"They were planning to do this through their attorneys, just to keep the deal fair and impersonal," Phil said, trying to hedge. But Walker wanted the offer negotiated in person. "Two o'clock. In the hotel executive suite," he instructed, immediately erasing Phil's ingratiating smile. *Persistence*'s sale price had skyrocketed, and Walker was ready to deal.

"Let's get to the point, gentlemen." Walker intentionally arrived five minutes late, his tan attaché case and wire-rimmed glasses adding a no-nonsense edge that he needed. He'd even worn a dress shirt and tie to draw attention away from the cast. This was his show, and he had waited long enough to end it. Before Phil Pittman had a chance to moderate the discussion, Walker took charge. He began smoothly, without registering the least sign of surprise that Mason Porter and his son-in-law were among the sizable group seated at the conference table with Phil. The number of members of their syndicate investors seemed to have grown as the bidding war for *Persistence* escalated. Mason Porter had enlisted the support of the yacht clubs from the St. Pete-Tampa Bay area as well as several boat builders, in order to amass sufficient funds to keep the locally produced boat flying the Bay-area banners. They would all benefit from having a local contender in international sailing competitions. But only two men there would find another aspect of the deal appealing.

"I'd like to see *Persistence* keep a familiar home base," Walker acknowledged graciously. "My boatbuilding roots are in the Tampa Bay area. But since I'm getting married this afternoon, I must be practical. I've considered several offers, and I've decided to give you a last-minute opportunity to match the one I'm most inclined to accept. But here's a souvenir just to whet your appetites and loosen your purse strings." As he spoke, he took a stack of glossy black-and-white photos from his attaché case, copies of the close finish in the fifth race, showing *Persistence* crossing the mark. To Porter and Phil Pittman he made a special gift, a photo showing the wire strippers and several inches of shroud cable with obvious crimp marks.

"You're forty thousand short," Walker said succinctly, aiming his comment directly at Porter. "For two hundred thousand *Persistence* is yours. No hassles. No further discussion necessary." Porter looked from the photo to his son-in-law, to Pittman, then back at Walker.

"I'll give you a few minutes to discuss this with your friends," Walker said diplomatically. "Unless of course, you'd simply prefer to come up with the money yourselves and spare the rest of these gentlemen any unnecessary complications. I'll be outside," he added, tucking the attaché case under his sling, then strolled out into the hallway to await their decision. Only he knew how dry his throat and damp his palms had become. If Porter and Pittman went for the squeeze play, Walker would come out of the deal far better than he'd ever dared to dream.

"We've finished talking," Pittman announced as he came out into the hallway to get Walker only minutes later. "We'll meet the price." He couldn't even look Walker in the eye as he made the pronouncement.

"Wise move," Walker acknowledged, taking a deep breath to steady his nerves.

"We'd prefer you don't make the actual amount public," Phil added.

"I'll have no comment, as long as the check doesn't

bounce," Walker replied. "You can drop the papers off at the boat. Ross will give you the pliers."

Phil hesitated as if he intended to say something more.

"I know you have too much class to ask for any commission out of this," Walker said, nailing him.

"Oh, certainly not," Phil replied stiffly. "I just wanted to wish you and Miranda my best."

"Thanks." Walker let it drop at that. Then he nodded at Pittman who stood there a moment and returned to his colleagues.

Walker pressed the call button and boarded the elevator. In a hundred solitary games of chess played in his factory loft, he had spent countless hours shifting pawns and knights, bishops and queens. Sometimes he sent them out as decoys; others moved in carefully planned sequence to close in, threaten and capture the king. This game had been played on a grander scale, and the board had spanned from the Gulf of Mexico out into the Atlantic. Now in a quiet meeting on the eleventh floor, he'd ended it. Checkmate. With a single victorious war whoop that shook the elevator walls, he was on his way.

MIRANDA TOOK A TAXI, a dented old white station wagon driven by a white-shirted Bahamian, to the marina where Jack Flint had his diving shop and bait house. This one last detail had been gnawing at her since Walker first mentioned seeing her picture on Jack Flint's bait-house wall. Charlie and Walker's comments about adding a caption under the incriminating pliers had made her remember other rude captions that Flint had written about her and posted with her newsletter column and photo. When Miranda had the dispute with Flint in Tortola almost a year earlier, the pure evil in the man had stunned her. Since then she'd seen more sophisticated manipulators and heard more venomous insults. She wasn't any tougher, but she was less naive. She wasn't going to be victimized, not even indirectly. While Walker took care of his loose ends in the executive suite at Nassau's S.O.R.C. headquarters, she would take care of a loose end of her own.

Flint wasn't even in the shop when Miranda got there. Along one wall were compartments of various-sized snorkels and swim fins, and the odor of cigar smoke and fish made the small room oppressive. A mound of pink-hearted conch shells, polished and marked for sale, sat on the counter next to the cash register, so any diver could have a souvenir if he was unsuccessful on his own. Miranda spotted her picture among several other pin-ups—crude cut-out jokes from men's magazines, naked women in provocative poses and last year's girlie calendar. Without hesitating, she pulled out the tacks and took her picture down.

"Can I help you, honey?" The voice behind her was familiar, and more friendly than the last time she'd heard it. When she turned toward Jack Flint, he stared at her a moment before one side of his mouth slowly arched into a sneer. "Oh, it's you again." He stood blocking the doorway, looking her up and down. "And you've been pokin' your nose in my business again, I see." He oozed the words like an oil spill on clear water. "Give me the picture, lady or I'll bust your a. . ."

"You keep your foul mouth closed and get out of my way. The only thing I'll give you is my attorney's name so you'll recognize it when you're invited to court," Miranda fired back. "Now back off, while I'm still feeling charitable enough to let this end here and now." She started toward him, but Flint didn't move. His birdlike dark eyes skittered over her nervously.

"If you keep me waiting here, I imagine I could get curious enough to take a close look at your rates and the condition of your inventory. I'm sure the tourist bureau and the Bahamian charter operators would appreciate a well-researched article like this one." She waved the dog-eared clipping menacingly under his nose. "But I think you should understand that detaining a person against her will constitutes kidnapping. That's a felony. Move, Flint," she ordered him.

This time he backed out, with Miranda steadily keeping in step with him.

"If you think you got me worried with your big talk, you got it wrong," Flint bellowed angrily. "You ain't got nothin' on me. You and your attorney can take that article. . ." Miranda didn't wait for him to finish. She'd already backed him across the dock, but seeing Flint so close to the edge was simply too tempting to resist. With a quick shove to the center of his chest, she set him teetering off balance, his arms flailing like a windmill. Then almost in slow motion, he arched over the water, hesitated and did a backward swan dive into the clear turquoise of Nassau Harbor.

"My reflexes are getting better and better," Miranda boasted as she turned to see Walker, his tie flapping and cast bobbing in its sling, as he raced along the dock toward her. Nearly breathless, he slowed to a lope before making a full stop in front of her.

"I was afraid you'd come here," he said, panting. "I got out of my meeting and Charlie told me you'd taken off in a taxi. When I found out which marina you'd headed for, I knew you weren't off arranging canapés for any reception." He put his good arm around her and drew her close to his side as they walked off, totally ignoring the sputtering and cursing issuing from the figure bobbing in the water between the dock pilings.

"I had a little old business to tend to," Miranda said sweetly, as she ripped the newsletter into shreds and let the pieces flutter away.

"My business went swimmingly, too," he joked. "They went for the deal," he reported as they strode off.

"Great. That's one problem solved," Miranda said, hugging him. "Now that you're going to be solvent and world renowned, that only leaves several hundred lesser issues for us to work on."

"And some we haven't even thought of yet," Walker quipped, grinning. "I'm sure you'll keep me humble."

"I'll certainly give it a try."

"I THOUGHT WE AGREED this would be a simple ceremony with a few friends," Miranda whispered in Walker's ear as he carried her ashore onto the grassy bank of Paradise Island.

"Your dad said he wanted to make the occasion memorable," Walker answered nonchalantly. "He and

Sibyl didn't want anyone to feel slighted. When you and I agreed to have it here, part of the reason was because of the wide open spaces. Under the circumstances, this seemed to make sense."

Seventy-two competition sailing yachts had been assembling in spectacular array, their brilliantly colored pennants flying and their decks lined with hundreds of crew members while Walker rowed the dinghy from *Persistence* to the shore. Wearing deck shoes and bathing trunks, he managed to get Miranda on land dry and safe before joining her there. Then Howard Vaughn helped him get into his jacket and trousers for the ceremony.

The embankment overlooking Nassau Harbor was the perfect site for a traditional wedding, although Miranda and Walker had used a few liberties in defining "traditional." But when it came to inviting a few friends, Howard Vaughn and the Albrechts had included the entire S.O.R.C. field.

At the top of the terraced hillside stood The Cloister, an arched stonework colonnade shipped in pieces to Paradise Island from Europe to add a classic elegance to the resort community. Once part of a fourteenth-century monastery, the structure stood without roof or stained-glass windows amid low leafy trees and clusters of flowering shrubs. Below, nearer the water's edge, under a lacework wrought-iron gazebo, the musicians who played for this wedding were far from typical. With belllike sounds, a steel drum accompanied the progress of the bridal party. Dennis, Lloyd and Jack Davis played along, wood blocks and harmonica, dulcimer and drums combining in a magical island sound that filtered out over the water where most of the guests remained aboard their vessels. *Persistence* was anchored among them, her sails lowered and her lifelines festooned in bright flowers.

"This is just the way we planned it, give or take a few hundred guests." Walker tried to sound reassuring, but Miranda could see the anxiety in his eyes. He was afraid he'd let her down again.

"The important ingredients haven't changed," Miranda said, straightening his tie, and giving him an approving look. "Don't worry, Walker." She stood on tiptoe and kissed him lightly. "We can handle it."

At that moment, the elegant, stately father took his daughter's arm and handed her a cascading bouquet of tropical flowers while the musicians played a delicate native version of the wedding march. Walker preceded them up the hillside where the minister was waiting, dutifully ignoring the wet shoes and sockless feet of the groom. That the best man was a short, balding sail maker and the maid of honor's post was filled by a young man in a wheelchair didn't affect the poetic beauty of the occasion. Standing in their midst with her dark hair rippling and her dress of embroidered gauze billowing gracefully about her long tanned legs, Miranda provided the touch of grace that made any incongruities seem insignificant.

"Friends..." the minister began with a faint English accent, "we are gathered here today with this man and this woman who love each other and wish to stay with each other as husband and wife."

Walker gave Miranda's hand a gentle squeeze as he drew in a long, deep breath. Miranda turned her head slightly to see something she might never see again. Walker Hall—intrepid sailor, sure victor of the S.O.R.C., superb boat builder and the newest member of the business community on Tortola—was crying. His palm was damp and his complexion sallow. In the middle of the lovely wedding vows, Miranda felt her smile waver, then gradually become a broad grin.

Then it came time for her to answer the question, "Do you, Miranda Calvert Vaughn, take Walker Hall as your lawful husband?" She had to respond with a soft, musical laugh, "I certainly do."

She fought for a bold future until she could no longer ignore the...

ECHO OF THUNDER

MAURA SEGER

Author of **Eye of the Storm**

ECHO OF THUNDER is the love story of James Callahan and Alexis Brockton, who forge a union that must withstand the pressures of their own desires and the challenge of building a new television empire.

Author Maura Seger's writing has been described by *Romantic Times* as having a "superb blend of historical perspective, exciting romance and a deep and abiding passion for the human soul."

Available in SEPTEMBER or reserve your copy for August shipping by sending your name, address and zip or postal code, along with a cheque or money order for—$4.70 (includes 75¢ for postage and handling) payable to Worldwide Library Reader Service to:

Worldwide Library Reader Service

In the U.S.:
Box 52040,
Phoenix, Arizona,
85072-2040

In Canada:
5170 Yonge Street, P.O. Box 2800,
Postal Station A,
Willowdale, Ontario, M2N 6J3

ECO-A-1

ANNE MATHER

Anne Mather, one of Harlequin's leading romance authors, has published more than 100 million copies worldwide, including **Wild Concerto,** a *New York Times* best-seller.

Catherine Loring was an innocent in a South American country beset by civil war. Doctor Armand Alvares was arrogant yet compassionate. They could not ignore the flame of love igniting within them...whatever the cost.

Available at your favorite bookstore in June, or send your name, address and zip or postal code, along with a check or money order for $4.25 (includes 75¢ for postage and handling) payable to Worldwide Library Reader Service to:

Worldwide Library Reader Service

In the U.S.	In Canada
Box 52040	5170 Yonge Street, P.O. Box 2800,
Phoenix, AZ	Postal Station A
85072-2040	Willowdale, Ont. M2N 6J3

HIF-A-I

You're invited to accept 4 books and a surprise gift Free!

Acceptance Card

Mail to: Harlequin Reader Service®

In the U.S.
2504 West Southern Ave.
Tempe, AZ 85282

In Canada
P.O. Box 2800, Postal Station A
5170 Yonge Street
Willowdale, Ontario M2N 6J3

YES! Please send me 4 free Harlequin Superromance® novels and my free surprise gift. Then send me 4 brand new novels every month as they come off the presses. Bill me at the low price of $2.50 each—a 10% saving off the retail price. There are no shipping, handling or other hidden costs. There is no minimum number of books I must purchase. I can always return a shipment and cancel at any time. Even if I never buy another book from Harlequin, the 4 free novels and the surprise gift are mine to keep forever.

134 BPS-BPGE

Name (PLEASE PRINT)

Address Apt. No.

City State/Prov. Zip/Postal Code

This offer is limited to one order per household and not valid to present subscribers. Price is subject to change. ACSR-SUB-1

Just what the woman on the go needs!

BOOKMATE

The perfect "mate" for all Harlequin paperbacks!

Holds paperbacks open for hands-free reading!

- **TRAVELING**
- **VACATIONING**
- **AT WORK** • **IN BED**
- **COOKING** • **EATING**
- **STUDYING**

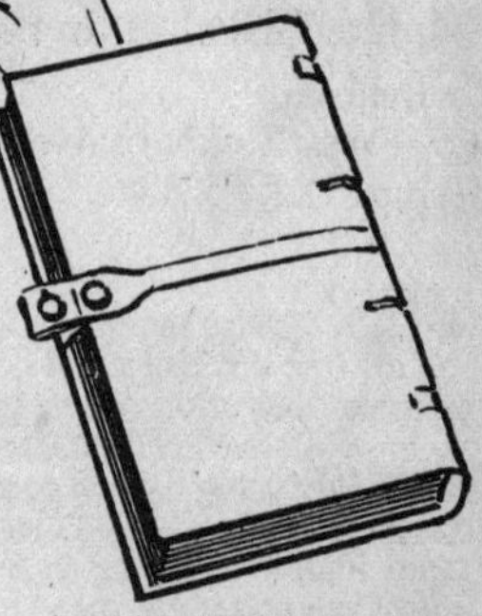

Snaps closed for easy carrying.

Perfect size for all standard paperbacks, this wonderful invention makes reading a pure pleasure! Ingenious design holds paperback books OPEN and FLAT so even wind can't ruffle pages—leaves your hands free to do other things. Reinforced, wipe-clean vinyl-covered holder flexes to let you turn pages without undoing the strap...supports paperbacks so well, they have the strength of hardcovers!

Available now. Send your name, address, and zip or postal code, along with a check or money order for just $4.99 + .75¢ for postage & handling (for a total of $5.74) payable to Harlequin Reader Service to:

Harlequin Reader Service

In the U.S.A.	In Canada
2504 West Southern Ave.	P.O. Box 2800, Postal Station A
Tempe, AZ 85282	5170 Yonge Street,
	Willowdale, Ont. M2N 5T5

MATE-1R